3 9082 14518 9851

D0886562

DEATH BY TART ATTACK

DEATH BY TART ATTACK

Tamar Myers

First world edition published in Great Britain and the USA in 2022
by Severn House, an imprint of Canongate Books Ltd,
14 High Street, Edinburgh EH1 1TE.

Trade paperback edition first published in Great Britain and the USA in 2022
by Severn House, an imprint of Canongate Books Ltd.

severnhouse.com

British Library Cataloguing-in-Publication Data
A CIP catalogue record for this title is available from the British Library.

ISBN-13: 978-0-7278-5035-5 (cased)
ISBN-13: 978-1-4483-0891-0 (trade paper)
ISBN-13: 978-1-4483-0892-7 (e-book)

All Severn House titles are printed on acid-free paper.

Typeset by Palimpsest Book Production Ltd.,
Falkirk, Stirlingshire, Scotland.
Printed and bound in Great Britain by
TJ Books, Padstow, Cornwall.

This book is dedicated to Ellie Schwartzberg,
the wisest woman I have ever known.

ACKNOWLEDGMENTS

I would like to thank my publisher, Kate Lyall Grant, at Severn House for the opportunity to write this book. I would also like to thank my editor Sara Porter for her wisdom and skilful guidance. I also wish to acknowledge my copyeditor Anna Harrison for a bang-up job, and of course, the art department for a scrummy cover.

In addition, I am very grateful to my literary agent of twenty-eight years, Nancy Yost, of Nancy Yost Literary Agency. I want to give a shout-out to the entire team there, most especially Sarah, Natanya, Cheryl, and Christina.

Lastly, I would like to acknowledge my full-time secretary, Alex. He is totally incompetent. He is utterly incapable of typing a single word, no matter how vigorously he pecks at the keyboard. Then again, it's perhaps understandable, given that he is a three-ounce parakeet. However, he does cheer me on all day by saying 'I love you, sweetheart' and 'I'm a happy bird'.

ONE

I am a hoarder. Don't get me wrong: I don't hoard stuff; I hoard memories. My mind is so cluttered with memories, both good and bad, that it is hard for me to be in the present. There are times when I live in my head so much that I forget that I have feet and lose my balance – both literally and metaphorically. Frankly, it's the unpleasant memories that I tend to fixate on the most. It has taken me a long time to come to grips with my status as a memory hoarder, but now that I have, the next bad memory that pops into my head, I vow to promptly pitch from my psyche. But that's easier said than done. Bad memories tend to recirculate, like unclaimed luggage on an airport conveyor belt.

As if that's not bad enough, there are the times that an awful memory will appear in the flesh and knock one for a loop. That's what happened the September that I turned sixty, and my ten-year-old started high school. My worst nightmare rode into town with the sound of thunder, toting hellfire and brimstone, and my family dynamics were irrevocably altered.

But now, I've gotten way ahead of myself: so far ahead, in fact, that most of the story has been left behind. Usually, the only thing that gets this far out in front of me is my extraordinarily long, narrow nose. Fortunately, my probing proboscis does come in handy for stabbing pickles in the bottom of a jar.

This story begins the day that I heard a racket coming from Hertzler Road that was even louder than my husband's snoring. Given that it was one o'clock in the morning, I was in bed, clad in my long, cotton, flannel nightgown (the sexy number that had a small pink bow attached to the zipper pull at the neckline). I threw on my long, cotton chenille robe, crammed my tootsies into my skillet-sized, fuzzy, polyester slippers, and ran to the dining-room window to see what in tarnation was going on.

Now, I am not waxing hyperbolic when I say that what my eyes beheld, my mind simply could not believe. I'm sure such a phenomenon has happened to you before, hasn't it? At any rate, I did the logical thing, which was to close my eyes, and then open them again for confirmation. Unless one is a masochist, pinching oneself should never be one's go-to option.

Unfortunately, what I beheld the second time was the same as the first. A seemingly endless line of heavy earth-moving equipment was rumbling slowly down the rural route that fronts my farm. The Amish here use horses to pull their farm machinery, and the Mennonites use tractors, but these machines were of the type and scale that I have only seen in cities when skyscrapers are built. I ran back to our bedroom as fast as my rubbery legs could take me.

'Aaron,' I shouted. 'Wake up!'

My sweet husband, Gabriel Rosen, turned on his reading light. '*What* did you call me?'

'*Barren,*' I said. 'As in, I was barren as the Gobi Desert until your periwinkle pollinated my hollyhock.'

The dear man sighed. 'Mags,' he said, 'you called me by your first husband's name again, didn't you?'

'Yes, but bear in mind that he tricked me into marrying him, and since he was already married, technically he never *was* my husband.'

'In that case the two of you were just shacking up.'

'Oh pot, quit calling thyself black,' I said. 'Your sister told me all about your college conquests. Romeo Rosen is what everyone called you. Now hie thee to yon dining-room window and tell me what you see.'

My long-suffering, and forgiving, husband crawled out of bed and lumbered into the dining room. For a moment he stood at the window rubbing his eyes with the heels of his hands.

'Well?' I demanded. 'What on earth do you think is going on?'

'We're either both imagining things, hon, or the world as we know it is about to end. There's only one way to find out!' He ducked into the kitchen and grabbed a massive, high-powered torch from a pantry shelf. 'Come on, let's go find out.'

That said, Dr Gabriel Rosen, the love of my life, and a well-respected member of the Village of Hernia, Pennsylvania, charged outdoors and down the driveway. Moi, ever the dutiful wife, followed faithfully in his stead. Although we may be rubes and country bumpkins, we are not without a minimum of technology.

In this case, our appearance caused two exceedingly bright security lights to click on. It was only then that I remembered that while I, a conservative Mennonite woman, was properly clad from head to toe, the Babester was only wearing the same set of nightclothes in which he had been born.

TWO

I t was a given that the men in the slowing, passing vehicles would notice my husband's baby-making equipment. It is, after all, considerable. The drivers blasted their horns, and their passengers leaned out the windows and shouted obscenities. Meanwhile, Gabe stood there, transfixed and gobsmacked, in his altogether, until the taillights of the last of the vehicles disappeared into the early morning mist a quarter mile down the road. When he turned to me, he didn't seem at all upset or embarrassed. He was excited.

'While I'm getting dressed, you run and ask Freni to watch Little Jacob. Then I'll get the car started. We're following those folks.'

Follow them we did, all the way to Hernia, population, 2,172. That figure, incidentally, would be much higher if one took into account the fact that more than a few of our citizens are two-faced. At any rate, the route that these behemoth earthmovers took had them come to a full stop, approximately four miles south of my place. At that point they turned right and inched their way across the two-hundred-year-old stone bridge that spans Slave Creek.

This historic landmark was built back in the days of oxcarts and isn't meant to carry such heavy loads. All vehicles over two tonnes are required to enter town from the opposite side of the village. Not only were the drivers of these machines going to be heavily fined, but they were also going to be the recipients of a first-class Magdalena Yoder tongue-lashing (of course, one delivered in my usual mild-mannered Mennonite fashion).

'If they so much as harm one stone on our bridge, there will be all hectare to pay,' I said.

Gabe laughed. 'Oh hon, I'm sure that it's not a sin to say "heck".'

'Tell that to the bar of soap that Mama made me eat.'

'*What?* She made you eat a bar of soap for saying one word? And what happened to just washing your mouth out with the soap?'

'She made me eat a sliver of soap every time I said a bad word.' I shrugged. 'So I guess I must have been a very naughty girl.'

'Me like,' Gabe said. 'Tell me more.'

'It's not funny, Gabe. Every time I got the soap treatment, Granny whacked me with her hairbrush as well. Still, that didn't stop me. Either I was a slow learner, or the Devil really had his hooks into me.'

'You were just being a kid rebelling against a strict upbringing. Tell me some more of your so-called swear words.'

'No! That would be wrong now, just like it was then.'

'Not if you're trying to educate me – your heathen husband.'

Although I knew that Gabe was teasing me about the way I was raised, it felt good to talk about it with someone whose perspective differed from the norms of my Amish-Mennonite Community. All these decades after the fact, I still felt that I had been unfairly punished.

'I said the "D" word,' I said. 'Not the one that holds back water, but the word that describes mending socks. It got me two slivers of soap and three whacks with the hairbrush.'

'Tsk, tsk, why look at you, Satan's little sidekick,' Gabe said. 'I've never been prouder of you than right now.'

I hung my large horsey head. 'But dear, it gets much worse. One day when nothing was going right for me at school, I shouted out "cheese and crackers". The whole class heard me. Miss Entwhistle, my third-grade teacher, got the vapours and was sent home for the rest of the day. Of course, this resulted in our class being sent home as well, and the entire village learning that one Magdalena Portulacca Yoder, was a nine-year-old blasphemer.

'For this transgression Papa took me out to the barn and gave me a couple of gentle flicks with the buggy whip. I mean really soft – like this.' I tapped his sleeve to demonstrate. 'Then Papa snapped that whip in the air so that it cracked like lightning, and told me to holler bloody murder. Granny Yoder took pity on my

afflicted flesh and spared me her hairbrush, but Mama guessed
what her husband had done, and made me eat half a bar of that
dreaded soap. I went to bed with a stomach ache, and the next
morning, and for the next three days, I defecated bubbles.'

We were just one vehicle from the bridge by then, and Gabe
laughed so hard that *he* nearly ran into a stone wall along the
passenger side of the car. If it weren't for my long, gangly left
arm, and the keen vision in my pale, watery-blue eyes, I might
have had to give my Dearly Beloved a tongue-lashing. But as
soon as I wrenched the wheel from his hand and straightened
our trajectory, he slammed on the brakes. Now I don't mind
being face down in my dearly beloved's lap, mind you, but
normally it takes a bit of coaxing.

'Sorry about that,' the Babester said. 'That flatbed in front of
us doesn't have any brake lights.'

The offending truck was transporting a *crane*, of all things.
Now if idle hands are the Devil's workshop, then surely a building
crane is the Devil's favourite tool. In my opinion no structure
needs to be more than two stories tall, given that being a crane
operator is one of the most dangerous jobs that there is, and
we've all seen photos of fallen cranes which, on their way down,
have sliced through buildings like a knife through a sponge cake.
Not only that, but aren't skyscrapers an affront to the Almighty?
Just look what happened to the Tower of Babel. Those folks tried
building their way up to Heaven too, and God smashed that tower
to smithereens.

Apparently, the Good Lord didn't want this idolatrous piece
of machinery to even enter our peaceful village. After an interminable series of stops and starts, it became obvious the driver
couldn't manage the sharp right turn onto our narrow bridge.
The road ahead led steeply uphill, and there was not a spot within
ten miles that came to mind where a rig that long could turn
around safely. The best way out of this predicament was for a
skilled driver to straighten this monstrous truck, and then back
it up as far as the intersection of Hertzler Road and Bontrager
Road, where his chances were better. Although both roads are
paved, they are also flanked by drainage ditches.

'Wait here,' I said to the Babester, and then hopped out of the
car before he could stop me.

While I may have a face like a mare's, and my chest is a carpenter's dream (flat as a board), the Good Lord had seen fit to bless me with a pair of long legs and sturdy ankles. The fact that they blend into each other seamlessly, from calve to ankle, is why this phenomena is sometimes referred to as 'cankles'. At any rate, I hitched up my modest skirt (which fell to mid-calf), loped over to the cab of the truck, reached up with one of my long and gangly, but strong, farm gal arms to grab the vehicle's side mirror, and hoisted myself up onto its running board. Upon peering into the cab's open window, I gasped with disbelief.

'Why, you're just a baby!' I said.

'I am *not*,' the boy said. 'I'm sixteen.'

'Don't be ridiculous.'

'Then I'm *almost* sixteen,' he said, and bit his lip.

'Try again, dear, before I call the police.'

'I'll be fourteen next week?' With his rising inflection, he could have been a secret Canadian.

'Good heavens, I've got sturdy Christian underwear that are older than you.'

'Gross.'

'You do know that it's illegal for you to be driving this monstrosity.'

The boy burst into tears. 'My d-d-ad m-made d-d-o it. D-d-don't you think that I'd rather be home in bed? But he said that if I d-d-idn't d-d-rive for him tonight, he wouldn't give me this awesome summer job with his construction company.'

There are times when I can literally feel the tentacles of an evil presence starting to close in on me. Not that this kid was evil, but he was only a few steps away from Satan Himself.

'Tell me about this awesome summer job,' I said. Meanwhile the Babester, a.k.a. Dr Gabriel Rosen, was desperately flashing our car's lights in a failed attempt to get me to run back to him with a report. Instead of doing my husband's bidding, I did the best I could for the kid, which was to give him a 'thumbs up', and a lopsided, horsey-faced grin.

The boy, whose name was Rodney, wiped his runny nose on his pink and blue T-shirt. 'D-dad is the CEO of this, like, massively awesome amusement park that is going to be built over there.' He sniffed, and pointed with his chin in the direction of my beloved Hernia. 'It's gonna be the largest amusement park in the world, and it's gonna be Christian. All of it straight from the Bible. And I get to be the water boy.'

At that the Devil showed up to dance a long, slow number with me. He whispered in my ear that He planned to strangle me, by enveloping me in a web of microscopic roots that eventually squeezed all the oxygen from my lungs. Already I found it difficult to breathe, and I had yet to ask the name of this impending amusement park.

'What's going to be the name of this Christian amusement park?'

The boy's eyes glittered in the dark, as they were still filled with tears. 'Have you ever read the Book of Revelations?'

'It is Revelation, without the "s",' I hissed. Note that I hissed with an "s", and not without one, as some rich and famous, male, mystery writers are wont to do.

'Yeah, well, maybe. Anyway, the park's gonna be named Armageddonland, like, you know, in that first book in the Bible.'

I sighed. 'Armageddon is mentioned in Revelation, which is the *last* book – wait just one pea-picking minute! Those folks were here about five years ago, and I told them to get lost. I told them that no Amish person worth their buggy was going to sell valuable farmland to bring in a flood of nosey tourists. And the Mennonites won't stand for it either.'

'Huh?' The poor lad sounded stuffy from crying.

'That's right, young man. We're not about to allow a commercial travesty to ruin our peaceful community.'

'But my dad's a Mennonite,' the boy Rodney said.

'*What?*' I managed to hiss without an 's'. Harlan Coben would have been proud of me.

'Well, he *was* a Mennonite, until he committed pigamy with that lady from Hernia.'

My ears burned. 'Pigamy?'

'Yeah, you know, like having two wives at the same time.'

'That's *big*amy, dear.'

'Yeah, well she was a Mennonite too. Owned a motel or something. She made a real stink when she found about my mother and my sister – I wasn't born yet. You'd think my dad would forget about the pigamist lady from Hernia, but he still talks about her all the time. Magdalena this, and Magdalena that. Finally my mom couldn't take it anymore, so he split and took me with him.'

'Rodney,' I said, my voice seeming to echo in my skull, 'is your last name Miller?'

'Yeah. Are you psychic or something, lady?'

'Definitely something,' I said. 'Is your dad's name Aaron Miller?'

'Yeah.'

'Is your mother's name Katherine, and is she from Minnesota?'

'Wow!' he said. 'I mean like, crazy wow! You're really good at this stuff.'

I like to say that flattery will get one everywhere with me – just not *there*. But as much as I would have loved pretending to be a psychic, the Bible clearly forbids us from involving ourselves in such pursuits. That's because the Devil and His minions lurk in the shadows around the edges of the rational world. It was enough that the Devil's hot breath was still blowing in one ear.

'No, Rodney,' I confessed, 'I am not a psychic; I *am* Magdalena Yoder, the inadvertent adulteress whose innocence your father stole, on what was the happiest night of my life.'

'Awesome!' he said.

'*Excuse me?*'

'Well, I ain't never met such a big sinner as you before. Mind if I get your picture on my cell?' He started digging into the pocket of his jeans.

'I most certainly do,' I said. I leaned in and tried to slap his hand away from his pants. He moved away, so I leaned in further. Suddenly someone grabbed my ankles and hoisted my feet into the air. Then as if I was a collapsible wheelbarrow, I was shoved headfirst into the cab of the lorry and ended up with my face pressed against the young man's thigh.

THREE

'**W**ell, if this isn't a case of child molestation, then nothing is!' The speaker was an older man outside the truck, on the passenger's side, and his voice was somewhat familiar.

I scrambled to a sitting position. It wasn't an easy task for a fifty-nine-year-old woman in a long nightgown, topped with a long terrycloth robe, and wearing fuzzy slippers the size of Great Britain. I must have looked like nine cats trying to claw their way out of a gunny sack.

At last I was properly upright, but breathing heavily. I'm sure that my face was red, if not from exertion, then at least from anger. But then I saw that my accuser was none other than my ex-husband (or pseudo-husband, as I call that bigamist), and I felt the return of a very ugly emotion, one that I had worked very hard to eradicate over a decade ago. I felt hatred.

'Aaron Miller! How dare you come back to Hernia! We had an agreement.'

'Why, Magdalena Portulacca Yoder Miller Rosen, as I live and breathe,' Aaron said smoothly. 'You are a sight for sore eyes. Besides, haven't you heard? Agreements are meant to be broken.' His voice had deepened over the years, but it was still as smooth as silk.

I opened the cab door and climbed carefully down, determined to give the man a tongue-lashing. But when I stood face-to-face with him in the moonlight, just a few feet apart, I became curiously tongue-tied. Aaron Miller bore an uncanny resemblance to the Gabriel Rosen I had fallen in love with, and married, twelve years earlier. Aaron's hair was still a lustrous black, his waist trim, and his hips narrow.

The Babester, although still a handsome man, had undergone a few changes over the time we'd been married. His hair was streaked with silver, which caused Gabe to refer to himself as a Silverback Gorilla – well, truth be told that had to do with the silver hairs on his *back*. At any rate, my dear husband's waist had thickened and much to his dismay, he had grown what he called 'love handles'. But like I said, he was still a handsome man; he just looked like one might expect a sixty-year-old American male to look.

'I don't mind you undressing me with your eyes, Magdalena,' Aaron said, 'but stay away from my son. He's just a child.'

I found my tongue. 'You're the one who pushed me into the cab, you-you—'

Aaron laughed heartily. 'Oh, come on, Mags, I'm only kidding you.'

'Sexual abuse is not a laughing matter,' I snapped.

'Yeah, Dad,' Rodney said. 'Miss Yoder and I were only talking.'

'Oh, lighten up, you two,' Aaron said. 'We've got a bigger problem than political correctness here. We have to find a way to get this truck across that pitiful pile of stones and concrete that you Herniaites refer to as a bridge.'

I bristled with indignation. 'Our bridge is over two hundred years old – well, some of it, anyway. I guess the parts that collapsed and were carried away are also that old, as are their replacements. Stones are stones, after all. They were all created five thousand years ago when God spoke forth the earth. My point is that our bridge is venerable; it has served our town well. It was meant to accommodate horse-drawn wagons and carriages, and has done an admirable job of accommodating *most* vehicles with combustion-powered engines. It was never intended to accommodate this amount of tonnage.'

'Wow!' Rodney said. 'She's just like you described, Dad. Long-winded like our preacher. And she don't know science neither. She thinks the world is only five thousand years old.'

'She *does* know grammar,' I said, 'which you would do well to learn.' I turned to his father. 'Aaron, how did you pop up so suddenly? I don't see any trucks stopped on the bridge.'

He shook his head. 'Nope. The rest of the convoy made it across without raising as much as a dust mote. We've halted the length of Main Street, waiting for my boy here to get across. I'm parked just over there – so I trotted on back to check on him. Then lo and behold, to my everlasting joy, my gaze fell upon my first love. If memory serves me right, I was six, and you were five—'

'Aaron!'

He winked. Or blinked. The moonlight was bright, but my heart was racing so fast that things in general were a bit blurry.

'OK, we'll walk down memory lane soon enough,' Aaron said. 'But now Rodney's going to get this rig across the bridge and—'

'*I'll* tell you what you'll do,' I said. 'You'll get someone other than a boy to get this behemoth backed up far enough for it to turn around, and then that licenced individual will drive it back from whence it started. It will not *now*, or *ever*, cross our bridge!'

I'd stamped a fluffy foot on the pavement to emphasize my dictum. Unfortunately, I quite forgot that I was wearing fuzzy slippers, and not my usual black brogans. The pain that shot up my right leg set me to hopping about on my left leg and moaning. Thank the Good Lord that at this hour there were no tourists about, for they might have concluded that I was engaging in some Old Order Mennonite ritual or dance. For the record, we do *not* dance, and there is only one place where I allow myself to moan. And there, only once.

I was still making a fool of myself in this way when the Babester seemingly appeared out of nowhere and punched Aaron Miller in the face. He did it with such force, and so swiftly, that Aaron was nearly knocked to the ground. If it had not been for the guard wall behind him, Aaron might have staggered backwards so far that he ended up in Slave Creek. Instead, he sat abruptly down on the rock wall, dazed, and obviously in pain himself.

'What the heck was that for?' he moaned.

'It's payback for whatever it is you did to my wife.'

Aaron touched his cheek gingerly. 'You mean that you didn't see me manhandle my ex-wife and shove her into the cab of my truck?'

The Babester advanced on Aaron, who remained seated. 'Is that what you did?' he demanded. 'You manhandled her?'

I leaped between the two men, the two loves of my life, which didn't do either of my slipper-clad feet any good. 'Sweetheart,' I purred (to my current husband), 'I deserved to be manhandled in this case; I was halfway through the truck window hollering at Aaron's cub.'

'I ain't no cub!' Rodney sounded disturbingly like his sister

Alison. Gabe and I adopted Alison ten years earlier, after Aaron
and his wife had abandoned her. Alison's existence is something
else that I was unaware of when I married the first time.

'Hollering about what?' Gabe said.

'They're here to build Armageddonland!'

'Yeah?' my Jewish husband said.

'Darling,' I said. 'You really *are* clueless, aren't you?'

'Refresh my memory,' Gabe said.

'They want to build an apocalyptic theme park, based on the
Book of Revelation,' I said.

'The Book of Revelation isn't in my scriptures,' the Babester
said.

'Uh-huh,' young Rodney said. 'The Book of Revelation is in
every Bible.'

'My husband is Jewish, dear,' I said.

'Then he's going to Hell,' Rodney said. There wasn't a trace
of malice in his voice. In his mind, he was merely stating a fact.

'The funny thing,' Gabe said, 'is that Hell isn't mentioned in
my Bible either.'

'That's because *you* people have only *half* of the Bible,' Aaron
said. Unlike his son, Aaron's sole intent was to be contentious.

Mennonites, along with the Amish, are by doctrine pacifist
peoples. They are exempted from military service (serving in a
civilian capacity instead), and they do not lift a hand when
physically assaulted. My ancestors were massacred by the
Delaware Indians at the Northkill Amish Settlement in 1757
because they would not defend themselves. Aaron Miller
was born and raised a Mennonite, and has Amish ancestors, as
do I. But clearly, the man who knowingly engaged in bigamy
and subsequently abandoned his daughter had abandoned the
teachings of our fathers. Since my Dearly Beloved was not averse
to fisticuffs, some serious intervention needed to be done.

My first thought was to feign a heart attack. Being married to
a cardiac surgeon, I'd been well versed in the symptoms that I,
as a woman, should expect, should I experience one. But I try
not to lie – although I have been known to embroider the truth
from time to time (which is not the same thing, mind you).

Fortunately, the Good Lord has seen fit *not* to endow me with
talent of any sort. Although I am a member of the choir at Beechy

Grove Mennonite Church, I have been repeatedly asked to sing 'solo' – so low that no one can hear me. Perhaps that's because the sound of my singing has been described as a mashup of nails on a chalkboard, an angry goose, a busted bagpipe, and a cat in heat.

Psalm 100 declares: 'Make a joyful noise onto the Lord all ye lands.' A joyful noise is exactly what I make every Sunday morning, and I am not ashamed of it. The fact that my singing curdles the milk in the Stutzman's dairy, puts the hens off laying in a five-mile radius, and caused Old Man Lehman's mule to kick down the door of his stall and run all the way to the Maryland border, ought really to be none of my concern.

Now where was I? Oh yes, I decided that the best way to prevent a physical escalation between my current husband and my ex was to exercise my vocal cords. Ergo, I threw back my horsey head and let forth with my rendition of our beloved national anthem, 'The Star-Spangled Banner'. Of course, I began my full-throated assault near the end of the song where that dreaded, impossibly high note coincides with the word 'free'. Multitudes of performers have been known to duck the challenge by suddenly changing keys or dropping down an octave. Not me.

I hit that note with a sound that I pray I never hear again. Two seconds later something soft bounced off my head and landed on the ground in front of Aaron. Rodney, being young and agile, scooped it up.

'Dad!' he exclaimed. 'Look! It's a bat. She killed it with her screeching.'

'Drop it, son,' Aaron said. 'It could be diseased.'

'Or maybe it's just stunned,' Gabriel said. 'Magdalena once momentarily paralyzed a team of runaway horses by singing "Mary Had a Little Lamb" to them.'

Of course that wasn't true, but since Gabriel meant it to be helpful to me, what he said can't really be counted as a lie.

'Either way, we should be going, son,' Aaron said. He turned to leave.

'Not so fast, dear,' I said. 'I'm still the mayor, so listen up. First, you have to take the kid with you, and have one of your more experienced drivers return in the morning to get the truck unstuck. Without damaging either the bridge or the wall! But as

I said before, he will not be taking this vehicle across our bridge. Go the other way to the Bontrager place.'

'And second?' Aaron said sarcastically. 'I know there is more that you're just itching to say.'

'And second,' I said, 'don't think for a minute that your Armageddonland is a *fait accompli*. We citizens of Hernia are simply not to going to permit such a travesty to be built next to our village.'

Aaron grinned, and in the light of the moon his teeth gleamed an unnatural white. 'You were always underestimating me, weren't you, sweetheart? Doll Face, this killer of an amusement park is going to be set on the one-hundred-and-twenty-five acres that used to be my uncle Bob and aunt Mable's farm, out there on Skinny Branch Road. That's where we are headed now, honey-buns.'

'Hey, buddy,' the Babester growled, 'watch the endearments.'

I could hardly believe it. Bob and Mable Bontrager had been two of the nicest members ever to grace the doorway of my church. I'd known them my entire life, just like I'd always known Aaron. But somehow I'd never connected the dots between Mable *Miller* Bontrager and Aaron's father. I suppose that might have been because Mable was the youngest of twelve siblings, and Aaron's father was the oldest. But there you had it: Bob and Mable, who were childless, and lived well outside of our village limits, had left their estate to the nephew who had run off to Minnesota and pursued a very different lifestyle. And not that I mean to gossip, but Bob originally hailed from Kansas, and from the very beginning there were rumours that Bob might really have been *Barbara* Bontrager in men's clothing. But who am I to judge?

I flashed Aaron my victory grin. 'Too bad for you that you didn't do your homework, you Judas. If you had, you would have discovered that I am on the Bedford County Planning Commission.'

The problem with Aaron's victory grin is that his teeth are straighter and whiter than a row of Chicklets chewing gum pieces. The British would call them 'American teeth'.

'Oh, you poor, naive, country bumpkin,' Aaron said. 'The planning commission did approve this development. They did so last year, by a five to three vote when you were organizing your annual goat festival. Don't you recall the anonymous donor that gave every member of the committee a ten-thousand-dollar grant to use as they as they saw fit?'

'No, I never got any money – oh, you snake! You bribed the committee when my back was turned.'

Aron's grin widened to reveal more teeth than a body has a right to own. 'They weren't bribes; they were discretionary funds for local improvements. You're just angry because you weren't at the meeting the day I doled them out.'

At that point I was quivering with rage. 'You won't get away with this,' I squeaked, for I sounded as if I'd been sucking on a helium-filled balloon. 'You're going to be sorry, Aaron Paul Miller. Before I'm through with you, you're going to wish that you were dead.'

FOUR

You already know that my name is Magdalena Portulacca Yoder Rosen, but perhaps you don't know that I was born and raised on a dairy farm four miles north of the Village of Hernia, Pennsylvania. Hernia, by the way, sits in a valley in the Appalachian Mountains, between the long and narrow Buffalo Mountain to the east, and a lower range known as Pigeon Hills to the west. Today the Village of Hernia incorporates my farm, but there is a good reason for that: I am its mayor.

I am an Old Older Mennonite. We're the ones who still wear little white prayer caps on neatly pinned up braids. There are more forward-thinking Mennonites, whom you might pass on the street but never recognize. Some Mennonites have Amish ancestors (I do), but some don't. What all Mennonites and all Amish have in common is that they are non-violent and they strive to be humble. I, in fact, am quite proud of my humility.

That said, the reason I became mayor of our village, and have been mayor for nigh on twenty years, is that I am by far its wealthiest citizen. It is moi who paid for its sewer system, to bury our utilities, for weekly garbage removal, and for a liveable wage for two full-time law enforcement officers. I also built a library next to the school complex, and – well, modesty prevents me from saying more.

But make no mistake about it. I did not inherit millions of dollars! I was a mere lass of twenty when my parents were killed in a car crash in the Alleghany Tunnel, squished to death between a truck full of pasteurized milk and another one carrying state-of-the-art running shoes. They left my eleven-year-old sister and me a small dairy farm, and a lot of debts. I was unable to manage the dairy herd by myself, so I sold off all the cows but two, and then – I know the idea had to have been Heaven sent – it occurred to me to turn our 200-year-old farmhouse into a full-board inn. That meant that boarders would get three square meals a day, all cooked by my elderly kinswoman, who is an authentic Amish woman, and whose mother tongue is Amish. Amish, by the way, is a dialect based on the Swiss German that my cook's ancestors (and mine) imported in 1738.

In other words, my establishment was to be a quasi-authentic Pennsylvania Dutch inn, except for *one* thing. The enormous, and almost instantaneous, success of the PennDutch Inn, as I call it, is because of a theory that popped into my thick skull after listening to some friends recount their tales of trips to Europe. It is as follows: tourists will pay big bucks to endure great discomfort, just as long as they get to view it as a cultural experience. Think about it. Visit just about any cheap, chain motel in America, and the rooms will be large, with private baths, an easy chair, a closet with hangers, an ironing board, a coffeemaker, quite possibly a small fridge, and sometimes a microwave. And of course, there will be a television.

Are you having hot flashes? Then crank down the air conditioning. Are you cold-natured, even in the summer? Turn on the heater. Well, it's a good thing that you're in America then, isn't it?

By contrast, the rooms in some European hotels are so small that you have to plop your suitcase on the bed so that you can open it to retrieve a fresh set of sturdy Christian underwear. By then you need to use the loo, so up comes the suitcase again, and out comes a robe, because you will have to toddle down a dimly lit hallway to use a common toilet. In that horrid little closet, you try to line the seat, but instead of a roll, all you find are little squares of waxed paper, more suitable for hot-cross buns than your own home-grown buns. And don't even think about controlling the climate in your room; air-conditioning is almost unheard of, and if you complain that it's too cold in October, the manager will tell you that no one, *but no one*, gets heat until November.

But look at the bright side! You're in Europe, seeing European things. So, I reasoned, why not come to the PennDutch, pay exorbitant prices, have a pseudo-authentic Amish experience, and be just as miserable without the jet lag experienced from flying to Paris or London. Even if one is the romantic type, who wishes to visit Rome in order to get her rear end pinched (not an Amish desire, I assure you), I can arrange to have her back into one of my neighbour Janet's beehives. For a fifty-dollar fee, of course. A mere 200 dollars gets one the privilege of mucking out my horse stalls and cow barn. Three hundred dollars lets one rake out the chicken house and put down fresh straw. Collecting the eggs will cost five bucks apiece. Weeding and hoeing in the vegetable patch is an activity guests vie for, as it is back-breaking work in the sun. The base price is 200 dollars a day for a single row. On hot days the price goes up with temperature. And of course, guests must clean their own rooms and communal baths, for an extra fee, or they don't get to eat.

Why would any sane person put up with this . . . one might call it nonsense? Because there are people in this world with money to burn, and once word got out of my quirky establishment's existence, my little farm became the inn place – pun intended. The filthy rich, and the very famous, from all over the world just had to say that they too had endured abuse at my hand, so to speak. To have stayed at the PennDutch Inn, was like having gained access to an exclusive club from which the hoi polloi were excluded.

Then the unthinkable happened: someone was murdered in my inn. A normal person might guess that this would put a damper on business, but *au contraire*. Who knew that there are folks out there that request rooms where murders have happened? And there were plenty of murders. Death seemed to follow me like that fictional woman from Cabot's Cove. I started receiving letters and emails telling me that I was possessed by the Devil, and that *I* was the Grim Reaper. However, my best friend Agnes, who is a nominal Christian at best, came up with a theory that I like much better. Perhaps our omniscient God, knowing that these victims will soon be murdered, is directing them to the PennDutch to die because our all-knowing God also knows that I am capable of solving their murders.

But oh, have I ever digressed. Now it's time to return to the bridge and my confrontation with my ex-husband, Aaron Miller. Having just told Aaron that he was going to wish that he were dead because of his involvement with Armageddonland, it was time for me to make a quick exit into the night. Not just any exit would do, though. 'Head up,' I muttered to myself. 'Shoulders back. Flat chest out.'

But it's hard to make a strong exit when one's current husband is lagging behind one, all the while attempting to apologize for his wife's supposedly over-the-top behaviour, never mind that *he* punched Aaron in the face. And it's hard not to feel like an authority figure when one's pseudo ex-husband is demanding that his former wife apologize as well, or *else*. Or else?

Whatever. I stood my ground, as I covered ground, back to our car, and even when Gabe the Babester lectured me all the way home I merely nodded my head mutely. No, I take that back, because I slipped in a few 'yes, dears' just to get him to shut up, so that we could get back to bed.

But you can bet your bippy that I didn't sleep a wink. Quite sensibly both Gabe and I had turned off our cell phones upon retiring that night, and we'd both left them behind in our haste to follow the last truck in the convoy. Upon return to the inn, we discovered them lit up like Christmas trees. Not only were the villagers livid about the noise, but somehow they had managed to coerce our relatively young Chief of Police, Toy Graham, to harass me as well. And since I'm the sort of woman who needs to get an irritant out of her system before she can heal, I returned his call.

'Toy,' I said, 'no, I haven't been sleeping; I've been dealing with the source of this problem, face to handsome face. Strike the word "handsome", will you? I'm tired.'

'Uh – OK. So then you know that this company is planning

to build the largest theme park in the world, right outside of town?'

'Yes,' I said tiredly. 'I just found out tonight, probably around the same time you did.'

'Is there nothing you can do to stop it? After all, you're on the planning commission.'

I sighed. 'They did an "end run", and I was the end. They gave this forthcoming monstrosity their stamp of approval the weekend of our last Billy Goat Gruff Festival.'

Toy laughed. 'I never thought I'd hear you use football terminology. But can't you cry "foul" because you weren't there? Maybe force a revote?'

'No,' I said sadly. 'The bylaws state that there are no allowances to be made for absenteeism. But there is something that we could do that might change the outcome. It's a slim chance, but slim is better than nothing.'

'What's that?' Toy said so urgently, it felt like he wanted to suck the answer out of my phone.

'We could – I mean, we *should* – organize and protest. As soon as we hang up, we should call everyone we know, which between us is half the county, and get them to come out to the Skinny Branch Road building site at dawn tomorrow. When the people rise up to protect their peaceful way of life, then Hell, and its millions of visitors a year, will have to find a new home.'

'I'm on it,' he said, and hung up.

I immediately called my best friend, Agnes Shafor, née Miller. She happens to be distantly related to both Aaron Miller and me. She is also the most likely person I know to still be awake at three in the morning.

'I hope I'm not disturbing you,' I said.

'Don't be silly, Mags. I'm still trying to finish yesterday's crossword in *The Times*. What's a fourteen-letter phrase for "failed novelist"? Two words.'

'*Kirkus* reviewer.'

'Thanks! Now, to what do I owe the pleasure of your company in the wee hours of the morning? Did you and that stud muffin of yours have a tiff?'

'Agnes, I told you that name for him in confidence.'

'So? It's just you and me – or are you on speaker phone?'

'The FBI is listening, for Pete's sake!'

'You're joking!'

'Sadly not. That's what happens when you have oodles of high-profile murders at a quaint country inn. This isn't Cabot Cove, and I'm not Jessica Fletcher. Not that I ever watched *Murder She Wrote*, of course, because it was secular television. But believe me, my guests are more than happy to make comparisons.'

'Like what?' Agnes said. 'That everyone liked Jessica because she was never sarcastic, or made snarky comments?'

'That's not fair!' I wailed. 'I wouldn't say those things either, if I had a writer to put nice words in my mouth. Sometimes the Devil makes me says things that I regret later, or I'm tired and things sort of slip out, or people are just plain stupid, and need to be told the truth.'

'There you have it,' Agnes said. 'And that's what makes you the Magdalena Yoder that most people love. Just not everyone. Now, get down to brass tacks, and tell me the reason for your call. Because I want to get this crossword puzzle completed before the morning paper comes.'

'It's this: remember a development company that wanted to build a Christian theme park called Armageddonland, about five years ago?'

'Yes,' Agnes said cautiously.

'They're back. They rolled through the village last night with all manner of earth-moving trucks, and today they're breaking ground over on Skinny Branch Road. At what used to be Bob and Mable Bontragers' place.'

'No way! You know, I heard a lot of rumbling earlier, and I assumed it was thunder, but I never thought to look outside.'

'Agnes, you haven't heard the half of it. The man who's spearheading this project, the head honcho on the ground here, is Aaron Miller.'

In the time it took Agnes to process this information, I grew six more grey hairs (two on my chin) and the food in my refrigerator went bad. Finally she gasped.

'You mean your Pookey Bear?'

'My *ex*-Pookey Bear! And that expression of endearment has

been permanently retired. But yes, one and the same. And get this, he has a son who is seven years younger than Alison.'

'Whom he abandoned,' she said. 'But whom you lovingly took in and adopted,' she added.

'Well, this isn't about me; it's about our community. Aaron wants to turn the Book of Revelation into a theme park that will dwarf Disneyworld.'

Agnes laughed. 'That will be the day.'

'You don't understand. With the world the way it is now, an "end times" theme could become wildly popular, even with the unchurched. If Armageddonland pulled in just a tenth the number of visitors that Disneyworld does each year, that would be close to six million – well, five million, eight hundred thousand to be exact.'

'Holy Toledo!'

'Even a million visitors would destroy our way of life. New roads would have to be built, suburbs to house the workers, more schools, the traffic would get horrendous, and the Amish would probably sell their farms and move farther west to where they have relatives, as they have always done when they feel modern society closing in on them.'

'So it's bye-bye Hernia then,' Agnes said softly.

'Agnes!' I shouted into my phone. 'Wake up!'

'I'm still awake; I'm just sad.'

'No, I mean wake up to what needs to be done.'

'Oh Mags, you're not going to murder Aaron too, are you?'

'Ach! I've never murdered anyone! You hear that, Mr FBI? Maybe in my heart once or twice, but then everybody does, trust me. I bet that you've murdered someone in your heart as well, Mr FBI – or is it Miss FBI? Maybe Mrs? We all have someone that we can't stand, and wish that they'd disappear, which is the same as them being dead, isn't it? So if you know what I'm talking about, please do me a huge favour and cough, or scrape your foot along the floor, or make some little noise. It's important that we stay connected as humans at this basic level, when there is so much division and chaos in the world.'

My hearing is so acute that I can hear a bat belch at fifty paces. 'Agnes,' I said, 'was that you who just sighed?'

'No. Did you hear someone, Mags?'

'You bet your bippy. Hey, FBI person,' I said tersely, 'I know you think that you're just doing your job, but what you're doing is rude. Also, I thought you might want to know that two of your co-workers have complained about you having halitosis.'

'They have?' a soft female voice said.

'Mags, that was mean,' Agnes said.

Indeed it was. 'I'm sorry, Miss FBI, for lying and hurting your feelings, but take it from me, who's learned from experience, that a good mouthwash, used as directed daily, can be a gal's best friend.'

'Amen to that,' Agnes said.

'Thank you,' the soft voice said. 'I'll give you two some privacy now.'

'Wow,' Agnes said. 'That was interesting. Do you think she means it?'

'Who knows, but I'm innocent, so who cares? Anyway, Agnes, who is the biggest gossip in Hernia?'

'And that's important, why?'

'Just answer?'

'You know who it is: your new pastor's wife, Priscilla Utterall, a.k.a. Prissy.'

'Bingo. Listen, I need two favours from you. The first is to call Prissy – *tonight* – and I'm sure that she is still up, given that the convoy drove directly in front of her house. Anyway, tell her about Armageddonland, and how it's going to destroy our community, and that it's in the community's best interest if she calls everyone in the church membership book. Like tonight! Then she should call all the other pastors' wives in town and have them do the same. Oh, and everybody needs to know that tomorrow at dawn, out at the Bontrager place, on Skinny Branch Road, something very important is going to happen. Something that they'll all want to witness. And finally, I need—'

'Whoa! Hold your horses, Mags! Why can't *you* call Prissy Utterall? She's *your* pastor's wife, not *mine*! And what's this thing that she needs to witness? I want to see it too!'

'Agnes, I can't tell you what it is, but you're welcome to go out to the Bontragers' as well. Just be sure you're there by dawn. Now the other thing that I need is red spray paint. Do you still have some left over from when you tried to paint your front door last summer?'

'Of course. You know that project went nowhere when Hilda Heidlebaum accused me of being a member of the Communist Party of America and said that I was trying to solicit new members with a red door.'

I took a deep breath. 'Just in case you are still listening, FBI lady, my dear friend Agnes Miller is *not* a member of the Communist Party of America – or of any other country. Which is not to say that she isn't worthy of belonging to that organization, because she certainly is. Agnes is a founding member of Hernia's annual Billy Goat Gruff Festival and Parade, and twice served as vice president of the Hernia League of Ladies who Crochet Covers for Bibles.'

'For Overseas Orphans,' Agnes said. 'That's part of our name.'

'That's a bit unwieldy,' I said.

'But it's an important part of our mission,' Agnes said. 'Imagine the face of a little girl in Bangladesh who receives one of our delicate Bible covers with rosebuds in the corners, and the words "Holy Bible" formed by sprigs of lilac blossoms – crocheted, of course.'

'Will there be a Bible inside the cover?' I said.

'Magdalena,' Agnes said impatiently, 'baby steps. One can't do everything for the disadvantaged.'

'Agnes, I have to go now – as in right *now*. Please put those cans of red spray paint on your front porch. I'll be there to pick them up in fifteen minutes. No need to meet me at the door.'

'But Mags—'

'Bye, Agnes.'

FIVE

If you read your Holy Bible carefully, and prayerfully, as I do every morning, then I am confident that you will reach the same conclusion that I did: it is not a sin to speed. At least not on certain occasions. For instance, a twenty-five-mile-an-hour speed limit is definitely appropriate for day driving on county roads, given the frequency of horse-drawn buggies one might encounter. But at four in the morning the Amish are just waking up and will be spending the next two hours milking their cows and feeding their livestock. No Amish person would risk a valuable buggy horse by taking it out before dawn, unless it was absolutely necessary.

That said, it would have been a sin for me to poke along on an empty highway, feeling resentful because of the speed restriction. It's a fact that resentful feelings lead to sinful thoughts, so I did my level best to keep the Devil at bay by pressing my lead foot down as far as I dared. The fact that this made my tyres squeal several times, and left skid marks at the intersection of Gindlesperger Road and Hooley Lane, does not attest to my recklessness, but rather to the ability of my two guardian angels to protect me.

My early morning errand completed, I drove home a bit slower, but that was a mistake because I barely got home in time. My dear sweet Stud Muffin does not awaken quietly. I will spare you most of the details. Let's just say that I arrived at the first thunderclap, which gave me just two seconds to yank off my dress and dive under the covers.

When he was ready to get out of bed, my unsuspecting husband rolled over, and began to plant soft kisses on my forehead. Gabe is a virile man, whose beard grows noticeably in a twenty-four span, turning his face into a scouring pad. Instead of feeling aroused, I felt like I was being licked by a giant cat with a dry tongue. It was time to stop feigning sleep.

'Good morning, dear,' I said, between his facial assaults.

'Ah, there you are, sleepyhead,' Gabe said. 'Didn't want you to oversleep on the first day of your *cause du jour.*'

'But you never get up this early,' I said, 'and we got to bed so late last night.'

'Nonsense,' the Babester said. 'You love nothing better than a good fight, especially when you're on the side of right, which, of course, you always are. You just need a little help getting your engine started this morning, but I know just the remedy for that.'

I started to panic. 'But we did it last month!'

Gabe chuckled. 'Not that; the *other* thing.'

I put my brain on speed-dial, but all its circuits were either busy, or out of order. I hadn't a clue as to what Gabe's remedy could be. Unless it was eggs-over-easy, four slices of bacon, a rasher of cinnamon toast, and a pot of hot chocolate. Proceeded, of course, by a cup of strong coffee.

'Breakfast in bed?' I asked hopefully.

'That was last month too,' he said. 'After the *other* thing. No, what you need is to drive into town and have a proper visit with your cousin, Sam. That cavalcade of destruction drove right past his grocery store on its way through town. Eventually, there will probably be a huge supermarket built out there, close to Armageddonland, to service all the theme park employees. You know, in that new town they'll be building to house those employees – built on former Amish farmland, of course.

'But in the meantime, Yoder's Corner Market will be the closest food option for a lot of those guys and gals who will be living in makeshift housing. Sam is a wily businessman, who stands to rake in the money, and as such could be a loud and crafty supporter of Armageddonland.'

I threw off the covers. 'He wouldn't do such a thing! Sam is my double first cousin twice removed. Our people founded Hernia two centuries ago. It's in his blood!'

Gabe stared at me. 'What happened to your nightgown? And what's with wearing your sturdy Christian underwear to bed? Are you trying to send me a message? Do you want me to buy you another silk negligee, like the one I bought in Pittsburgh for our wedding night, but which you made me return? By the way, when I returned it, the saleslady found the little note that you'd pinned inside: *This garment is sinful*. She had a good laugh, but frankly, I was embarrassed.'

I could feel my cheeks burn. So much had happened since our wedding night that I really didn't have to wear long flannel nightgowns *all* the time. Maybe just for five minutes once a month. Anyway, had I been wearing a negligee when the convoy had driven past, I would not have been able to run out fast enough to witness its passing. However, if pretending to be enthusiastic about these disgusting scraps of cloth would satisfy Gabe's curiosity about my current mode of dress, I could play along. Contrary to what many people think, 'thou shalt not lie' is not one of the

Ten Commandments. Instead that oft misquoted verse commands us not to 'bear false witness against thy neighbour'. As in a court case.

'Surprise!' I shouted and threw the bedclothes off entirely. For those who've not tried it, be forewarned: even mere prevarication can tie up an invaluable number of brain waves. This explains why I forgot that I'd hastily jumped into bed still wearing my sensible black brogans.

Gabe stared harder. 'Now this is going to take me a minute to puzzle out. Hmm. If sturdy Christian underwear equals negligee in "Magdalena speech", then clodhopper shoes must have some corollary in the foot world. Let me see, you want to paint your toenails.'

I threw a pillow at the Babester. 'I'm not a harlot!'

Gabe laughed. 'Not every woman who paints her toenails is a harlot. Your sister paints hers.'

'You're quite right,' I said. 'Harlots get paid. Now guess again.'

'Uh, your feet were cold, and you thought shoes would do a better job than socks at keeping them warm.'

I shrugged. 'But maybe it means that I want you give me a foot rub.'

My dear husband laughed. 'Is that all, babe? Anytime. Just say the word.'

I clambered out of bed. 'I'll take you up on breakfast – but maybe in the kitchen this morning. And you might want to put *something* on first, in case the bacon grease splatters.'

'What about Little Jacob?' Gabriel asked, which just shows what a good father he is.

'Don't worry about him; Freni will spoil him with food, and she'll make sure that he catches the school bus. The Amish might not believe in education higher than the eighth grade, but our Freni is immensely proud that her adopted grandson is only ten, and already a freshman in high school.'

'As are we,' Gabe said. 'Our hearts are bursting with pride at the little genius we old farts have created, when it could have gone so wrong. You getting pregnant at age forty-nine. And me fifty-one.'

'But it didn't go wrong,' I said, 'so we should just focus on the positive – such as our relationship, and live every day with thanksgiving in our hearts.' Of course I knew that was much easier said than done, especially since 'Worry' is my middle name.

'Sounds like a plan,' Gabe said, and smiled. He had seldom looked as attractive as he did in that moment. I was sorely tempted to kick off my clodhoppers, undo the many clasps of my sturdy Christian underwear, and hop back into bed.

Despite the fact that I should have been camping out on Cousin Sam's doorstep, trying to get any information that I could on Armageddonland, Dr Gabriel Rosen and I had a lovely breakfast. True, he botched the eggs-over-easy, but he then managed to turn the disaster into quite tasty scrambled eggs, with extra sharp cheddar cheese melted inside. He certainly redeemed himself, and had he suggested the mattress mambo again, I might even have agreed to it. I say this despite the fact that by then it was daylight, and the Good Lord intends for us to endure the horizontal hootchie-cootchie, and the pillow-case polka, etc., only in the dark.

As I was running my long, crooked index finger around the inside rim of the toast plate, trying to pick up the fallen cinnamon and sugar sprinkles, the front doorbell rang. The PennDutch Inn has two primary doors: the formal front door, which guests use the first time when they register, and the kitchen door on the side, where family and friends show up. Sometimes the latter knock; sometimes they just walk in. There is also a third door, a private one, that opens from the master bedroom onto a small patio, but that's not relevant here. That particular morning we had no guests, which meant that the only person who might use the front door was the pastor's wife, Prissy.

'What excuse do you want me to give her?' Gallant Gabe said.

'None will be necessary, dear,' I said, and ran a long, crooked pinkie around my gums to dislodge any chunks of food larger than a small suitcase.

'So I'm not to answer the door?' my Sweet Patooty asked anxiously. 'Both cars are in the driveway. The sun is already up, and you know how she loves to gossip. Women of her ilk believe that a bed should not be used for *anything* past sunrise, least of all sleeping.'

'No, dear,' I said. 'I'm actually expecting her. I'll be waiting in the parlour.'

'Oh hon, you're up to something again,' he moaned, but the bell rang incessantly, so off he went.

The chairs in my parlour are uncomfortable by design. This is so that my guests will not laze around on their backsides, and hopefully perform more chores. At any rate, I barely had time to seat myself on the least torturous, straight-back chair when my pastor's wife burst into the room.

'The Devil has arrived in Hernia,' she practically shouted, as she waved her phone at me. 'Here, look at this.'

I gasped at what I saw. All the trucks we'd seen last night carrying the heavy equipment had been vandalized, including the one that had been stuck on the bridge. Not by men, it would seem, but by the Devil. The number 666 had been spray painted, in red, on every vehicle. Even some of the pieces of heavy equipment that the trucks had been carrying had been likewise vandalized with that auspicious number. That number, by the way, is extremely significant to conservative Christians who believe that the events in the Book of Revelation are real prophecy which will indeed come to pass. In the 'End Times' the number 666, also called The Mark of the Beast, will be stamped on the forehead of every man, woman, and child who are not true Christians, and who have followed the 'false prophet'. They are the ones doomed to spend eternity in a lake of fire and brimstone.

I grabbed Prissy's phone and showed it to Gabe. My Dearly Beloved frowned and sat next to me.

'I expected some pushback from the community,' he said. 'But not this soon, and not like this. You don't suppose these vandals are from that church across town with the super long name? You know, the one that handles rattlesnakes in their services?'

'I wouldn't rule anyone out,' I said, shaking my head.

'Harrumph,' Prissy said, and folded her arms across her chest.

'Harrumph?' I said delightedly. 'People actually say that in America?'

Prissy frowned. 'I was disagreeing with your assertion that the vandals could be anyone. No Amish or Mennonite would have done that. We are a law-abiding people.'

'There are exceptions to every rule,' my Jewish husband said.

'Here, here,' I said. 'Have a seat, Prissy, and tell us all about it.'

Prissy glanced around the sparsely furnished room. 'Well,' she said, 'I know not to sit on that rocking chair, even though it's the most comfortable seat in the room, because your dead granny still sits in it. Magdalena, you should know that there's no such thing as ghosts. That's not scriptural.'

'Harrumph,' I said. 'Granny prefers to be called an Apparition-American now.'

'And tell Prissy her slip is showing,' Granny hissed. For the record, only a few people are privileged to hear, or see, Granny.

'I will not,' I muttered.

'What?' Prissy said, as she plopped on an armchair that was stuffed with horsehair and ancient springs that threatened to erupt through the faded chintz fabric.

'The Prophet Samuel was a ghost,' I said. 'It's in the Bible.'

'Ha! You read it wrong; I should know, because I'm a minister's wife. In any case, I thought your granny had been exercised, and that an Indian ancestor had come to take her place.'

'Ah, that. She'd been ex*orc*ised, but it was only temporary. Granny didn't actually make it all the way to Heaven, because her hold on earth is too strong. As for the other ancestor, he'd been kidnapped by the Delaware Indians as a child and adopted by them.'

'This is all very fascinating, I'm sure,' Prissy said, 'but quite heathen in its content. Magdalena, you fail to live up to the spiritual standards of a deacon. I'm afraid that I'll have to report this conversation to the reverend.'

'Oh yes, please do,' I said.

Prissy scowled. 'Was that sarcasm?'

'*Au contraire*,' I said. 'I was giving you my blessing to vent. It isn't healthy to keep judgemental thoughts all bottled up inside.'

'Well, I never!'

'Just tell us about your adventure this morning,' Gabe said calmly – and wisely. 'Don't leave anything out. We already know about Aaron Miller and his plans to build Armageddonland, but how did they react when clergy and virtually half of the town showed up to protest?'

Although he hasn't maintained himself quite as well as Aaron Miller has, my Pookey Bear is still a handsome man. And maybe it's because he's a doctor, but when Gabe speaks, one can hear the authority in his voice.

Prissy grunted. 'Before I answer that question, where was the mayor? Huh, Magdalena?'

'The mayor already did her bit at two in the morning,' I said. 'The dear gal needed her rest.'

'Boogers,' Granny said. 'When I was your age I could butcher a pig, chop three cords of wood, plough a field with a mule, do the laundry by hand, and birth a baby all before noon.'

'Yeah, yeah,' I said.

'You're muttering again,' Prissy said to me. 'So anyway, about five hundred of us concerned citizens showed up at the crack of dawn. It turns out that we'd all been alerted to this so-called Armageddonland by an as-yet-unidentified woman. We represented all the churches in Hernia, except that we were almost evenly divided in our opposition to the construction of this sensationalistic, commercialistic mockery of the Book of Revelations.'

'There's no "s" on Revelation,' Granny hissed. 'As the preacher's wife, you should know that.'

I couldn't help but smile. Incidentally, I was the only one in the parlour who could hear her.

'What's the matter with you, Magdalena?' Prissy demanded. 'You look like you're constipated.'

'No, I'm fine,' I said. 'I just find it hard to believe that churches in Hernia would support this theme park. It's going to change our way of life forever. Our young people will be seduced into working for it, and who knows, someday soon, it could even mean a Walmart and a movie theatre where Kaufman's Feed Store stands today.'

Prissy blanched. 'My granddaughter dragged me to a movie that was supposed to be about Noah, but it wasn't anything like the story of Noah in the Bible. In the movie there were naked' – she glanced at Gabe – '*breasts*, and a naked you-know-what on a man.'

'You mean a turkey neck?' I said.

Prissy covered her face with her hands. 'You truly are a wicked woman, Magdalena,' she said.

'I'm a married woman,' I said, 'and my husband's a doctor, for crying out loud. Certain similarities cannot be denied. Now back to Skinny Branch Road. I'm guessing that it was the Lutherans and the Presbyterians who sided with us Mennonites, while on the other hand the Baptists and Methodists—'

'You got that right,' Prissy said.

'And the snake-handlers?' Gabe said.

Prissy pulled a man's white handkerchief out of the depths of her bosom. To be fair, she was modestly dressed, and showed no cleavage, but the Good Lord had somehow seen fit to allot Prissy my share of breast development. At any rate, after retrieving the cloth, she honked loudly into it several times. Gabe later remarked that somewhere nearby a lonely goose must have honked in reply.

Prissy sniffed. 'The snake-handlers are behind Armageddon all the way. "Bring it on," Reverend Splitfrock said. His members cheered.'

'It figures,' Gabe said.

Prissy stuffed the man's handkerchief back into her bosom and leaned forward. 'Magdalena, you may be a sinful woman, unworthy of being a deacon in our church any longer, but none-theless, the Lord has blessed you with a good mind.'

'Hear, hear,' my sweet husband said.

'And just like the Lord used King David, who was an adulterer, it has occurred to me that, despite your many faults, the Lord can use you to save Hernia from this intrusion on our way of life. You are, after all, the mayor, and our wealthiest citizen – and, uh, the village's benefactress. I am sure that Reverend Utterall will agree with me when I say that you have been "chosen".'

I hopped to my feet like I'd been shot out of a cannon. Given their enormous size, I never have to worry about stumbling forward.

'Get. This. Straight. Prissy,' I hissed like a bag full of snakes. 'I am *not* an adulteress. I didn't know that Aaron Miller was married. If you want my help to save Hernia, then you have to help me redeem my reputation. *Capiche?*'

'I don't speak French,' Prissy said.

'It's Italian,' Gabe said. 'It means: do you understand?'

Prissy crossed her arms and smiled. 'So that rumour is true too, huh?'

'What rumour?' I demanded. 'This *is* my natural hair colour. For the record I believe that dying one's hair is a form of lying. Women who believe that lying is a sin should not judge others while pretending that their hair is what God gave them, when it actually came out of a bottle.'

'What utter nonsense,' Prissy said. 'Anyway, I was referring to the rumour that you were involved with the mafia.'

Gabe and I gasped in unison.

'The mafia?' I said.

Prissy pursed her lips. 'How else can one explain your inordinate success in a business that is – well, so ordinary.'

'Her clientele are far from ordinary,' Gabe snapped. I'd rarely seen him so angry.

Out came the white handkerchief again. Although Prissy dabbed eyes, she may have been waving it as a flag of surrender.

'I really didn't mean to offend you, Magdalena,' she said. 'I was merely trying to ascertain how well connected you were. But with the Lord on our side, it doesn't really matter, does it?'

'It would seem that God has championed many dead people,' Gabe said quietly.

Prissy stood as well. 'Yes, Magdalena, I will do my best to polish your tarnished image in exchange for you leading the charge in this battle for the soul of Hernia. Capris?'

Gabe and I exchanged glances.

'You can bet that my wife will beat the pants off of them,' he said.

'No need to get vulgar with your sexual references, Mr Rosen,' Prissy said.

'I meant that she'll whip them soundly,' my Dearly Beloved said, sounding quite annoyed.

'Or refer to violence either,' Prissy said, wagging a plump pink finger in Gabe's direction.

'Oh, boogers,' Granny said. 'If I could get out of this chair, I'd grab this woman by one ear and drag her off to the woodshed for a proper thrashing.'

'Granny!'

'Don't start preaching to me, Magdalena. It's in the Bible, you know, about how sparing the rod spoils the child.'

'Yes, but Prissy is not a child. Yes, she's rude, and arrogant, and presumptive, but she has to be at least sixty.'

Prissy, who had not heard Granny's half of the conversation, was less than amused. '*What?* I'm thirty-five, Magdalena! OK, maybe I'm thirty-nine, but hardly a day over. I'm certainly *not* sixty.

'And it's you who has the reputation of being rude and arrogant, not me! I'm just a quiet, retiring preacher's wife.'

'She's as quiet as a cat in heat,' Granny said.

'Prissy, *dear*,' I said as calmly as I could, 'I will do my best as mayor to rally the community and organize those of us who still want to preserve our traditional way of life. As you know, I have excellent relations with our Amish brethren, and I was speaking to Bishop Yoder this morning. He's my second cousin. Bishop Garber is my second cousin once removed, and Bishop Blough is my third cousin thrice.'

Prissy appeared gobsmacked. Although my pastor and his wife are Old Order Mennonites like I am, they do not hail from Hernia, but from the State of Kansas. Perhaps they had their own tangled genealogies, perhaps not. I'd never bothered to discover if they had Amish roots.

'My grandparents were born Amish,' I said. 'My parents left the Amish and joined the Old Order Mennonite Church because my father wanted to buy a car to use in emergencies. He believed that the practice of riding in the cars of non-Amish, the so-called English, was hypocritical.'

'Hmm,' Prissy said. 'Weren't your parents shunned by the community for leaving the faith?'

'Yes, of course. At first. Even their own parents had to turn their backs when they passed by. But eventually both sets of parents, and eighteen of their adult siblings, eventually left and became Old Order Mennonites. They became the nucleus of our Beechy Grove Mennonite Church, although some became so liberal that they joined the General Conference Mennonite Church. That's what Agnes belongs to.'

Prissy shuddered. 'I'm sure that some of *those* Mennonites are good people, but since they don't wear modest clothing and prayer caps like we do, how is one to know that they're even Christians? Their women sometimes wear pants, for crying out loud.'

'Tch, tch,' I said, but I felt a brief surge of affection for her, knowing that we finally agreed on something.

'Well,' Prissy said, nodding her head sagely, 'this explains everything now. I can see why, despite your manifold failings, the church record shows that you have repeatedly been elected a deacon. I'm just surprised they haven't made you Pope.'

'Is that sarcasm?' Gabe said.

'Do Mennonites have popes now?' Granny said.

I grabbed one of Prissy's arms and steered her to the door. 'I'm so sorry you have to be running off now, dear. Drop by again, just as soon as water runs uphill.'

Prissy didn't resist me physically, but she did have a parting shot. 'Your beloved cousin Sam was at the building site.'

'Sam Yoder? The owner of Yoder's Corner Market?'

'Oh yes, and he was distributing coffee and pastries to the workforce. What do you think about that?'

'I'll think about it after I have a chance to talk to Sam myself,' I said. 'Not everything is as it first appears.'

'Harrumph,' Prissy Utterall said. 'I couldn't agree with you more.'

SIX

Sam Yoder and I are more than just double second cousins, twice removed: we were childhood friends. Ever since he was six yours old, Sam has flirted outrageously with me. And not that it's any of your business, Sam is the only man, besides my husband, my pseudo-husband, and my doctors, to have had an intimate connection to my lady parts. The reason for that is because Sam delivered my son, Little Jacob, on the floor of his grocery store, ten years ago. Rail-thin, Sam has been unhappily married to his six-hundred-pound Methodist wife Dorothy for thirty-five years, but neither of them is interested in a divorce.

When I walked into Yoder's Corner Market on Hernia's Main Street later that same morning, the one that the convoy of the trucks had passed through, the establishment was filled with little groups of Amish women, huddled together, and gossiping in their native Amish tongue. I knew most of these ladies by name, and of course they knew me – at least by reputation. I nodded at them, and in most cases they nodded back.

The store has expanded over the years, and Sam now has a proper office, one with a door, through which one has to be buzzed for admittance. While I admire his caution, nonetheless, it irritates me that I have to announce myself every time I arrive, as if I was your everyday Jane or Sally, and that he puts me through the third degree.

'Who is it?' he said that day, even though he could see me clearly through his cashier-style window.

'It's your conscience, Sam. Let me in, and we can review your latest missteps.'

'Ah, tis you, Magdalena, the one who got away. Enter, fair lady, before my heart bursts from my chest.' He buzzed open the door.

I scooted in. 'That would *not* be a sight for sore eyes, Sam, so try to keep yourself intact. I'm here to chase down a rumour, not to do a clean-up on aisle four – so to speak.'

Unlike some bald men, Sam is not handsome. His oversized head is knobby, and the lenses in his round, wire-framed glasses, distort the size of his eyes, making them appear much larger than they actually are. It's been said that Cousin Sam resembles some popular depictions of space aliens. That, of course, is downright silly, since aliens couldn't possibly exist because the Bible makes no mention of them. But come to think of it, the Bible doesn't mention kangaroos either, and what's more, it doesn't answer the question about how any of Australia's fauna managed to find their way on Noah's Ark, given that Australia is an island continent.

But back to Cousin Sam. He looked as tired as I felt. In fact, he looked worse. He looked like he'd been run over by one of the earth-moving vehicles, which then backed up, and ran over him again.

'I heard that you were in the catering business this morning,' I said.

'Yep,' he said. 'You want some coffee? I've got a fresh pot right here.'

'No, thank you. What I want is to know why you're aiding and abetting the destruction of our way of life here in Hernia. Sam, you were born here too. This is all you've ever known. Your store has a predominantly Amish clientele – I mean, the Good Lord knows that anyone with a car is going to choose to drive the twelve miles into Bedford and shop at a real grocery store. But the Amish rely on you for their staples and their dry goods.

'This tourist attraction is going to change all that. It's going to bring an enormous amount of development to the area: an increase in population, new housing – wait, that's what you're counting on, isn't it? You want to grow your business exponentially. You're not satisfied with being Yoder's Corner Market. You want to grow your business into a proper supermarket, and you want to do it before the chain stores move in.'

Sam smiled. 'Is that too much to ask? Surely you, Magdalena, innkeeper extraordinaire, would understand. Ever since my Dorothy went on that cable TV show, *Game of Bones*, and lost four-hundred-and-sixty-five pounds, the romance has gone out of our marriage.'

'Oh,' I said.

'Would you like me to explain?' Sam asked.

'No,' I said.

'And don't be jumping to conclusions, because it's not that I no longer find her attractive, now that she's a mere shadow of her former self – Dorothy still has that winning personality that I fell in love with.'

'Oh?' I said again. 'I reckon a wolverine with its tail caught in a trap would be sweeter than Dorothy.'

'Yeah,' Sam said. 'Isn't she a peach? That's why I married a Methodist, you know. I couldn't find a Mennonite woman with a firecracker personality like that, except for you, and you wouldn't have me. You have always been the love of my life, Magdalena.'

I sighed so hard that all the dust molecules in his office lifted and, thankfully, momentarily obscured his mournful face. Then I waited for the dust to settle before I strove to drive home my point.

'Samuel Nevins Yoder, I love you like a brother, but we will never, *ever*, be kissing cousins. What's more, I fail to see what any of this has to do with you wanting to upgrade your business, to go from owning a corner market to a fully fledged modern supermarket.'

Cousin Sam went over to the little interior window of his office and pulled down the shade. Then he locked the door.

'I need the money,' he whispered, 'to pay for Dorothy's surgeries.'

'*What* surgeries?'

Sam flapped his arms. 'Magdalena, when one loses that much weight – well, right now if my Dorothy were to jump off Lover's Leap on Stucky Ridge, the odds are that if she caught an updraft, she could soar like a condor.'

'I see,' I said, and I certainly did. Skin loses elasticity even on bean pole arms such as mine.

Of course, the safest, and simplest, solution for *most* women is to dress modestly in elbow-length sleeves, as the Good Lord intended us to do. When the Babester takes me to Pittsburgh restaurants in the summer, I've seen women in sleeveless tops who apparently have little regard for their fellow citizens. When they raise their arms, they would appear to have bags of white mice swinging from those appendages. It is enough to make me lose my appetite.

'So you understand,' Sam said.

'Yes, but I don't approve; it makes you a traitor to your community. You know that the Amish will be tempted to sell their land by the generous offers coming from Armageddonland people, but the community will be fractured, because there will be holdouts, and relocation for the takers will not be easy. As for the Hernia of your grandparents, and parents, and you growing up – that will disappear. Forever.'

Sam removed his glasses and rubbed his eyes with the balls of his hands. 'Life's a pile of road apples,' he said, using our colloquial term for horse manure. 'Why does nothing ever work out for me?'

I leaned forward and patted him on the knee. 'But is that a *true* statement? Your beloved Dorothy was the winner of *Game of Bones*, and not only did the two of you win a two-week trip to Manchester, England, but she lost all that weight. Now she can get out of bed.'

'But I preferred her fluffy,' Sam moaned. 'And now that she has her figure back – well, sort of – her eye has begun to wander. I'm afraid my zippy, straight-shooting, Methodist gal from Bedford is going to leave me.' He moaned again.

I patted his knee again. In fact, I allowed my long, shapely fingertips to rest gently on the tip of his bony knee.

'Sam, if the surgeries are successful, and she can shed her excess – uh, her gliding suit, then why do you want to enable her?'

'B-because if I don't help her, and she finds someone who does, then I've lost her for sure.'

I held a split-second board meeting with Me, Myself, and I. The vote was unanimous.

'Sam, dear,' I said, 'I will loan you the money for Dorothy's surgeries *if* you promise to have nothing to do with the Armageddonland people ever again. And that includes building a supermarket way out there to service their employees. And by the way, I will loan you the money to get started on a supermarket that is to be built right here in the village of Hernia. For *our* people. Plus, the loans will be interest free.'

'But you hate Dorothy!'

I gave his knee a playful, sisterly slap, and winked. Believe me, what I was about to say was all in jest.

'Now, now, hate is such a strong word. Abhor is more sophisticated, don't you think? I merely abhor Dorothy Lynne Yoder.'

How was I to know that the woman in question had her own key to Sam's office, and was standing right behind me? In any case, what I should have remembered is that Methodist women, unlike Old Order Mennonite women, are not averse to growing talon-like nails. In some cases they go so far as to attach artificial nails that resemble panther claws, and this was the case with Dorothy Yoder. For the record, when these claws are dug into the side of one's neck, squealing like a stuck pig is an appropriate response. Sticking pigs, however, is never appropriate.

'Magdalena Portulacca Yoder,' she roared over my squeals, 'you brazen hussy, you. I saw you stroking my husband's knee!'

I jumped to my feet in order to free myself of the daggers. Also, I think faster on my feet.

'That's right, Dorothy,' I said. 'I'm here to steal your husband. Sam has been the apple of my eye since kindergarten.'

'Really?' Sam said, sounding sadly way too hopeful.

'Truly,' I said to Dorothy. 'I have a potato at home that looks just like Sam's head. All the bumps are in the right places. Little Jacob made a pair of spectacles for it out of craft wire, and then took the potato head into school to use in his diorama of downtown Hernia. He got an A plus.'

'Ha,' Dorothy said, 'I don't believe that for a minute.'

'Fine with me,' I said. 'Anyway, I can't think of a finer man than Sam. Yoder's Corner Market is the nerve centre of Hernia, where folks gather whenever there's a crisis. It's where the Amish come from miles around to do their shopping. Even the non-Amish, the so-called "English" often shop here, rather than drive the twelve miles into Bedford. Also, Sam lends a sympathetic ear to everyone who walks into this store, and if asked, he offers wise counsel.'

'I do?' Sam said.

'Quiet,' I said. 'Your husband,' I continued, wagging a finger at Dorothy, 'is the bulwark of the community, he is the glue that holds us together, he is beloved by all. Men want to be him, and women just plain want him. No doubt even some of the Amish women ogle him from beneath the brims of their bonnets.'

'They do?' Sam said, sounding a mite alarmed.

'Shh,' I said. My wagging finger began jabbing at the air. 'So you, Dorothy Lynne Yoder, need to get your ducks in a row and make up your mind. Are you going to rein in your roving eyes, and keep them permanently trained on the scrawny, little, knob-headed, dare I say pot-bellied, bird you have in your hand, because he's the genuine article, or are you going to cast about for a complete unknown, who may well cast you aside when the going gets tough. You already know that Sam loves you, whatever size you are.'

Dorothy cocked her head. 'Sam,' she said, 'do you love this sleazy slattern?'

'Sleazy slattern?' I hissed.

Sam raised his hands defensively. 'Yes, but in a sisterly way. It's you, Sugar Lips, that I adore, with my heart, soul, and body.'

'And with all your earthly possessions,' Dorothy said. 'Right?'

'Of course, Sugar Lips.'

'In that case, I promise to keep my sugar lips inside our bedroom door and give you all the sugar my Sweet'ums can take.'

'I think I'm going to puke,' I said.

'Then use your pocketbook,' Dorothy said. 'I can't believe that a millionaire like yourself would get her purse at a department store. You should buy a brand name handbag at an exclusive boutique where celebrities shop.'

I held aloft my dilapidated, zipped, faux leather pouch in which I carry some essentials. 'My, my,' I said, 'that was three terms you used for this sack. But whatever you call it, I don't feel the need to make a statement with it, nor does it need to be so large that I can smuggle Sam out of his office in it.'

'Good one,' Sam said. 'But could we try it just once?' A look from Sugar Lips put the kibosh on his suggestion. 'Well, now that we've agreed to stop Armageddonland, how do we make it happen?'

'That's one of the reasons that I'm here,' I said. 'You see, since they already have the zoning approval to build on the old Bontrager farm, we can't actually stop them. But they're going to need more land than that to create the space Aaron mentioned. The parking area alone will require more than the Bontrager farm. This means that they will have to expand north of Skinny Branch Road, up towards the turnpike.

'So, what we need to do is meet with the area Amish bishop and convince him of the dangers that Armageddonland poses.'

'That should be an easy sell,' Sam said.

'Right, and then we ask him to tell his member families not to sell their land to these outsiders. Sam, we both know Bishop Amos Hooley, but I think that he would be more comfortable hearing this from you – I mean, since you're a man.'

He nodded. 'Does this mean that you won't even come with me?'

'I think that it's better that I don't,' I said. 'But I suggest that you take Toy with you.' Police Chief Toy Graham was an Episcopalian, who originally hailed from Charlotte, North Carolina.

Dorothy fluffed her hair as she pushed out her chest. 'Maybe the bishop only thinks he's uncomfortable with outside women, because he hasn't met a *real* woman. Unlike someone in this room, I have had experience being on a nationally televised game show. And unlike someone in this room I have a well-modulated voice, with no discernible accent. Plus, the camera operators, and the make-up people, were all constantly remarking on how symmetrical my face is.'

'That's nice, dear,' I said kindly, 'but if you dress like a hootchie-cootchie mama, you'll scare the bishop's horses and cause an old man to faint. Do you fancy giving mouth-to-mouth to a bearded Amish bishop?'

'Good point,' Sam said softly.

'Where does a Mennonite woman even learn the term "hootchie-cootchie"?' Dorothy said.

'From my guests, dear,' I said, 'most of whom are quite worldly, like you.'

'You'd be surprised what Cousin Magdalena has learned from them over the years,' Sam said. It didn't take an overactive imagination, such as mine, to hear the pride in his voice.

'Give me a break,' Dorothy said. At least she no longer had her claws dug in my neck.

'Sam, the Amish shop here at your store, and you, being as personable as you are, you know most of the patriarchs. Don't you?'

'Well, at least to exchange a few words,' he said.

'That's good enough. Here's a list of their addresses, which I keep by the way, in my community relations file. Since they don't have phones, please drive out ASAP and talk to Bishop Hooley, and then drop in on some of these men.'

'*Now?*'

'Yes. Even as we speak, the theme park folks could already be making their pitch to some cash-strapped farmers.'

'What will I do when he's gone?' Dorothy whined. For the record, the woman normally spends her days in their private quarters above the store watching television, while Sam minds the store. Not once, to my knowledge, had she ever expressed separation anxiety.

'Dorothy,' I said, 'are you a good actress?'

'Don't be daft, Magdalena. Of course I am. Those reality shows are about as real as your dreams. We were handed scripts

the day before each shoot that told us where, and how much, to
emote. I know that your kind of Mennonite probably doesn't
watch much TV, but people are saying that I might win an
Emmy Award for the most convincing crying – like in ages, or
something.'

'Awesome,' I said. 'I could care less.'

'You mean, that you *couldn't* care less, right?' she said.

'Whatever. Now, here's what you do: scrub your face, and put
on a skirt, and a long-sleeved blouse or sweater. Button it to the
neck. Then go down and work the cash register while Sam's
away. See how many customers you can fool into thinking that
he's finally hired a sensible Mennonite woman from – say,
Summersville, or Bedford. Make a game of it. See how good an
actress you are when there's no script. Afterwards, if you sent
the footage from the security camera to a Hollywood agent, well,
who knows, you might even get an audition.'

To say that Dorothy Lynne Yoder was excited is a bit of an
understatement. She hugged me so hard that she nearly broke
my thorax. While holding me thus she jumped up and down,
then she twirled me in circles, and finally she slung me between
her bare legs in what was surely some heathen Methodist dance
move. The entire time she was laughing hysterically.

By the time she released me, I felt like she'd had her way
with me. It was all I could do to stand and look either Dorothy,
or Sam, in the eye.

'Oh Magdalena,' Dorothy wheezed, 'that's a fabulous idea. I
don't know why my Sugar Lips never thought of that.'

Sam shrugged. 'How was I to know?' Then he clapped his
hands. 'OK, ladies, let's get this show on the road.'

SEVEN

When I hired Chief Toy Graham, he wasn't even dry
behind the ears. He was a pretty boy with a delightful
Southern accent and impeccable manners. He has
since matured into an incredibly handsome man, but sadly, both

his accent and his courtly manners have become – how should I put this? Now one would almost think that Toy was born *north* of the Mason-Dixon Line. It is only when he gets truly excited, that one hears the melodious tones of his native North Carolina.

In the old days, Toy would have rushed around his desk and pulled out the chair for me. Then he would have made a big show of trying to scoot me back in, even though I haven't mastered the art of lifting my behind and allowing the gentleman this honour. Women of my heritage, where the man is to rule over his wife, as per Genesis 3:16, were never shown this courtesy. Ergo, I would immediately plop my patooty down, which forced poor Toy to shove my chair back into place with me in it. I didn't behave this way to be rude; I just didn't know what was expected of me. Eventually this ruined both the chair and the floor. Come to think of it, perhaps this is why he abandoned the practice.

Many men that I know don't even stand when a woman enters a room, unless she's carrying a platter of food intended for a buffet table at a church supper. Then it's only to be the first in line. Just after he signed his second contract with us, Toy stopped jumping to his feet every time I entered the room. It was around the same time that he began calling me by my given name, instead of 'ma'am'.

Today I found him pacing. 'Dang it, Magdalena,' he said, which is perilously close to swearing, if you ask me, 'I didn't get a wink of sleep last night, thanks to that ex-husband of yours.'

'Tell me about it, dear,' I said, in the dulcet tones for which I am so well known.

'Yeah, well, as a private citizen, at least you can turn your phone off. Calls of complaint about the noise kept coming into the station all night long. They only now just stopped.'

'Give thanks for small blessings, dear. That's what I always say.'

'Let me know when that happens,' he said. 'Magdalena, are you going to let me vent, or not?'

'Vent Vesuvius, erupt if you must!'

'I must,' he said. 'When that last truck got stuck, unable to make the turn onto the bridge, the others parked their rigs in the middle of Main Street, and stayed there, with their engines running, until the stuck vehicle got turned around.'

I growled in exasperation. 'I told Aaron distinctly to wait until morning to deal with that truck!'

'Yeah, well when I issued that fool, Aaron Miller, and his crew, tickets, you wouldn't believe the guff he gave me.'

Uh-oh. Toy had just said the biggest 'F' word of them all. There are three of them, you know: *flatulence*, *fornication*, and *fool*. In Matthew 5:22, Jesus said that calling someone a 'fool' put one in danger of hell fire. Just because Toy was an adult, and a long-lapsed Episcopalian who did not read his Bible on a daily basis, was not enough reason to give him a pass.

'Tut, tut,' I said. 'Although I must say that it's a bit ironic, don't you think?'

'What is?' Toy said.

'Only the fact that the folks who caused you to have a sleepless night are bringing a facsimile of Hell to Hernia, and you just used a word that the Good Lord stated, in the Gospel of Matthew, might well gain you admittance to the genuine article.'

'I said *what*?'

'Don't expect me to repeat it, dear. It's a one-way trip to that destination, and if I had to choose, I'd take extreme cold over extreme heat. Theoretically, one can always pile on more down comforters, and put more logs on the fire to stay worm. But as for fighting extreme heat? After one's air-conditioning has broken down, and one has stripped nude, and is lying in an icy mountain brook, then that's it.'

Toy laughed heartily. 'I see that you've thought about this a lot.'

'We don't keep magazines in the bathroom anymore.'

He laughed again. 'But as you know all too well, I don't believe in Hell.'

I sighed. 'Then as much as I'm against Aaron Miller and company building Armageddonland in our county, if it does get built, then I advise you to visit what will undoubtedly be their number one attraction: that eternal lake of fire. You might rethink things then.'

'Doubt it,' Toy said. 'So tell me, what is your plan to stop them? I know that you didn't drive into town after a bad night's sleep just to convert me?'

'As much as I hate to admit it, I had another agenda. We need to organize in order to keep Armageddonland contained – at the very least. I've already spoken to Sam. He's on his way now to speak with Bishop Hooley and some of the elders in the Amish community. The plan is to convince them not to sell any of their farms to Armageddonland. I'd like you to ride along with Sam.'

As I spoke to Toy, his demeanour changed to one of solemnity, perhaps even melancholy. Although Toy was an outsider, an *Englisher*, he'd quickly established a good rapport with the Amish community. This was despite the fact that the Amish are trad- itionally loathe to turn to law enforcement to handle any crimes, short of murder. They prefer that every other law infraction be arbitrated, or adjudicated, by church elders. But the Amish are sinners, just like the rest of us (Romans 3:23), and they are capable of violence and sexual predation. Because he had a good relationship with the people he served, Toy had twice been alerted to incidences of spousal abuse in the Amish community. Once even a preacher turned himself in to Toy for having abused all six of his daughters.

Then one beautiful April afternoon last year, the Amish of Hernia literally turned their backs on Toy. It was the day that he married Steven Lantz, a former Old Order Mennonite. Their marriage came as a shock to everyone in Hernia, including me. I like to think that I am no longer a naive woman, thanks to the variety of guests who have paraded through my inn, but I didn't even know that Toy was gay. All these years when he said that he was a 'confirmed bachelor', I took him at his word. In fact, and I divulge this shamefully, at times my loins have even quivered when his hand accidentally brushed against mine.

Anyway, six of our nine village council members had imme- diately demanded that I fire Toy Graham. 'But on what grounds?' I'd asked. Gay marriage is legal, even here, and Toy's employ- ment record is exemplary. I had absolutely no grounds to dismiss him. Janice Kurtz, whose capacity for judgment even exceeds mine, brought up the idea of using the morals clause in Toy's contract with the village.

'Homosexuality is a sin,' she'd hissed, and then quoted two verses from the Holy Bible to prove her point.

'What did Jesus have to say about it?' I'd asked. No one had answered, which meant that either they hadn't read their Bibles, or that they were Janice supporters. Since Toy was the best police chief that Hernia had ever been honoured to have, it was time to put a stop to this insurrection.

'Jesus never even mentioned gay people,' I'd said.

'Maybe that's because there weren't any gay people back then,' Doreen Detweiler had said. She and Janice, both Methodists, were best friends and backyard neighbours. And Doreen, by the way, was on her third marriage, which is a record for Hernia.

'You may be right, dear,' I'd said patiently. 'I'll have my husband look into it and see if the Chinese had invented the Gay Virus already by that time. Now moving right along,' I'd told the council, 'Chief Toy Graham is keeping his job. That's final. And how do I know that it's final? Would anyone like to answer that question?'

More silence.

'Anyone? Anyone at all? How about you, Janice, dear?'

'Oh Magdalena, stop showing off,' Peter Livingood had said. 'We all know that you're Mrs Moneybags and that you pay his salary. You don't need to rub it in.'

I'd smiled benevolently at my team. 'In that case, all's well that ends well. Have a blessed summer!'

Except for myself, Janice Kurtz was the last person to leave the high school library, where we'd held the meeting. When she reached the door, Janice had turned and jabbed the air with a stubby forefinger.

'You'll pay for this,' she'd said. 'We'll never accept this.'

Accept it? I was never thinking about accepting his marriage to another man; I was only thinking about keeping Toy on as our chief of police, for crying out loud. The fact that the man is gay should have no bearing on how well he does his job, but marriage is for procreation. Unless it involves a heterosexual couple past child-bearing age, because that too is OK. And no one would deny an infertile heterosexual couple of any age to tie the knot. But two people of the *same* gender, solely because they love each other, and want to care for each other for the rest of their lives? I'm not sure that's a convincing argument. I mean, just because it's legal doesn't make it Biblical.

Chief Toy was well aware of the mood around the village. When I stood across his desk from him the morning after the truck invasion, he looked more like a boy who had just received a whipping than an officer of the law. It was clear that my request to go with Sam to talk to the bishop reminded him of how much he had been rejected by those with whom he had previously developed a good relationship. My head understood why the community had a problem with his marriage. But my heart wanted me to throw my gangly arms around him, and give him a sisterly hug.

'Magdalena,' Toy said, perhaps sensing my distress at his despondence. 'I know that you have got to be conflicted right now. You interpret the Bible literally, so therefore you have to believe that I have entered into a forbidden relationship. That in fact, as a gay man, my lifestyle is sinful. But I can tell by your cow-like expression that you are contemplating giving me a hug, with those long, gangly arms of yours. Am I right?'

'Why I never!' I said, and stomped a hoof. 'Cow-like indeed. Cows are passive, and my face is always anything but. And whoever even thinks of the word "gangly" these days? Do you subscribe to a magazine that specializes in the use of arcane words?'

Toy smiled. 'But you did want to give me a motherly hug, didn't you?'

I stomped my other foot. '*Motherly?* I'm not that much older than you. *Sisterly*, maybe. And yes, I thought that maybe you could use a quick bosom bump to boost your morale. I still think that you're the best man for the job, Toy, and you don't have to worry about the Village Council. They'll do what I say, as long as I pay your salary. But have you thought about the two of you – uh – hmm – sort of downplaying your relationship a little? I mean, just until the community can adjust.'

Toy's perfect features hardened. Practically literally – but not, of course, since 'literally' is currently the most misused word in the English language. But his face did look to me like it had been cast out of a high quality resin.

'Just what do you mean by *downplaying*?' he asked, his lips hardly moving.

'Well, we require our officers to live locally, so naturally you'd need to stay here. However, since Steven Lantz's law practice is in Bedford, there is no reason that he couldn't relocate, and then you could visit him at his new house or apartment on weekends.'

Toy's eyes narrowed. 'Let's flip this around,' he said. 'Steve and I are legally married, as are you and Gabriel. How would you feel if I suggested that Gabe move to Pittsburgh, and that you visit him on weekends? After all, there is a sizable Jewish community there, and he is a fish out of water here, being one of a kind. From what I heard, no one in the community approved of your marriage, and in fact, they still don't.

'Face it, Magdalena, according to the scriptures that you are so fond of quoting, your husband is going to spend eternity in Hell. Yeah, that's right, boss, even a lapsed Episcopalian like me, can pick up a few useful titbits now and then. Like what it says in John 14:6, about nobody reaching God, who *art* in Heaven, unless they go through Jesus. You and Gabe will definitely be spending your afterlives apart.'

I had no comeback. He was right. I'd made the choice to love someone who might never choose to be 'saved', and would always be an outsider even if he was married to a woman whose ancestors founded Hernia. Toy, on the other hand, was an outsider, who had married a local, but whose lifestyle was the antithesis of our community standards. On the other hand, both Toy and Steven claimed that they had been born gay, and who was I to argue?

What I didn't want to do was cry in front of him. Magdalena Portulacca Yoder has not allowed herself to cry since she was six years old, and Mama caught her licking the outside of the honey jar. Little Maggie got such a whipping that the bruises on her thighs turned not only black and blue, but yellow and purple as well. No siree, when I felt the first tear roll down my cheek, I hightailed it out of Chief Toy's office and out onto the street.

Outside in the sunshine, I began to gather my thoughts. That is to say, I would put a lid on my emotions, grow a stiff upper lip (oh, to be English!), and drive the three blocks to my best friend Agnes's house. There the two of us would fine tune my plans to hold back the assault on our way of life from the Armageddon folks, and maybe even exchange a few words about Toy (over whom Agnes also had a 'boy-Toy' crush, as she brazenly put it). Agnes and I have known each other since we were babies in diapers, and as long as we're not arguing, she always makes me feel better.

Alas, I never made it to Agnes's that morning. Before I even got to my car, I received a text from Gabe telling me that I was: NEEDED URGENTLY BACK HOME. So, I pressed the pedal to the metal and made it back in record time, which meant I broke the speed limit. And that's a sin, by the way. Therefore I shouldn't have been surprised to find trouble waiting for me at home.

EIGHT

It's been said that I have a fertile imagination. I disagree. Nevertheless, as I covered those four miles at breakneck speed, I envisioned my dear Freni dying; our home disappearing into a sinkhole; a gas explosion leaving our house but a pile of kindling wood; the Babester falling down our impossibly steep stairs, and fracturing a hip; and our sheep in the meadow, and our cows in the corn, even though we don't have any sheep.

But when I pulled into our long gravel drive and caught a glimpse of the small blue car with the vanity license plate that read HERNIA on it, that's when I really began to panic. That car belonged to our twenty-two-year-old daughter Alison. She was supposed to be pursuing her studies at the University of Pittsburgh School of Medicine. This could only mean that she'd been expelled from the school; that she had gotten pregnant, probably with twins; had been diagnosed with a terminal disease, and come home to draw her last breath in the loving arms of her parents; or, worst of all, had gotten married without telling us, and cheated me out of being mother of the bride.

I said a quick prayer, and ran, possibly even shrieking as I went, in through the back door. There I found Freni, Gabe and Alison, sitting around the kitchen table. Their expressions were expectant; not sorrowful.

'Ach, Magdalena,' Freni said, 'hurry up is one thing, but to squeal the tires, that is too much, yah?'

'Someone stole my wings,' I said.

Freni shook her head, which took quite an effort, given that she has virtually no neck. 'Always with the riddles, this one.'

'What's going on?' I demanded. By then I'd already enveloped Alison in my long, gangly arms. If she was contagious, I was bound to get whatever it was that she had – except for pregnancy. Even naive Mennonite women seldom get pregnant via limb-to-limb foetus transfer.

Gabe cleared his throat. 'This is my doing, hon. Last night, after you fell asleep, I took the liberty of calling our daughter and asking if she could come out this morning for an emergency family meeting.'

I frowned. 'But *why*? What can she do about Armageddonland?'

'Armageddonland?' Alison said. 'I don't get the joke?'

'It's no joke,' Gabe said. 'Your birth father is building the world's largest amusement park based on the Book of Revelation. True believers will be able to take gondola rides over Hell, to get their kicks watching people like me writhing in eternal agony.'

'Yah?' Freni said. 'Then maybe you should convert.'

Gabe patted Freni's arm affectionately, even as he rolled his eyes. 'There is no mention of Hell in my Bible. It was the Greeks who introduced both the concepts of Heaven and Hell following Alexander the Great's conquering of Judea.'

'Ha,' I said. 'There's no mention of Alexander the Great in *my* Bible!'

'Wait a minute,' Alison said, 'is this for real?'

'Yah,' Freni said, 'as real as the nose on your mama's face.'

'No way!' Alison said, and then seeing how serious the rest of us were, she laughed hysterically.

I gave her a good two minutes, by my watch, to settle down, and then I tapped my foot rapidly against our hardwood kitchen floor. The girl didn't even notice me, as she was too busy rocking back and forth, clutching her stomach while howling like a coon dog that'd caught the scent of game. So then I clapped loudly as close to her face as I dared.

'Alison! This isn't funny. The theme park that he's building will be larger than Disneyworld. Millions of people will visit it. He's inherited Bob and Mable Bontragers' place. Even if we manage to keep it limited to the northern side of Skinny Branch Road, the impact will be felt here. Our infrastructure will be negatively impacted, and our landscape will be ruined by this eyesore. Also our young people will be lured away by minimum-paying jobs that this theme park needs in order to operate, so they will not be joining their fathers and mothers in the time-honoured, and God-sanctioned, business of farming.'

Alison wiped the tears from her eyes and sighed dramatically. She might have been twenty-two and in medical school, but she was still a girl.

'So, Mother, what do you want me to do about this theme park – which I still find funny as all heck. What are they going to have? A ride called Hell?'

'Yes,' Gabe said.

'Ach!' Freni said, and wrung her stubby hands.

'Wow!' Alison said. 'It doesn't surprise me that someone eventually thought up such a weird idea, but to put it so close to a quiet little village, it's almost like they have it in for us. I mean, for *yinz*.' 'Yinz' by the way, is the plural of 'you' in Pittsburgh.

Yinz, shminz, the idea of retaliation had not occurred to me. Yes, I had discovered that Aaron was a bigamist, and I was the one who'd revealed that fact to the community, and to the registrar's office where we'd gotten our marriage certificate eleven months earlier. Later, I also testified in court against him. But the fact that Aaron then sold his farm, and left Hernia with his tail tucked between his well-muscled legs, that was on him. Wasn't it? So then, why on earth would it even pop into his devilishly handsome head that I should be punished?

I nodded as I thought through what Alison had said. 'He always could hold a grudge,' I finally agreed. 'He probably still blames me for letting him seduce me, a *virgin*, and then turning against him when I discovered that he had another wife. He came very close to hitting me on several occasions.'

'Yah,' Freni said. 'That man had a temper.'

'We used to play together as children,' I said. 'When I was five, and he was eight, I accidently let go of a string attached to one of his toy boats over in Miller's Pond. Kids had a lot more freedom back then. Anyway, he waited an entire year – an eight-year-old waiting a year, if you can imagine – and then he threw my new birthday dolly, in her satin dress, as far as he could into the water.'

Alison squirmed. 'OK,' she said. 'You don't have to convince me about how awful he is. But I hope you know that has nothing to do with me.'

Despite five hundred years of inbreeding that bred out the 'hugging' gene, I grabbed Alison and pressed her to me. 'Oh, daughter of mine,' I said, 'of course you are entirely unconnected with anything your father did to me. Just so you know, I don't believe that there are any such things as "good" or "bad" genes. And by the way, your Miller grandparents were two of the sweetest, kindest people ever to walk this earth.'

'Thanks, Mom,' Alison said.

'Well, it's the truth,' I said. 'Anyway, there's something else that we need to tell you.' I looked at Gabe. 'Do you want to tell her, or should I?'

'Don't do this,' Alison said. 'I've always hated it when the two of you hem and haw. Just come out with it, whatever it is.'

'You have a biological brother,' I said. 'His name is Rodney, and he's here. Well, not in Hernia, exactly, but out at the building site.'

Much to my surprise, Alison's face lit up. 'No way! A baby brother. I've always wanted a baby brother – oh, don't get me wrong, Mom and Dad, I already have one. Little Jacob *is* my brother, but if my dad – I mean, my ex-dad, remarried, and had a kid, well, there's a chance the baby might look a little like me when he grows up.' She laughed. 'Who knows, he could even be a kidney donor if I need one.'

'Sweetheart,' Gabe said tenderly, 'this is no baby. He was driving a big rig past our house last night.'

Alison recoiled. '*What?*'

'He's fourteen,' I said. 'At least he will be fourteen next week.'

She shrugged. 'So the man who *was* my father cheated on the woman who threw me out. But this boy is still my half-brother, and I still get a kidney out of this revelation.' She laughed sardonically. '*Revelation*. Get it?'

Neither Gabe nor I said anything. After a long silence Alison spoke up.

'*What?* What aren't you two, the most uncensored parents in the world, not telling me? Spit it out, before I explode!'

'Yah,' Freni said. 'Spit. Maybe I explode too. Then who will clean up the mess?'

'Alison, sweetheart,' Gabe said, as he put his arms around our daughter, 'Aaron Miller did not cheat on his wife. Rodney Miller is not your half-brother; he's your full sibling.'

Alison's eyes narrowed. 'But that would mean that she was pregnant with this boy when they threw me away at age nine. I was in foster care for three years before you rescued me. I bet she'd had an ultrasound that showed she was having a boy, and that's why they decided to clear the nest of the girl that they never wanted. Oh, right now I hate that man so much that I could kill him!'

If steam really could come out of someone's ears, I could have cleaned my reading glasses by holding them next to her head. I was tempted to tell her something about hate being an unhealthy emotion, but now was not the time. Besides, who was I to lecture anyone on their emotional health?

'I understand how you feel,' I said instead. 'When I found that your birth father was married to your birth mother, I hated him too. You wouldn't believe the thoughts that went through my head.'

'I could,' Gabe said.

'Yah, me too,' Freni said.

I gave them both the stink eye, in a kindly, Mennonite way, of course. 'It was early September, just like it is now, and the poison ivy back along the woods was in full growth. I put on rubber gloves, cut a large bunch of that noxious weed, and rubbed them in your birth-father's underwear. Every single pair.'

'Ouch,' Gabe said.

'And?' Alison said.

'He was a slow-learner. It took him five days to figure out he'd been sabotaged. In the meantime he'd invented the Itchin' n' Hitchin' Britches Dance.'

Alison laughed heartily, and to my surprise, Freni joined her. When I was growing up, Freni had often lectured me on the spiritual damage that results from taking revenge on one's enemies. Either time had mellowed her, or knowledge of Aaron's son had tipped the scale a little bit in my favour.

'Mags,' Gabe said loud enough to make the ladies stop laughing, 'now that I know what you're capable of, you can't be pulling that trick off again.'

I shrugged. 'Maybe I will, and maybe I won't. That all depends on you, doesn't it, dear?'

'Go Mom,' Alison said, as she dissolved into peals of laughter.

'Then two can play that game,' my Dearly Beloved said. 'I can just as easily get hold of poison ivy and rub it in your sturdy Christian underwear.'

'Ach!' Freni squawked. 'Such talk is of the Devil.'

'Moving right along,' I said, 'do you think that you'd like to meet him?'

Alison flinched. 'Who? This Rheumy kid?'

'Yes, him. And his name is Rodney, dear.'

She gasped softly. 'You're serious, aren't you?'

'Serious as a heart attack.'

'What's he like?' Alison said.

'Well, for starters,' I said, 'he sort of looks like you, and—'

'In a boy sort of way,' Gabe chimed in quickly.

I frowned at Gabe for cutting me off. 'But in short I would describe him as a spunky little kid who's being bullied by his father to do things that are really beyond his ability to grasp.'

Alison smiled. 'I like the spunky part.'

'Yah,' Freni said proudly. 'That is you. Spunky like a young mule.'

'Thank you, Grandma Freni,' she said. Of course eighty-year-old Freni wasn't her real grandmother, just a distant cousin of sorts. However, after Freni's grandchildren moved to far off Iowa with their too-tall mother and their hen-pecked father, both my children adopted the bereft old woman as their honorary grand-mother. It was an arrangement that benefitted them all.

'I can ride out to Skinny Branch with you to meet your new brother, if you'd like,' Gabe said.

'Thanks, Dad, but no thanks,' Alison said. 'This is something I need to do by myself.'

'Can I at least give his father a call to let him know you're coming?' I asked. 'I have his number on my phone.'

'You *do*?' Gabe said.

'Well *maybe* I do,' I said. 'He might have changed it years ago.'

My Pookey Bear glared at me. 'My question is: why didn't you delete this number after you found out that you'd been played by a bigamist?'

'I was busy!' That was certainly not a lie, not if taken at face value. I'm always busy; I organize our closets in my sleep. I'd organize our neighbours' closets as well, if they'd let me back in their houses.

'Dad, Mom, quit fighting,' Alison said. 'Dad, I'm sure there's nothing for you to be jealous of. I bet he's gained a ton of weight, and his head looks like a peeled hard-boiled egg.'

'He certainly has a yolk for a brain,' said the love of my life.

Since it is my aim here to be utterly honest, I must confess that I was a mite irritated by the above statement. Perhaps if I'd kept a cooler head I might have steered a more pragmatic course in the weeks and months ahead, and been able to keep my past, and my community's future, from becoming so dangerously entangled.

NINE

I was biting into a warm cinnamon bun slathered with cream cheese icing when I heard someone climbing up the back steps to the kitchen door. I could tell by the footsteps that it was my best friend Agnes. I crammed as much of the pastry as I could into my mouth, and then placed the plate, which contained seven more buns, on the seat of the chair beside me. I then shoved that chair up against the table as far as it would go. The Good Lord willing, Agnes would have a cold, and not be able to smell the delightful scent of warm yeast dough and cinnamon wafting out from beneath the table's edge.

The dear woman is a 'yoo-hoo friend', meaning that she need not knock or ring the bell to enter. She is only one of three people who enjoy this special privilege. Sam and Toy are the other two.

'Yoo-hoo,' Agnes trilled, slamming the screen door behind her, and then stopped dead in her tracks. 'Fee-fi-fo-fum, I smell the scent of cinnamon buns.'

I turned to the side, so she wouldn't see me desperately trying to chew a wad of bun that might well have choked me. It wasn't that I didn't want to share with Agnes, but she had been nagging me for weeks to help her resist temptation in regard to unnecessary calories. Besides, those buns were really meant for Little Jacob when he got home from school.

'Magdalena, look at me!' Agnes said.

I turned.

'Now say something,' she ordered.

'Tum-ting,' I said.

'Aha,' Agnes said triumphantly. 'You've got a cinnamon bun crammed into your mouth, haven't you?'

I nodded sheepishly. But before I could defend my seemingly rude behaviour, my best buddy grabbed the chair next to me and plopped her patooty down on it, landing squarely atop the plate of fresh, warm cinnamon buns. A normal person might have reacted by leaping to their feet and expressing irritation over their soiled garment, but Agnes didn't even seem to notice.

'Hurry up and swallow, Mags. I have something to tell you.'

I masticated madly, and with great relief, but as I did so, I noted with some alarm that Agnes was painted up like a Presbyterian. Or maybe a Methodist. No real Mennonite would be caught dead, or alive, painted up like a circus clown. I swallowed several times: first to get the roll down, and second to minimize the number of harsh words in my critique of my bestie's attempt at applying make-up.

'Agnes, dear,' I said, 'you look like a trollop.'

'Why Magdalena, how rude of you.'

'No, I'm just stating a fact. You look like a strumpet, in need of a trumpet, and possibly a crumpet, what with that iridescent gold eyeshadow, bright red rouge, and hideous orange lipstick. Are you headed to a ladies of the night convention?'

'No, bestie,' Agnes said, without missing a beat, 'because if I were, you'd be coming with me, so you wouldn't have to ask.'

'Touché, dear,' I said. 'What's the occasion then?' I gasped softly. 'It's *them*, isn't it?'

Agnes paled, which only made her rouge more obvious. 'Them?' she squeaked.

'The enemy – Aaron Miller and his construction crew.'

At that poor Agnes blushed so deeply it was hard to tell that she was wearing rouge. 'A woman has the right to make herself feel pretty,' she said, 'and if you don't like it, then you can just take a long walk off of a short pier.'

'Well, I never!' I huffed.

'It's about time you thought about it then, isn't it?' Agnes said. 'That long, horsey face of yours could stand to use some improvement. Some contouring around your cheekbones should help to shorten your equine profile, and maybe some artificial lashes to minimize that reptilian look you have become so comfortable with.

'Of course, as we both know, there's not much hope for those withered old lips of yours, given that they look like a pair of long-dead guppies. Of course, the real trouble is your holier-than-thou hair, all fifty-two feet of it. Magdalena, Magdalena, let down your long hair.'

Believe it or not, I was familiar with the fairy tale of Rapunzel. It was a favourite of mine, and I used to daydream that I was her. Then I started to worry about how much it would hurt to have a man climbing up my locks, and if he did so, would it cause hair loss. That's when I asked Gabe to tug on my tresses with all his might. Wouldn't you know that my doctor husband just laughed and refused to do that one small favour? Now where was I? Oh yes, I'd just learned that my dearest friend, Agnes Miller, could give as good as she got.

I stood. 'Agnes, dear friend, arise, and clasp me to your bounteous bosom. Only you, of all my friends, would have the courage to tell me the truth about how I look. I've always known that I have a horsy face and withered lips, but the reptilian eyes – now that's a new one. Anyway, Gabe's always telling me how beautiful I am, but I know that he can't really mean it. I have mirrors, after all. Because even though my eyes are reptilian, they still can see my reflection.'

'Stop it, Mags!' Agnes rose, and the cinnamon buns rose with her, as they were stuck to her bum, plate and all. 'I need to tell you something of great importance – something quite serious. And in private.'

'We are alone, dear.'

'Where's Gabe?'

I pointed to the door of our bedroom. The PennDutch Inn was originally a large farmhouse, and as such, lacked a master suite. When we built one off the back, we designed it so that the door to it was off the kitchen, rather to any of the public rooms. I knew that my husband, who is retired, was probably glued to his eighty-five-inch television set and would not poke his head out until lunchtime. All the same, there was fun to be had in playing along with my friend's wild imagination.

'He could come out at any time,' she said. 'We need to relocate.'

'Let's tiptoe to the parlour,' I whispered.

'Mags, are you making fun of me?'

'Shh.'

Agnes sighed, but went along with my foolishness. One of the functions of a good friend is to humour your buddy, is it not? Of course Agnes knew not to sit on Great Granny's lap. Even though she has neither seen, nor heard, my stern ancestor, she's known a great number of people who have – people who've made more reliable witnesses than Yours Truly.

'Now what's this all about?' I said, after we'd both selected our seats.

'Not so fast, girlie,' Granny said. 'Do I smell cinnamon buns?'

'Oh, my word!' I said. 'I plum forgot. Agnes, you've been sitting—'

'Silence!' Granny hissed. 'Tell the woman to come sit on my lap.'

'But you hate it when anyone sits on your rocking chair.'

'Do it,' Granny snapped, 'or I'll moan.'

Sometimes when Granny moans at her lowest frequency, even folks who can't hear her speak pick up the vibrations and feel uncomfortable. Some have likened the feeling to what one might expect from a dental drill in the hands of a first semester dental student. Still, there are others who claim that Granny's moaning is more akin to a case of severe heartburn. A few misguided souls have even compared the sensation to that of sexual fulfilment.

'Mags, what's going on?' Agnes demanded. 'What's the old lady up to now?'

'Why, that does it!' Granny said. 'You march that whipper-snapper over here right now and make her sit.'

'Yes, ma'am,' I said, and turned to Agnes. 'Please, *please*, be a dear and go sit in Granny's chair. She wants you to, I promise.'

'I don't believe it.'

'If you don't, she'll moan.'

Agnes got up and totted over to the rocker by the fireplace. I held my breath as the plate of buns bobbled along with her, still mashed to her backside. Thank heavens I'd been heavy-handed with the cream cheese icing. As she squeezed her generous buttocks into the confines of Granny's ancient chair, I could hear them both sigh.

'Now then,' I said to Agnes, 'tell me this top secret business of yours.'

'I got a call from you-know-who this morning.'

'That's wonderful, dear,' I said. 'And how is the President?'

'Not him, silly,' Agnes said, sounding a bit annoyed. 'Aaron Miller called me.'

'Why you?' I asked. 'I mean, what about?'

'He was letting me know that Armageddonland Enterprises is holding a televised news conference this afternoon at two o'clock, up there at the old Bontrager place. They will be announcing their vision for the theme park, and all the benefits that it will bring to the people of Hernia, and to Bedford County, and America in general.'

'Right,' I said, 'like the benefit of emptying your wallet so that you can have fun watching other people burn in Hell.'

'Yes, something like that,' Agnes said. 'Anyway, they were going to hold off on this big announcement for another three months or so, until after they'd broken ground and had at least poured some foundation, but then some Devil-worshipping terrorist vandalized their vehicles with the Mark of the Beast. Aaron said that he thought this was a sign from God, and that they should make their intentions known today via the press. All the major networks will be there to cover his remarks, along with dozens of cable news shows.'

'Not if I can help it!' I hollered.

'Get real,' Agnes said softly. 'There is nothing you can do

about stopping the news conference. But there is something we can do to cause a distraction.'

'I'm all ears – the older I get, the bigger they grow.'

'Ain't that the truth,' Granny said between grunts. Apparently dear Agnes was starting to feel a mite heavy.

'Well,' Agnes said with a smirk, 'why do you think that I'm all dolled up like a trollop?'

'Hmm. I assume that it has nothing to do with trolloping. Am I correct?'

'That isn't even a word, Mags, and you're correct. I gussied myself up so that I might get the attention of one of the news anchors, and get him, or her, to interview me as a local. I'm someone who has a lot to say about this intrusion on our way of life, and on the immoral character of the man who is the face of this venture.'

'Agnes, you go girl! I am so impressed. I mean that truly. I always knew that you were spunky, but you have really outdone yourself this time. Are you planning to go alone?'

'Yes,' she said, and smiled. 'I was going to ask you to come with me, but then I decided that I too am a strong, and competent, woman.'

Granny coughed.

'You certainly are, dear. And just remember that in this era of so-called Fake News, a good Christian must still always tell the truth. That said, I see nothing wrong with embroidering the truth a tad, in order to make it a wee bit more – uh, dramatic. You know, to drive home a point.'

'Liar, liar, sturdy Christian underpants on fire,' Granny said.

'Mags, I'll do just fine. I just thought it was important that you know about this big press conference, because no doubt you are going to be immediately inundated with calls from concerned citizens.'

'Let's hope so,' I said. 'I mean that I hope that they care enough to call. But thank you so much for letting me know, and actually trying to do something about it. Tell me, what is Prissy doing to stop this horde of invaders?'

'Well,' Agnes said, 'she plans to show up this afternoon with a horde of her own: the Mennonite Women's Sewing Circle. The combined total of your Beechy Grove Mennonite, and my First

Mennonite, is over one hundred and fifty. If only half that number show up to protest, that's still a good-sized herd – I mean, horde.'

'Boogers,' Granny said.

'Well, give me a call and let me know how it goes,' I said.

Agnes took that as her cue to leave and stood. This time the plate of cinnamon buns detached from her buns and remained on Granny's rocking chair. If Granny had had anything to do with that, I couldn't tell, since Agnes's not inconsiderable girth had blocked my line of sight. As far as I know, Apparition-Americans are incapable of interacting physically with the corporeal world. Thus I must conclude that too much of the icing had been absorbed, either into the buns, or into Agnes's skirt, and what had initially made them sticky was no longer a factor.

When Agnes and I were both back in the kitchen, I handed her a damp tea towel.

'Agnes, dear, I don't know how to break this to you, but you've been sitting on cinnamon buns ever since you arrived.'

Agnes smiled. 'Duh. I wanted to see how long you could keep up the charade without laughing. I've got to hand it to you, Mags, you're pretty good – good enough to have to buy me a new skirt. This one has a few snags in it anyway.'

'Will do,' I said, as I threw my gangly arms around her and hugged her tightly to my pitiful bosom. I know, I said before that I'd been bred not to hug, but I was referencing *real* hugs. The hug I gave Agnes was a 'Mennonite hug' wherein one pats the other person's back repeatedly, as if trying to induce a burp.

'And another thing,' Agnes said, as she pulled herself lose enough to breathe, 'I want a baker's dozen of those rolls to take home next time I visit.'

TEN

Alison returned from the enemy camp minutes after Little Jacob was let off by the school bus. Although he is only ten, our son is a senior at Hernia High School, and will graduate in another six weeks. Next year he plans to attend the

University of Pittsburgh as a pre-med student and follow in his father and sister's footsteps. That means that Gabe will have to move into the dorm with him, because I am not allowing my little boy to live on campus, unchaperoned, with sexually active people that are twice his age.

At any rate, Little Jacob was enjoying a fresh batch of cinnamon buns and a glass of milk as his afternoon snack, when his big sister walked in. The joy on his face is something that I wish I could have captured in a bottle.

'Ali-belli!' he shouted, spraying milk everywhere. Proving that he was flesh and blood, he knocked over his chair on his way to hug her.

'L.J.!' she shouted and squeezed him so tightly that he begged for mercy.

'Are you on semester break?' he asked incredulously.

'Nah, I just missed you, kiddo.' She tussled his dark curls.

'How long are you staying?'

'For dinner – maybe. I can't promise, because I have a lot of studying to do.'

They turned to me with exaggerated long faces, and I returned their look. 'Try leaving here without eating, missy, and you'll be arrested. I have my connections, you know. And for the record, Alison, you don't look good in orange.'

'Mom's right,' Little Jacob said. 'Not about the orange part, but about her having connections. She's still the boss of Chief Toy, even though she doesn't approve of gay marriage.'

'Good for her,' Alison said. 'About being the boss, I mean. Say bro, do you mind if I talk to Mom alone for a minute?'

'But you just got here!'

'I know, but next time I'm here, I'll spend all of my time with you. I won't even look her way.'

'What about Dad? Will you look his way?'

'Maybe just to say hello,' Alison said. 'Same thing goes for Freni. The rest of my time is yours. I promise.'

'All right,' Little Jacob, my twelfth-grader said, in the voice of a ten-year old.

Nonetheless, he went back to his snack, while my daughter and I went out to take a stroll across the pasture, where I keep my two dairy cows. There is a song that goes: 'Nothing could be finer than to be in Carolina in the morning.' But I submit that nothing could be finer than to amble across a Pennsylvania pasture on a late-summer day when the sun is shining, the birds are singing, and the smell of cow manure is in the air.

A largish pond occupies the middle of the pasture, and I've situated a log bench on its north shore. We women made that the goal of our walk.

'Where is Dad?' Alison wanted to know almost immediately.

'He's either at the library in Bedford, or else in the basement of the courthouse, researching old deeds and covenants. Not *everything* has been scanned and stored on computers, and even records that have been electronically preserved, are sometimes illegible. Your dad is looking for anything that we can use to at least put a temporary injunction of restraint on these folks.'

'Good. I hope he finds something.' She brushed a fly away. 'Mom, my entire day was a waste; I never did get to meet Rodney.'

'*What?* Tell me about it.'

'Well, I saw Aaron,' she said, referring to her birth father by his given name. 'I was taken to see him straight away by a bimbo.'

'A what?'

'Isn't that what your generation used to call a woman dressed like a – hmm – a tart?'

'Sad to say, I missed out on that delightful word. It must be because there aren't that many Mennonite and Amish bimbos – except for your Auntie Susannah. But I always thought of her as a slattern *par excellence*.'

'And I bet she's proud of that distinction. Anyway, when I asked to see my brother, Aaron said that Rodney had gone into Bedford with one of his workers to pick up some supplies. In the meantime, he would show me the plans for Armageddonland and take me on a tour of where the various components were going to be located.'

'Tell me everything!'

'Mom, how long have they owned the old Bontrager house?'

The warm September afternoon suddenly turned chilly. 'Uh, they must have acquired it about a month ago. I'd heard that there was some remodelling going on out there, but that was to be expected. But it was just painters and wallpaper hangers – that kind of thing. No one ever saw what looked like a private vehicle in the driveway. Why did you ask?'

'Because Armageddonland snuck one past you. The entire interior of the house has been turned into office spaces – well, except for a huge area just when you walk in. That place is now a showroom, occupied by two very detailed models of the theme park. One model depicts the exterior of the pavilions and various kiosks, and the other, which is even larger, is of the interior. It's horrible, Mom, it's just horrible. As a Jew, I was utterly offended.'

I pulled Alison close. I don't remember my parents ever hugging me. On the other hand, Prissy has accused me of hugging my children too much. The last time that Prissy made that remark, I was tempted to hug her as well – maybe even until her lips turned blue. And not a Mennonite hug, either, but a proper Jewish hug, with no back slapping.

'Alison, dear, did you tell Aaron that you officially converted to Judaism when you were eighteen? That what he's constructing would have folks watching your people screaming in agony for all time?'

'Of course I did.'

'*And?*'

'His response was that I was still alive, so that it wasn't too late for me to renounce my faith and go back to being a Christian.'

My heart was broken. This was, of course, all my fault. I had married a man of the Jewish faith, and it was his influence that had steered her towards choosing Judaism over Christianity. I too believe that the Bible condemns non-believers to eternal torment. The words are as plain as the Yoder nose on my face. I was raised to believe that every word in the Holy Bible should be interpreted exactly as they are read, and that they come directly from God's mind. To make allowances for historical context, or influence from other cultures, is blasphemy.

I am in my sixtieth year. Jesus is my saviour, and the saviour of the world; I cannot see it any other way. Yet I cannot under-stand how a truly loving God would torture billions of unbelievers, past, present, and future on a tricky matter of faith. I mean, what about the millions of indigenous Americans on both continents who never even heard of Jesus before 1492?

'Mom,' my daughter said, pulling herself from my embrace, 'have you been listening?'

'Yes, dear. Of course, I've been listening, and it breaks my heart that I've put you in this situation.'

'Stop it, Mom!' she said vehemently. 'You didn't do anything. I am who I choose to be; you and Dad are the exact parents I would choose if I could order you out of a catalogue – a catalogue of crazy people.' She poked me in the ribs and laughed.

I poked her back. 'Takes one to know one, Dr Rosen.'

'Ah – ah, not yet. I've got a ways to go.'

'Yeah, but you'll make it with flying colours. Probably graduate at the head of your class.'

'Anyway, back to Aaron. He was lying to me the entire time about Rodney's whereabouts. He'd already shipped my brother back to Minneapolis, to his mother. The only reason he was here last night was to get your attention, so that you would call me. Aaron as much as said so. He said he didn't think he stood a snowball's chance in Hell – sorry, Mom – of seeing me, if he didn't dangle Rodney as bait.'

I jumped up from the bench with such force that I sent a nearby flock of sparrows into flight. The nerve of that man, preying on my daughter's emotions like that, and telling her a bald-faced lie. And this from a man who was building a theme park based on Hell.

Alison tugged at my skirt until I sat. 'Mom, please, I just want your thoughts on what to tell Little Jacob. Do I let him know that I have another brother out there, one to whom he is not related? I don't want him to be hurt by this disclosure – you know, feel jealous because Rodney and I have the same birth parents. Because that means nothing to me, but L.J. is only ten.'

'You've got a valid point, dear,' I said. 'I guess the question is did anyone else besides your dad and I meet Rodney? Was he gone before Prissy and her group of protestors showed up there at six this morning? And even if he was, one can never be sure that Aaron's crew will keep their mouths shut in the weeks and months ahead. The one thing that I have learned about gossip is that, like water, it follows the course of least resistance. If one of the crew strikes up a friendship with someone from the village, and then is at a loss for words, he might think that having driven the boss's son to the airport is something worth talking about. Maybe even something to brag about.'

'Yeah,' Alison, 'you're right. But let me tell Little Jacob, OK?'

'Sure, dear.'

I got up. The afternoon was waning and my two cows, Udder Joy and Pleasant Creams were headed to the barn to be milked by Freni's teenage grandson as I was between clients, who would otherwise pay big bucks for the privilege. My two previous Jerseys, Fleischig and Milchig, I'd sold to a neighbour so that he could breed them with the expressed intention of building up his herd. Most visitors don't realize that in order for a dairy cow to produce profitable amounts of milk, their calves must be separated from them, and then either bottled-fed, or slaughtered. In my opinion, either course of action is traumatizing for both mother and offspring.

At any rate, after giving birth myself, and raising my own son up from infanthood, I felt it only fair that my cows have the experience of raising their calves – but only *after* they have spent two years as working cows. Do I feel guilty about still keeping dairy cows? Yes, and no. My cows are kept in a large green pasture, bordered by a shady wood. The central pond allows the cows to take a dip on hot summer days. I also share the milk with the poor and shut-ins of Hernia after it has been pasteurized at Showalter's, which is a large dairy farm over by Summerville. When asked why I don't drink soy or nut milk, I always give two reasons. The first reason is that since these so-called milks don't come from teats, they aren't proper milk in my book. If you don't believe me, just try to find an udder on an almond; it will take you half a day until you find it. The second reason is that cow's milk has more protein that the aforementioned liquids.

As we strolled back to the house, arm in arm, I asked Alison what she thought about Agnes's performance at the press conference that afternoon. I'd heard from half a dozen church ladies, including Prissy, that dear Agnes had been more than just defensive of our way of life here in Hernia. Apparently she'd stepped over the line and was 'in your face' offensive to a reporter from one of the major television networks. She accused him of being religiously prejudiced against progressive Mennonites, because he wasn't interested in interviewing her. Instead he had his cameraman focus on the more interesting Old Order Mennonites and Amish in their recognizable garb. Then when Aaron Miller came to the reporter's defence, dear sweet Agnes exploded with righteous wrath and called him a traitor to his people. She even went so far as to shout that he was the Second Coming of Judas – a moniker which doesn't even make sense. Still it does show just how worked up poor Agnes was.

To me, the most distressing thing that I heard was that there were many in that assemblage who muttered their support of my friend's tirade. Some even clapped, quietly of course, to show their support of Agnes. Admittedly, some of Armageddonland's opponents were 'English', for example Presbyterians, Lutherans, and what have you, but it was the behaviour of the Amish and Mennonites that bothered me. We were supposed to be the *gentle* people, the *pacifists*, and not who approve of name-calling. Needless to say, I felt ashamed on Agnes's behalf.

'And how did Aaron react?' I asked Alison, although I'd already been told, in half a dozen different ways. However, since my daughter had literally been at his elbow, I wanted her viewpoint.

'Aaron called Agnes an "ignorant old busybody" and "Magdalena Yoder's lackey".'

'Then what happened?' I asked, while remaining remarkably calm, for I knew what was coming next.

'Then Agnes slapped Aaron. She may be short and round, but she can exert quite a lot of force. Aaron was knocked into me, and I fell backwards, knocking over Levi Schrock. He's Aaron's foreman. So the three of us went down like dominoes. At first there was dead silence, and then the crowd cheered like you wouldn't believe. Some of the younger ones – English kids only – even started chanting "Agnes Samson" over and over again.'

'Boy, will that go to her head,' I said.

'Yeah,' Alison said, and gave my arm a gentle squeeze, 'but remember, Mom, she doesn't have anything else. Not since her nude uncles died. At least you have Dad and us kids. And Freni.' She pointed to the heifers that had already reached the barn. 'And them. Not to mention that you are the Mayor of Hernia, so you have lots of friends.'

'As well as enemies,' I said.

'Right,' Alison said, but she said it with sarcasm, like she didn't believe that I had enemies, which of course I did. 'Hey Mom, I've gotta scoot. I want to get back to school before dark. I know that I'm just a kid by your standards, but I still don't like night driving in a big city like Pittsburgh.'

'All right, dear. Call me when you get in?'

'You got it.' Then off she went, skipping like a girl the rest of the way to the parking area between the house and the barn.

Raising Alison had been both a challenge and a joy. To have one's first experience with motherhood involve a teenage girl might be compared to having to drive a stick shift big rig on one's first day of driving lessons. But we learned on the job together, and we both hung in there, and although I am her mother first, she is also my friend now that she is an adult.

Still, as I watched her drive away, I felt a sense of unease. It was like the late-afternoon shadows were trying to envelop me, and wrap me tight in one dark, impenetrable blanket of dread. I walked faster, keeping in front of the advancing shadows, but they sped up, chasing me to the house. I knew that was superstitious nonsense, that these were thoughts unbecoming a Christian. Alison was going to be just fine. She was going to call me when she reached her dorm.

ELEVEN

But Alison didn't call. After what I presumed to be a reasonable length of time, I called her, but was sent straight to voicemail. So I texted her, but got no response. I waited another reasonable length of time – from a mother's perspective – and called again. This time I got a recording telling me that her 'message box' was full. My next step was to break one of the cardinal laws of motherhood: I called Rachel, her closet friend.

'Mrs Rosen, is that you?' Rachel said. In the background I could hear lots of chatter.

'This is my phone, dear,' I said, 'but it's my alter-ego calling. Do you know where Alison is?'

'Yeah, Mrs Rosen. She's in the bedroom with Nate. Do you want me to disturb them?'

Nate Shapiro was a 'drop-dead gorgeous' medical student from New Jersey whom Alison had been dating for more than eighteen months. They were 'unofficially' engaged, which Gabe told me was an expression that, in their particular case, was something that I didn't want to dwell on too much. I should simply accept their explanation, at face value. They were supposedly waiting until they'd completed medical school until they took their relationship to the 'next level'. But Agnes, perennial pessimist that she is, was willing to bet her house that Alison and Nate were already doing the hospital bed ballet.

'Of course I want you to disturb them, dear. What kind of a mother wouldn't want to wrest her daughter from the clutches of he who is named in One Corinthians 5:11?'

'Uh, Mrs Rosen, that's not the new Harry Potter book, is it? I thought she was done writing those.'

'It's the Bible, dear, and the word is fornicator.'

'Come again?'

'No, you come on, Rachel Morgenstern! You're almost a doctor. You know what the word "fornication" means. Now you march right in there and tell my daughter to get her petite patooty out here, and pronto. And tell her that she better be fully dressed when she does it, too. Capiche?'

'Mrs Rosen, she's already dressed now.'

'TMI!' I cried.

'I don't see how that's too much information,' Rachel said calmly. 'Everyone at these study sessions wears clothes. It would be distracting if they didn't.'

'Did you say study sessions?' I squeaked.

'Tomorrow we start the end of year exams. I shouldn't be saying this to you, but I'm sure glad I wasn't in Alison's shoes today. I mean all that stress of having to drive home and deal with family problems, and then drive back again. She barely made it back for tonight's cram session. Hey, I better shut up and go drag her away from the session that's taking place in my room.'

'No, don't!' I shouted. 'And never tell her about our conversation. If you do, I'll – I mean, how would you like a top-of-the-line iPad? The very best that money can buy? Brand new, of course.'

'My lips are sealed,' Rachel said, so we rung off.

I was still brooding about that late-night conversation a week later. There are times when my mind grabs hold of a topic like a dog does with a rawhide bone, and it just won't let the subject go. I was still hurt that my supposedly adult daughter had neglected to notify me that she'd arrived safely back on campus. However, rather than call her and talk about it, I'd laid awake half the night, having two-sided conversations in my head.

The next morning found me sipping my third cup of very strong coffee on the front porch. There are several rocking chairs on the porch which I seldom use, as I view 'porch sitting' as being on the shady side of decadent. But the Psalms did spend a lot of time extolling the wonders of nature, and yea, my front yard does offer enough variety of flora and fauna to soothe even my troubled soul.

Only one maple tree remains following the violent storm of five years ago, but it is old, well-shaped, and beautiful. That morning a pair of grey squirrels were running up and down and around its massive trunk. I preferred to think that they were merely playing tag, which kept them, and their activity, in the realm of cuteness. The grass was thick and lush that time of the year, and a male robin, with his bright red breast, was hopping about in it looking for worms. Closer to the road a large flock of starlings foraged for whatever it is they eat. Starlings, by the way, are not native to America. One hundred of these birds were introduced in 1890 by Shakespeare enthusiasts, and today there are about two hundred million of them in the country. At any rate, as I sat there, sipping my coffee, a small orange cat leapt out of nowhere, and landed in their midst. The birds rose as one organism and swirled in the eastern sky in a tight form-ation called a murmuration. Eventually the birds disappeared over the neighbour's farm. Meanwhile the orange cat, which had been unsuccessful in his hunt, sat for a moment to lick his paws and wash his face. Then he jumped into the drainage ditch which parallels the road, and he too disappeared from sight.

I was peacefully pondering the beautiful, and seemingly choreographed, movements of the starlings, when I suddenly remembered that I had a guest arriving at any minute. For the record, now that I am a wealthy woman of some notoriety, I no longer advertise my rooms. In fact, the only guests that I rent to now, are people whom I, or a family member, wishes to meet. Little Jacob is really into sports and video games, so under supervision of his father, we occasionally have notable sports figures under our roof. And what is my opinion of these guests, you might ask? Boring!

My Dearly Beloved fancies himself to be an intellectual. He belongs to several high IQ societies, with MENSA being the *least* impressive one. I'm not saying that he's full of himself, or arrogant, just that the pedestal he's put himself on is so high, that should he ever fall off, the results could be disastrous.

My guests, of course, are generally people with whom I am in agreement. They include preachers whom I hear on the radio whose sermons are Bible-based, and whose viewpoints are correct. If I hear, or read of, an individual whom I think might have a snowball's chance in Satan's homeland, of saving my Dearly Beloved's immortal soul, I invite that person. To be honest, these brazen attempts of me to convert my husband usually backfire. Although Gabe is always polite to my guests, he is adept at thinking up excuses for having to take 'emergency' trips out of town, trips that invariably require taking Little Jacob with him.

That particular day I was waiting to greet just one couple, and they were Gabe's guests. While Gabe often took it upon himself in those days to greet his own guests, he was still lollygagging about in our bedroom that day, doing exactly who knows what in there. However, the purpose behind his dawdling was expressly so that I should be the one who welcomed the two FARTers.

Please do not think that I am a vulgar woman. I find the 'F' words to be very offensive. I am descended from the Amish, who are also known as the Plain People, and they eschew *fancy* dress. As a Conservative Mennonite woman, just one generation away from my Amish forbears, I too find *fancy* things quite undesirable. As to the other 'F' word, well in all confidence, I try never to pass gas inside the house, or any place else where someone might hear me.

Even one audible toot in the company of others is one too many to bear for a mature Christian woman with good manners. Thus, if necessary, I will hold these potty puffs inside me until I begin to float like a hot air balloon at a Thanksgiving Day Parade. At that point I will attempt to manoeuvre myself to the nearest door by grasping various pieces of furniture and pulling myself along, hand over hand. Once outside I can finally relax. If it is a cloudy day I blame the subsequent boom on an unseen overhead jet breaking the sound barrier. But if it's sunny outdoors, I will blame my two cows, or if need be, my chickens – if they are roaming about.

Now where was I? Oh yes, FART in this case is an acronym for Facts, Accuracy, Reason, and Truth. Tammy Faye and Jim Barker, from South Carolina, a couple of lawyers in their late thirties, are co-chairs of the organization, as well as its founders. They are also two of America's biggest liars in my humble opinion. They claim that they represent an organization that deals with facts – the unvarnished truth, as if there is such a thing. If that is the case, then why does FART question the existence of GOD? Well, I could hardly wait until I got my large, but nicely shaped, hands on this pair of atheists.

As it turned out, shortly after the starlings swirled away, a Porsche roared up my long driveway in a spray of gravel. Believe me, I could tell the make of the car even before it turned off Hertzler Road; I am no stranger to folks who spend big bucks on automobiles, and once succumbed to that temptation myself. I also knew exactly what these folks would say when they got out.

'You really should pave that road,' the man said.

'You really should drive slower on a gravel road, dear,' I said. 'Now you'll have to pick up all those little stones and put them back. Otherwise they might put out my husband's eye when he mows the grass.'

They man chuckled and held out his hand. 'You're obviously the famous Magdalena Yoder. Gabe warned me about you.'

I gave the fellow the once-over before taking the proffered paw. He was an extremely handsome specimen of manhood: full head of blond hair, bright blue eyes, strong brow and jaw, bulging biceps, etc. The complete list would read like something out of the romance novels my sister Susannah reads.

As for his wife, Tammy Faye, she was the human equivalent of a Barbie Doll whose make-up had been applied with a trowel. I am well acquainted with this doll, because Susannah, who was never allowed to own one, griped constantly about it when she was a girl. She even stole one, and manged it keep it for a week before Mama found it and in a fit of righteous anger tanned her hide. My sister claims that she might not have been so promiscuous and gone to prison for aiding and abetting a murderer, had she been allowed to own this toy. Her spurious claim is based on the fact that plastic Barbie had no sex organs, and her little outfits did not include prison clothes.

Unlike her husband, Tammy Faye was a redhead – a 'ginger' – as the Brits call it. I can only guess that the colour of Tammy Faye's fiery mane was natural, given her milk white complexion. Even then I can't be sure due to the amount of make-up that covered her face. Heavy black lines followed the contours of her green eyes, and her eyelids glittered with shadow the colour of spring grass.

'All this dust is bad for one's pores,' the human Barbie said, and offered me a hand with painted nails, the length of which would make an anteater proud.

'You know Cleanliness is next to Godliness, dear,' I said. 'I can't for the life of me figure out how you can perform your daily hygiene tasks with claws like yours. As for dust clogging your pores, when is the last time they had a chance to breathe? I wouldn't be surprised that when you finally rid yourself of all the gunk, you'll find that missing bunch of coalminers. I mean that charitably, dear.'

Tammy Faye gave a little snort. 'That's why we're here, dear, aren't we?'

'I beg your pardon?'

'Well, Jim and I are quite clean – *we* have indoor plumbing – but it's the subject of Godliness we'll be pursuing this weekend. Or rather, God*less*ness.'

I stuck pinkies in both ears simultaneously and squiggled them around to clear any blockage. Surely I had not heard right.

'*Excuse* me?' I said. 'Godlessness?'

Jim smiled, revealing a blinding array of capped teeth. 'Yes, and we really appreciate that your husband invited us. We're atheists who oppose the building of this monstrosity. Believe me, we hate the thought of it as much as you do.'

These were the Babester's guests; had they been mine, I'd have shoved them back into their expensive car and sent them on their way. I had known they were atheists when Gabe invited them, but the reality was unexpectedly disturbing.

'The Armageddon monstrosity,' Tammy Faye said, just in case we had several monstrosities hereabouts, and I didn't know which one it was that drew their ire.

'Get behind me, Satan,' I heard myself say.

'What was that?' Tammy Faye said sharply.

Jim laughed. 'Honey, she's worried that we might have contaminated her spiritually just by shaking hands. Miss Yoder, just because we're atheists, that doesn't mean that we're filled with Satan.'

'Or demons,' Tammy Faye said.

'That's right,' Jim said, 'because those things don't exist.'

'Then why does the Bible say that they do?' I said. 'Even Jesus believed in demons. He cast demons into a herd of pigs.'

'Miss Yoder,' Jim said, 'we didn't come here to argue religion with you. We certainly didn't come to try and talk you out of your beliefs. We came here to stop Aaron Miller from building Armageddonland, and if that goal is unobtainable, then we at least want to stop him from making yet another of his horrendous schemes a success.'

I was stunned. 'Did you say *another* of his horrendous schemes? Do you mean that this isn't his first scheme?'

'Surely you've heard about Texas Exodus?'

'Hasn't everyone? I read that the ten plagues, in ten different pavilions, were so effectively replicated that visitors to that park were warned not to experience two or three a day. Otherwise they might suffer post-traumatic stress.'

'Which many of them have,' Jim said.

'Yes, but still, even though I am one hundred percent against schadenfreude, I would still love to go out there, just to take their Red Sea Experience – even though that costs extra. Imagine enough water to fill sixteen Olympic-size swimming pools parting, dividing into towering walls many meters high, so that you and about one hundred participants, dressed as ancient Hebrews, can cross on dry land. Then as soon as the last one in your party crosses safely, you turn and watch as the water comes crashing down and drowns the Pharaoh's troops who have been hot on your heels.'

'So you *do* enjoy watching others getting their just desserts.'

'*What?* No, it's just that this particular ride – or whatever you want to call it – the reviewer said it is the most dramatic, heart-stopping thing that she'd ever seen. And it's straight from the Bible, you know.'

'And it's also straight from Aaron Miller's mind,' Tammy Faye said. 'And you can attest to the fact that he is a wicked man.'

I nodded, although it felt strange agreeing with an atheist. I wanted to learn more about Texas Exodus from these folks, particularly Aaron's exact role in its success. When Aaron initially turned his back on Hernia, the only capital he had was from the sale of his farm. That had been in his family for generations, and was paid off, but it would not have been enough money to get such an ambitious theme park like Texas Exodus off the ground. In order to chat these folks up I had to play nice, but that didn't mean that I had to like them.

'You know,' I said, 'I can't help but wonder where he got the seed money to start a project like that. It takes money to make money, as the saying goes.'

'Exactly,' Jim said. 'So take a guess.'

'Did he marry a succession of rich, but extremely old, widows?'

Jim shook his handsome head. 'That wouldn't have been out of character with him – no offense – but that would have taken too long. No, our investigation revealed that he used the fifty-thousand dollars that you gave him when he left Hernia after the dissolution of your bogus marriage.'

I swallowed hard. 'No one was supposed to know about that! I haven't even told Agnes. And I only did it as part of a deal where he promised never to set foot across the state line again.'

Tammy Faye snickered. 'You trusted a married man to keep his promise *after* he pretended to be single, and then robbed you of your most precious treasure?'

I wagged a finger from side to side at the impudent young woman. 'Your presumption is wrong, dear. Aaron did *not* steal the three-hundred-year-old family Bible that arrived here in 1738 on the *Charming Nancy*. I am not as stupid as I look. I keep that Bible safely hidden under a floor plank, and I'm not telling you which plank it is on pain of death.'

Jim Barker rolled his eyes. 'That's not what she meant. Anyway, Aaron Miller used that money to buy advertising time for a product he called Reconciliation Crème. It was essentially white, odourless crap, supposedly made with oils and herbs from the Holy Land, and sold for fifty bucks a miniscule jar. A glob of that rubbed over one's chest every evening before praying, and estranged family members, lovers and friends would all begin the process of reconciliation.'

'What a scam!' I hissed.

'Exactly,' Jim said. 'The literature that accompanied the tiny jar of ointment warned that the process would be slow at first, so more crème would be needed, and of course, much more praying would be required. But Miss Yoder, you would be surprised by the number of broken-hearted people who would be willing to pay any amount just to reconnect with someone whom they once loved, but with whom they are now on the "outs".'

'No, I wouldn't be surprised,' I said. 'As an innkeeper for many years, I've seen and heard it all.'

'I bet you have,' Jim said. 'Anyhow, that's how Aaron Miller made his first million.'

'Miss Yoder,' Tammy Faye said, sounding a mite on the sharp side, 'my Louboutins are killing me. Aren't you going to at least invite us up on your porch so that we can sit down? These are six-inch heels, you know.'

'And maybe offer us a drink?' Jim said.

'Come on up and grab yinz a rocking chair,' I said. 'Now what would yinz like to drink? We have sky juice, orange juice, and cow juice.'

'Uh, what is sky juice?' Tammy Faye said.

'Where does orange juice come from?' I said pleasantly.

'Oranges – I think.'

'You're absolutely right, dear! And sky juice comes from the sky. So what would that be?'

'I haven't a clue,' she said, shaking her pretty red head.

'It's water, dear. Water comes from the sky.'

'So what's cow juice?' she said.

'Oy vey,' I said, borrowing from my husband's lexicon.

'Cow juice is milk, sweetie,' Jim said to his wife. He turned to me. 'Miss Yoder, I'll take some orange juice with a hearty splash of vodka.'

'Sorry, no can do. We don't serve booze here at The PennDutch Inn.'

'Jesus drank wine,' Tammy Faye said.

'Jesus isn't here,' I said, still using my pleasant voice. 'If he were, I'd serve *Him* some of my husband's Sabbath wine.'

'If it's all the same then,' Jim said, 'we'll forgo sitting on your fine porch, and just head on inside. I'm anxious to meet Dr Rosen. Not only do we see eye to eye on the Armageddonland solution, but he seems like the perfect candidate for membership in FART.'

'And I'd like you to show us to our rooms,' Tammy Faye said. 'I had to get up at four this morning to do my face and still have time for breakfast, so a nappy-poo about now would be divine.'

I gulped. Over the years I've had many an argumentative, cantankerous, Doubting Thomas stay at my establishment. However, to my knowledge, I'd never hosted a pair of out-and-out atheists, died-in-the-wool God-deniers – in other words, empty vessels waiting to be filled by the Devil and his thousands of spirit followers. Just the thought of atheists sleeping between my clean, Christian sheets was enough to give me the heebie-jeebies. I shivered at the thought.

'I'm not sure you'll be comfortable here,' I said. 'The rooms are sparsely furnished, and they are all upstairs where there is no air-conditioning. You're sure to sweat when you sleep.'

'Wonderful,' said Jim. 'Tammy Faye and I are no strangers to heat. After all, we come from the South. Besides, a little sweat never did a body any harm.'

'Speak for yourself, Jim,' Tammy Faye said. 'A Southern lady never sweats; she merely perspires. And there are only two activities that cause a proper Southern lady to perspire, Miss Yoder, and one of them is gardening. Do you wish to a have pair of atheists performing the mattress minuet while they self-marinate on your bed?'

'My land 'o Goshen!' I cried, as I slapped both cheeks in mock surprise. 'Who knew that I was a secret Southerner?'

'She's mocking us, Jim,' Tammy Faye said.

'Of course she is, darling,' Jim said. 'But that's only because she hasn't given us a fair shake. Once she's heard what it is that we can do to stop the Miller menace, she'll stop acting like a child and invite us inside.'

I prayed for courage, swallowed my pride, and invited them inside. I would give them the upstairs room with the best ventilation and offer them a fan. But if I heard so much as a bedspring squeak, Gabe's atheist guests were yesterday's history. As long as I had anything to say about it, no demon child was going to be conceived at the PennDutch Inn.

TWELVE

I led Gabe's guests directly to the parlour. That was the logical place for them to wait while I went off to fetch my husband. At the PennDutch we don't have a more casual space, such as a living room, or family room. And if we did, I certainly would never allow guests in it.

'Make yourselves comfortable,' I said slyly. 'Tammy Faye, you might wish to try the rocking chair.'

Tammy Faye recoiled and gave me the fisheye. 'You're asking me to eject that sweet old woman?'

'*What* sweet old woman, dear?'

'Aw shucks, Miss Yoder, you're playing games with me now. I'm obviously referring to that lovely woman in the rocking chair. Why I declare, the two of you could be sisters.'

Granny cackled. 'Sisters! Did you hear that, Magdalena? Now introduce me to your charming guest.'

'Very well,' I said happily. 'Granny, this is Tammy Faye Barker, and that's her husband Jim. They're from South Carolina and they are guests of Gabe. They're both FARTers.'

Granny wrinkled her nose. 'Just so long as it doesn't happen on my chair,' she said.

I turned to Tammy Faye. 'The woman who just spoke – I presume you heard her, as well as saw her – was my great-grandmother, who died when I was ten. On the other hand, since you don't believe in the paranormal, perhaps you really didn't see her, and were trying to be funny. After all, you did describe her as both lovely, and looking a great deal like me. As it can't be both, dear, which is it? You have to decide. So tell me: is my granny an attractive woman, or do you see a woman whose face would not look out of place in an advert for brood mares?'

'Yes, Tammy Faye,' Jim said loudly. 'Answer Miss Yoder. Tell her what's going on. I want to know as well.'

Poor Tammy Faye seemed at a loss as to what to do. She couldn't stop staring at Granny Yoder, and although her lips were moving silently, she seemed unable to take a step in any direction.

Finally I gave her a gentle shove. 'This nineteenth-century chair is calling your backside, dear. It was made by my great-granny's daddy back during the early 1860s – you know, during what you Southerners call the War of Northern Aggression, but what we Yankees call the Civil War.'

Jim stepped forward and helped his dazed wife take her seat, and then he plopped his considerable patooty on Granny's lap. 'What is all this nonsense about there being a woman in this rocking chair?'

Poor Tammy Faye looked like she was about to get sick. A curious fact about Apparition-Americans, at least of Granny's sort, is that they cannot pass through a human body. Perhaps that safeguard is in place to keep them from entering a human body, and inhabiting it. In other words, haunting it. At any rate, poor Granny was trapped on her rocker for as long as the man from FART chose to stay put.

'Granny – although she is actually my great-grandmother – is what is commonly called a ghost. However, she much prefers the term Apparition-American, because she remains quite patriotic, she doesn't dress in a white sheet, and she doesn't sneak up behind people and say "boo".'

'Boogers,' Granny said. 'If I could leave this darn rocking chair, I'd throw on a white sheet in a Mennonite minute. Then, assuming everyone could hear me, I'd chase after your guests, and scare the living daylights out of them.'

'I think I'm going to be sick,' Tammy Faye said.

'In that case, dear, run outside to heave. These floors are genuine oak.'

'Boogers,' Granny said. 'The girl will be just fine. You go get that handsome husband of yours while I entertain these two.'

'Tammy Faye,' I said. 'I realize that your rigid way of looking at the world doesn't allow you the freedom to properly process what you're seeing at the moment. It will take time. But you are an educated woman, who has no doubt taken physics at some point in time during your education. Surely you remember that two objects cannot occupy the same space at the same time. Therefore, your husband cannot possibly be sitting on my granny's lap at the moment. Can he?'

Tammy Faye sucked air between her perfect teeth. 'It could be a magic trick. A hologram, or something like that. You know, a gimmick done with hidden cameras, their lenses disguised by the faded flowers on that hideous wallpaper.'

'Those aren't flowers, dear; they're cobwebs. My last guests were supposed to clean this room, but they were slackers.'

I was beginning to feel a mite sorry for Jim Barker who'd only been privy to half of what was going on. In a way, it was rather like a non-believer attending a Pentecostal Church for the first time. At least when I attended one of their services, I had the advantages of being a practicing Christian.

'Well, whatever you do, girlie,' Granny said, pointing a crooked finger at Tammy Faye, 'tell this big oaf to get off my lap. I can feel my right leg falling asleep.'

'Granny,' I said, 'you can't feel anything, and you know it.'

'Jim is not an oaf!' Tammy Faye said hotly. She turned on me. 'And you, Miss Yoder, why don't you just call your husband? I mean, don't you dare leave us alone with this – this, whatever she is.'

I smiled triumphantly. 'My point exactly, dear. Although you are at a loss to describe Granny in words that make sense to you, still, you can't deny that she exists. Before today, I doubt that you would have thought such a thing possible. Now, expand your mind just a wee bit further, and exchange the word "God" for "Granny".'

'I ought to wash your mouth out with soap,' Granny said angrily, 'and then box your ears for good measure.'

'That was a stupid attempt to try and convert me,' Tammy Faye said. 'I resist being pushed.'

'Call your husband,' Jim said.

'OK,' I said. 'Have it yinz way, but you'll—'

'They'll what?' asked Gabe. He was suddenly standing in the doorway, with an amused expression on his face. I had the feeling that he'd been eavesdropping for some time.

'Nothing, really,' I said. It was a teensy grey lie. 'Just that they'd miss out on some alone time with Granny.'

'Speaking of which,' Tammy Faye said, 'is that a real woman – or, er – a ghost – or what, on that chair?'

Gabe smiled. 'She's not a what – exactly. She's my wife's great-grandmother in spectral form.'

'This is all too much,' Tammy Faye said. 'Jim, these people are loony. I want to go home.'

She was halfway to the front door before I managed to grab her arm. 'Not so fast, sister. You have to tell my husband what you told me. Come into the dining room and sit. Would you like a cup of coffee? How about a blueberry tart? They were baked just this morning by a genuine Amish woman – she's the best baker in the world.'

Actually, I didn't give the distraught woman a lot of choice. I literally dragged her to my massive table, which was carved by my ancestor, Jacob the Strong Yoder, and plonked her down in a chair that was far more comfortable than any chairs in the parlour. By then Gabe had joined us, and I had filled him in on just enough to get him asking nonstop questions. I doubt if there is a woman with a heartbeat who wouldn't be absolutely captivated by having such a handsome man showing interest in what she has to say. Then when I returned with passable coffee and Freni's unsurpassably delicious tarts – well, like most folks, Tammy Faye was able to compartmentalize two disparate 'realities'. For the meantime, Granny Yoder was filed away in compartment B, and as long as I didn't bring up her presence, it was a given that the Barkers wouldn't. No one likes to have their belief systems challenged – believe me, I know.

I will not deny the fact that Tammy Faye was an attractive woman for her late thirties. I know from speaking with my own gynaecologist that this is supposed to be when a woman is at her sexual peak. I am not attracted by female pheromones, so Tammy Faye did nothing to fan my cooling embers of desire.

However, peaches are my favourite fruit, and she brought to mind a ripe peach about to burst. Tammy Faye's hourglass figure strained against the confines of her sleeveless shift with its deep scoop neckline. Her bare arms appeared to be smooth and silky, so alluring to a man unused to seeing so much exposed flesh. When she began to giggle and toss her ginger hair at my hunky husband, it was time for me to step in and get things back on course.

'Now folks, since you've caught my husband up on what you've already told me – about what Aaron managed to pull off in Texas – what say we move ahead to the case on hand. You said that you knew of a way to stop him. What is it?'

'Come on, Mags,' Gabe said, using his parenting voice. 'This isn't fair. The Barkers are *my* special guests for the weekend. I get to ask the questions which, I'm sure, they would have gotten around to answering on their own, if you would stop messing with them.'

'What?' I said.

The second he opened his mouth, I shoved a tart in. Please do not judge me harshly. As I said, it was a delicious pastry.

Jim Barker was only too happy to answer my initial question. No doubt he'd had his fill of his wife's giggling and hair tossing as well. Truly, she had a spectacular and seductive mane.

'Down in Texas the majority of the men on the construction crew were undocumented workers from various Central American countries. In other words, people that our government terms "illegal". Aaron Miller paid them at a rate far below what he would pay a union bricklayer, or roofer, and even then, he stiffed them out of their last two weeks' wages.'

Gabe said something that I cannot repeat, and which I found to be offensive to women. Or maybe to female dogs. Anyway, I said empathically that Aaron was the son of a skunk.

'And,' Tammy Faye said, 'we have every reason to believe that he will do the same thing here, because he is going to need a construction crew that he can push to the limit. You know, he'll have minimal safety guards, and he'll have his crews working crazy long hours, because they'll desperately need the money.

But this time we're going to film it all. We're going to interview some of his labourers, and air those interviews on a nationally televised documentary.'

'Shut the front door!' I said. It is not a Mennonite expression, but neither were the guests I learned it from.

'Get out of town and back!' Gabe said. 'Do you really think that such an exposé will derail this project?'

Jim raised a fist. 'It's bound to blow Armageddonland to kingdom come. Uh, pardon the religious reference.'

'And should there be any legal repercussions,' Tammy Faye said with a toss of that luxurious mane, 'remember that we're both lawyers.'

'Duly noted,' I said. 'And Tammy Faye, dear, if you're having problems with an itchy scalp, my neighbour Bob is sure to have some sheep dip on hand for his ewes. If that doesn't work, I could fetch some pine tar from the woods. That stuff works powerfully well, although after the treatment, it does take a little effort to wash out from colour-treated hair like yours.'

'My hair colour is natural,' Tammy Faye said.

'Harrumph,' I said. Yes, her hair was gorgeous, but either she was lying, or her brown roots were lying.

'Magdalena,' Gabe said, 'you look like a photograph of Ireland.'

'I'm a Protestant,' I snapped.

Jim had the temerity to laugh. Clearly he was unaware that my Amish ancestors had emigrated from Switzerland because they were being persecuted by the Catholic Church. In the old country they were burned at the stake, or dunked into a freezing pond, primarily because of their belief in adult baptism.

Jim caught his misstep just in time. 'Your husband meant that he thinks your green with envy. He thinks you're jealous of my wife for no good reason. Believe me, Tammy Faye is flirting with your man just as surely as the sun came up this morning, and if Gabe can't see it, it's only because he enjoys it thoroughly, and subconsciously, at least, he doesn't want it to stop.'

Now there are times when the urge to sin is just too powerful to resist. Instead of telling Satan to 'get behind me', I run into my temptation as fast as I can, practically knocking my better angel off her perch on my right shoulder.

'Two can play this game, dear,' I said to Jim. 'Hold the fort with some more stimulating conversation and I will be back before your wife can write Methuselah backwards in Biblical Hebrew.'

Then I raced to my boudoir, removed my organza prayer cap, and gently laid it aside. My hair has never been 'cut' since the day I was born. The ends have been trimmed, but never more than an eighth of an inch at a time. Consequently, my 'crowning glory', as the Bible calls it, reaches to my lower calves. I wear it loose only when I go to bed with my hubby. Every morning I brush it and braid it, coil the braids around my head, and pin them in place with a myriad of pins. Therefore it took me a few minutes to undo my do, and of course, brush it smooth, but when I re-emerged in the dining room, I was quite another woman. I was a sinful-looking woman, of course, perhaps even a seductress on the prowl. Who knew that unchecked jealousy could drive me so deeply into sin?

I walked straight up to Jim Barker. The startled man dropped a half-eaten tart in his lap when he saw me. I didn't dare look at the other two directly, although my peripheral vision informed me that they were still in the room and involved in some tête-à-tête conversation.

'Hellooo, Jim,' I cooed, as I tossed my hair to and fro. One has to fight inertia for that amount of hair, so I invested a good deal of energy into my moves, especially my fros.

Let it be known that it is best to practice such a manoeuvre in the privacy of one's bedroom, before attempting to employ it as a strategy to make one's spouse jealous. Better yet, an Old Order Mennonite woman should save the full spectacle of her Crowning Glory for her husband alone. One lesson that I did learn was that hair whipping violently into someone's face is sometimes said to be a painful experience, especially if the onslaught of keratin is forceful enough to overturn the creamer and knock the sugar bowl off the table.

'What the heck?' Jim yelled, as he jumped up.

'Magdalena Portulacca Yoder Rosen!' Gabe thundered. 'Are you out of your mind?'

'Brava!' Tammy Faye said, and clapped vigorously. 'I loved it. Do it again!'

That was the not the reaction I wanted from her. I was trying to mock her when I did it, as well as make a fool out of Gabe. Therefore, how could she love it? That could only mean that she was mocking me in return. There was naught for me to do now but run back to my bedroom, fall on my knees, and make my heart right with God. But in order to do that, I had to be *sorry* for what I had done, not just embarrassed by the outcome of my behaviour. Therein lay the rub. I was even more upset with that faux redhead, Tammy Faye, and that much-too-handsome husband of mine, whose head was denser than an igneous rock.

I wanted to cry, but tears don't come easily to me. I also wanted someone to follow me to the bedroom, to at least try to talk me down from my heightened emotions. I wanted that someone to be Gabe, who would then apologize for being so insensitive. Then after kissing me passionately, and holding me briefly in his strong arms, Gabe would leave again and inform the Barkers that I had 'taken a powder', and that they would have to return to whence they had come. After that a third party – perhaps my friend Agnes – would act as their liaison in our combined efforts to take down the despicable Aaron Miller.

Ergo, I waited patiently by our bed, all the while brushing my own lustrous locks, but no one came. When I peeked outside the bedroom door, I could hear that the three of them were still in the kitchen, and that they were laughing. Laughing! The nerve of them. While I had been stewing and suffering, they'd been laughing! I redid my hair, dressed as quickly as I could, and slipped out through the kitchen. I realize that it was puerile of me to stomp on my car's accelerator when I knew that my car would spray the Barker's vehicle with gravel. But as I have often said: I am not a perfect woman. I am a work in progress.

THIRTEEN

I drove straight to Agnes's house. If my best friend couldn't lend me a sympathetic ear, then no one could. Perhaps she would even have a bit of harmless gossip, maybe about someone who attends my church. If what I needed was perspective, then shifting my focus away from Tammy Faye and Gabe, just might do the trick. To put it succinctly, it was possible that I merely needed to find new victims to judge.

I was surprised to find Agnes busy setting a beautiful table for three. She'd brought out the china that she'd inherited from her mother, and the beautifully embroidered tablecloth she'd received as a wedding present when she married old Doc – may he rest in peace. Agnes even had a fresh flower arrangement on the table, despite being allergic to most types of pollen.

'Agnes, dear, what gives?' I said. 'Does the Duchess of Sussex even have your address?'

'Very funny, Mags. If you must know, I've invited Toy and his husband here to lunch.'

'But why?' I asked. Why would Agnes do that when she used to have a crush on young Toy? Maybe she still did. If I were to be unsparingly honest – maybe under torture, or hypnosis – I might even admit that the sight of his comely visage, or the sound of his melodious voice, used to cause my nether regions to tingle shamefully.

Agnes reached out and patted my arm fondly. 'Mags, you may find this hard to believe, but I've finally decided to move on with my life. Having been briefly married to Doc, I found out what sex is all about, which for me, wasn't much. And before you say anything about there being other fish in the sea, I'm tired of swimming. Just like you, I'll be turning sixty in a few months, but unlike you, I have the opportunity to finally live out the rest of my days without the complications that involve caring for a family.'

'But you'll be lonely,' I wailed.

'No, I won't; you'll be popping in uninvited, and unannounced, every little whipstitch. But basically, I can set my own hours now. I can go to bed when I want or stay up all night if I wish. I can eat what I want, when I want. I don't *have* to clean my house – but you know that I will. Anyway, realizing that I am no longer searching for anything to fulfil me, has actually fulfilled me. At last I have stumbled upon contentment. Isn't that weird?'

'Definitely weird,' I said, although I wasn't necessarily agreeing with her conclusion. 'But doesn't entertaining two *married* men make you the slightest bit uncomfortable? I mean it's one thing to know that gay marriage is the law of the land, that it's out there in the world, but to have it here in Hernia, much less in your own home, I mean speaking of "weird".'

'Oh Mags, you're prejudiced.'

'I am not! The Bible states very clearly in Leviticus 20:13 that two men should not fornicate with each other.'

'That's where you, Mags, misquote even your own copy of The New King James Version of the Holy Bible. It says that they should not "lie" together. Since you take everything literally, you tell me what that means. Does it say that they shouldn't be telling fibs together? Or maybe even if it is about sex, it could mean that they shouldn't be lying down when they do the deed, but sex while standing is OK.'

'Ach!' I squawked. 'That's an even worse sin; sex while standing leads to dancing!'

'Oh, loosen up. Take a few stitches out of your sturdy Christian underwear and breathe a little. You're constantly using dance metaphors to symbolize the sex act, so why don't you actually try your hand at a little actual dancing. Maybe you and your Babester could take a ballroom dancing class over in Bedford. Just be mindful of those feet of yours, on account of – well, as you've reminded me a million times, they're the size of snow skis.'

'Get behind me, Satan!'

'Satan's gone home for the morning.'

'Agnes!' I said, shocked to the core. 'I can't believe that you said that. Aren't you a Christian anymore?'

'Tch,' Agnes said. 'Of course I am. I'm just tired of your goody-two-shoes, judgmental attitude, where just about anything fun is a sin.'

'*Moi?* Judgemental?'

'Mags, I also read my Bible, and I also arm myself with Bible verses that prove my points. Try this one on for size: "Then David danced before the Lord with all his might." Two Samuel 6:14.'

I hate losing arguments just as much as the next person. Sometimes it's wise to quit arguing, even when you're right, for the sake of friendship. Agnes's point wasn't valid because King

David was dancing before the Lord in some sort of religious ecstasy. He wasn't shaking his bottom to the beat of a drum or simulating the act of procreation. Something else was on my mind, something more important for a change than being right.

'Agnes, dear, does your newfound state of contentment mean that you are stepping back from your commitment to stopping Aaron Miller from destroying Hernia by building a gargantuan theme park within shouting distance of our peaceful little village?'

Agnes's eye left twitched, and she reached for a strand of her hair behind her ear to twirl around her finger. These were both new behaviours, and to me they were clear indications that I had put her on the spot. My BFF was either going to lie, or else take a stand that would make me simultaneously proud of her, as well as more than a mite irritated.

'Well, you see, Magdalena, the last time I saw the doctor, she said that I have borderline high blood pressure, and she gave me this pamphlet, and in it I read that stress is a contributing cause. And before you say anything, yes, she also said that I could stand to lose fifty pounds – uh – well, maybe eighty, or something, but Rome wasn't built in a day, was it? One has to start somewhere, doesn't one? Besides, stress causes me to eat. Therefore, to preserve this newfound peace of mind, this feeling of calm and contentment that I have finally come to in this, this last trimester of my life, I have decided not to involve myself in civic affairs.'

'Civic affairs?' I could feel *my* blood pressure rising like the tide in the Bay of Fundy. '*When* did you decide this?'

'Last night. Although it doesn't matter, Mags, because my decision is final.'

'I see. But tell me, dear, does it have anything to do with you losing your cool and slapping the vilest man ever to be born of a woman in the history of Hernia?'

My sweet lifelong friend wiped a tear from a chubby cheek with a stubby finger. 'Mags, you know that's not who I am; I'm not a violent woman. I brush ants and bugs up on to a piece of paper, and then I escort them outside rather than kill them. I feel awful about having hit Aaron. Did you know that it even made the national news last night, and again today on my favourite morning show? "Mennonite Woman Wages War on Christian

Developer!" That's what they titled the segment. As if Mennonites aren't even Christians, at least not compared to Aaron, the "developer". It made me sick. My phone started ringing yesterday evening immediately after the broadcast, and I kept getting calls until I turned it off at eight and went to bed. I even got a call from Hollywood, from a game show, saying that they were looking for spunky people like me for contestants.'

'Did you give them my number, dear?' I asked hopefully. I will concede the point that a prudent Magdalena ought never to set foot in a den of iniquity like Hollywood, where I've heard that 'just about anything goes'. However, if any one citizen of Hernia has both spunk in spades, and what it takes to be a good Christian witness to those West Coast heathens, then it's clearly me. Besides, in all honesty, it's awfully nice to be wanted.

Agnes clucked like a disturbed hen. 'No, I most certainly did *not* give the talent scouts your number. So who are you now, Mags? Joan of Arc on a sacred mission to save Hernia, or a would-be starlet, who will soon be wearing scarlet? Shame on you, Magdalena Portulacca. Do you know what your problem is? You want it all. You want to keep one of your ginormous feet planted firmly in tradition – that's why you've clung to the Old Order Mennonite ways – yet your other colossal foot is extended so far in front of you that you're practically doing the splits. That, *dear*, is why you married out of the faith altogether.'

I socked my chest with a balled fist to get my heart beating again. 'Y-you take that back!'

'Which part, Mags?' Agnes sneered. 'You knew that you weren't supposed to marry out of the faith, but you did it anyway.'

'The part about my feet.'

'Don't be silly; you're always making fun of your foot size.'

'That's different. They're *my* feet.'

'Fair point. I take everything back. From now on to eternity. Isn't that what best friends are for?'

I spread my long, bony, but otherwise elegant fingers in resignation. We had always resolved our squabbles equitably, and on the spot, but this time it seemed as if she had really bested me.

'OK,' I agreed, because I did have one flimsy arrow left in my quiver. 'But are you going to get a cat?'

'*What?*'

'You live by yourself now,' I said. 'Aren't single women your age supposed to have at least one cat to keep them company while they sit on the sofa and knit?'

'Mags, you know I don't like cats, and I've never learned how to knit. Purl this, slip that – they sound like instructions for getting dressed.'

'Well, I still think you could learn to like cats if you tried harder. Anyway, when are your guests arriving?'

'Not for another two hours. Now tell me why you're here so I can resume cooking them a lunch they will never forget.'

'Only if we can sit on your patio and munch on something. I didn't get a chance to eat breakfast.' Agnes has a cookie jar in the shape of a floppy-eared dog. His red hat is the lid.

'I suppose you'll want a glass of milk to go with the butter-scotch chip cookies I just baked. And talk fast, because I'll need to get the casserole in the oven no later than an hour from now, and you tend to be long-winded.'

'Why I never!' I said.

After I had been comfortably ensconced in one of the patio chairs, and had downed a cookie, along with half a glass of cow juice, I told her all about Gabe's visitors, and the shocking revelation that they had shared concerning Aaron's shameful exploitation of undocumented immigrants.

'Good for him,' Agnes said when I was through with my rushed recital of Aaron's sins.

'*What* did you say?' A butterscotch chip cookie, which I'd dipped in milk, fell into my lap before it could reach my mouth.

'Mags,' Agnes said, 'put yourself in the place of these undocumented workers. Many of them have fled crime, or otherwise horrible conditions, in their home countries. They have families to support, just like many documented Americans. And like everyone else they need a place to sleep and food to eat. Aaron is simply meeting their basic physical needs – safety, shelter, and food.'

'Yes,' I said, 'but they're not here *legally*.'

Agnes snorted. 'Good one, Mags. Were our ancestors legal immigrants?'

'Of course, dear. The British wouldn't have allowed them to settle here if they weren't here legally.'

'Ah, the British. Were *they* here legally? Didn't they just take the land from the original inhabitants? In 1750 the original inhabitants burned your family's cabin to the ground, scalped one of your female ancestors, and then took two of your male ancestors as their captives.'

'So?' I said petulantly.

Agnes patted my arm fondly. 'My point is that the original inhabitants must have thought that your ancestors, and mine, were illegal immigrants.'

'Don't confuse me with facts, dear. It's been a trying couple of days for me. This morning in particular. All I need to know is if I can count on you if the going gets tough. I mean really tough.'

Agnes stood and noisily began to clear the snack items. I knew that she had to get ready for her luncheon, but she could at least have answered before placing three china plates, and two glasses, on a serving tray. But then she turned suddenly, her face red with anger.

'You offend me,' she said. 'I would die for you, Mags. If you don't know that by now, then I guess you never will. Give me a call when my services are needed to throw myself on a live grenade, or take a bullet for you, but until then, leave me alone. And for the last time, I am not getting a cat, a dog, a bird, or even a goldfish.'

'What about a guppy, dear?' I said, and off I scooted. As a compliment to my friend's baking talents, I grabbed a couple of cookies off the serving plate.

On my way back to the PennDutch Inn, I swung by Yoder's Corner Market to ask Sam how his talk went with the Amish bishop. Sam was expecting me, and was in his office in the rear, so I parked out back by the service door. Before I could take two steps away from my locked car (yes, ever since finding a rattlesnake on my seat, I lock it) I got a text from the high school that Little Jacob attends. The message came from the school nurse, and I was supposed to call her immediately. Also, it was a matter of some URGENCY. Since Gabe was scheduled to be home and available to take calls all morning, and he is normally the pushover when it comes to issuing parental permission, I had little choice but to assume the worst. I could just picture the Fruit of my Womb lying prone on the gymnasium floor, after having been run over by a couple of much bigger boys during physical education class. Of course, it would be my fault, having had the hubris to allow a ten-year-old boy to advance to a grade where his classmates were seventeen and eighteen years old.

What I didn't expect to find was my baby sitting in the unlit nurse's station, under the desk, with his knees drawn up to his chest, and wrapped in a fluffy pink blanket. His teeth were chattering so hard, one would think he'd fallen through the ice on our pond during the January thaw. Although frankly it was the stench of urine that betrayed my son's location the second Nurse Lehman opened the door to her office.

'M-m-m-mama,' he said, 'I'm s-s-so sorry.'

'Nonsense, dear. It happens to best the best of us.'

Little Jacob's eyes widened. 'Even you?'

'Even me. I was exactly your age too. Of course, I wasn't nearly as bright, so I was only in fifth grade.'

'W-what happened?'

'How about you come out of there, and I'll tell you on the way home?'

'But I don't want any of the kids to see me!'

I stole a glance up at the enormous, round, analogue clock above Nurse Lehman's desk. 'Everyone is in class now except for hall monitors. Give me a minute head start, and I'll frown at them. That should send them all scurrying for the nearest exit.'

Little Jacob giggled and slowly emerged from his hiding place. When at last he stood, I could see that he was wearing only a shirt beneath the ugly pink blanket.

Nurse Lehman has had lots of practice reading small minds. 'Here you go,' she said, as she handed me an opaque plastic bag. 'His shoes and pants are in here. And there's no need to get the blanket back here anytime soon. I buy them from the thrift shop for precisely these sorts of occasions. The money comes from my discretionary fund which, come to think of it, comes directly from you anyway. So one might say, *you* bought the blanket. How about them apples?'

My son's small face scrunched up quizzically. 'Nurse Lehman, you're a really nice woman and I like you, but sometimes I don't understand the things you say. Like about the apples, I mean.'

Nurse Lehman smiled broadly and winked at me. 'That's just a silly expression. The important thing you should have heard was me saying that your mother is a very generous woman. Without her generosity, our village wouldn't have half of the services that it does now. Where there is a need in Hernia, your mother steps right up and supplies it. No questions – well, very few questions – asked.'

'Yeah?' Little Jacob said. 'I wish she stepped up and supplied me with a bigger allowance. Just about everyone in my grade thinks that my family is rich, but what I want to know then, if that's true, is why do I get the smallest allowance of any kid in the high school.'

Nurse Lehman laughed. 'What did you do, Little Jacob? Take a poll?'

'Yes.'

Since I'd promised to frown at the hall monitors, there was no time like the present to practice truly frightening facial distortions. Forget what your mother said about upturned eyelids getting stuck in that position. That's a myth. It is a fact that frequent frowning can leave a lasting impression on an otherwise youthful visage. The fact that one can hold a garden pea in the crease between one's eyes can be an indicator that one needs an attitude adjustment. And if one can hold even the smallest potato anywhere against the top of one's face, while one is in an upright position, perhaps it is time to take a few of one's issues to the Good Lord in prayer.

When Nurse Lehman saw my expression she laughed even harder. 'Your mama's a hoot, Little Jacob.'

'And a holler,' I said.

'Unh,' my progeny grunted.

I stuck my horsey head out into the hallway. 'The coast is clear,' I trilled. 'Let's vamoose.'

FOURTEEN

I t is amazing just how effective the right motivation can be. My dear boy was so afraid of being seen while wearing naught but a blanket and a shirt that he literally ran down the hall in a blue streak. But once he was securely buckled into his place in the car, and we were out of sight of the school his demeanour changed yet again.

'Mama, you're not going to tell Daddy about this, are you?' It warms my heart when Little Jacob calls me 'Mama' instead of 'Mom', but he only does so when he's needy.

'Darling, like I told you, there is no shame in what happened. I was even older than you when I had an accident. Mrs Reiner was the meanest teacher you would ever hope to meet, and she didn't like me in particular. That morning she wouldn't let me leave the room, no matter how hard I begged and – well, I know we're not supposed to hate anyone, but after that I really hated Mrs Reiner. Sometimes when I remember that day, I have to forgive her all over again.'

'Mom, stop!' Little Jacob said. 'Nobody kept me from going to the bathroom. But it *is* about you. Of course. Everything is about you, isn't it? It's always about you!'

I pulled over to the side of the road and stopped the car. 'How is this, what happened today, connected to me?'

'Because, Mom, everyone in my school is pissed at me, that's why!' Little Jacob's face was bright red, and there were veins throbbing at his temples. My baby, whom I had borne and nursed in my semi-dotage, looked like a livid old man – like a United States senator from the other party who hadn't gotten his way. And what language! If I had used the 'P' word my Papa would have seen to it that I wouldn't be able to sit properly for at least a week.

Well, the Good Lord had opened my shrivelled womb and blessed me with a child when I was nearing fifty. No matter how ugly my son's angry face was, and no matter how unfair his accusations, it was incumbent on me to remember that Little Jacob was a gift from God. That meant that I should be grateful that we were even having a conversation at this moment.

'Hallelujah!' I said. 'Thanks be to God.'

Little Jacob looked startled. 'What are you thanking God for?'

'For you, dear,' I said. 'You are the most precious thing in the entire world.'

'I'm not a thing, Mom!'

'Of course not. My bad.'

'Mom, don't try to be cool, because you're not. It's just weird.'

'Gotcha,' I said. 'Anyway, you're the most precious person in the whole world to me.'

'Ha! What about Daddy?'

'Your daddy's precious too, but I made you; I didn't make your daddy.'

'What about Alison? You're always talking about how much you miss her being away from home.'

'Alison's precious to me as well.'

'So who do you love more? Me, or Alison?'

'I love you more.' By the way, I used to say that to Alison as well, when she was insecure about my love. Face it, we all have a favourite child – the Bible is full of examples. The Bible also shows us that serious problems ensued when acts of favouritism were shown to that child. Therefore, I have always tried to treat my children equally when it comes to showing them affection and giving them age-appropriate allowances and gifts.

'Yeah, Mom, what if there's another kid in the family?'

I laughed. 'Little Jacob, I'm almost sixty years old. I know that Sarah in the Bible had a baby when she was ninety years old, but that was a special case.'

'He's not a baby, Mom. He's Alison's younger brother, only he's older than me. And he's mean as a stepped-on snake. But just because he's Alison's brother, that doesn't mean he's part of *our* family, does it?'

I was momentarily speechless – a rare event for me. Who knows how long I sat there slack-jawed, with my mouth hanging open, trying to process my son's words until he spoke.

'Mom,' he said sharply. 'You're catching flies, ya know?' It was an expression I'd often used on my children, and I deserved to hear it used on me.

'Is this kid's name Rodney?' I asked.

'So ya know all about him,' Little Jacob said accusingly, and started crying again.

'I don't know all about him, dear. I just learned about him, and I was told that he had gone back to Minnesota to be with his mother.'

'Well, he's *not*,' Little Jacob said, 'because his parents are divorced. He's going to live with his dad and he's going to my school.'

I stared at my son. 'How do you know this? Did you meet him?'

'He punched me in the stomach, and said that next time he'd break my nose and give me a black eye.' My precious boy started crying harder.

'He *hit* you? Why?'

Little Jacob gasped a couple of times and wiped his nose against his sleeve before answering. 'Because I called his dad an adulterer.'

'Oh.'

'Well, he was. Wasn't he?'

'Yes.'

'And do you know what he called *you*, Mom?'

'An adulteress?'

'He called you a seduc . . . a seduc . . . hmm. A seducelress, I think it was.'

'A seductress? How dare he!'

'Yeah, and he said that his dad calls you Jezebel. After he said that, half the kids in my class were chanting, "L.J.'s mom is Jezebel. L.J.'s mom is Jezebel".'

I fished a handful of facial tissues out of my brassiere and wiped his still runny nose. 'And where was your teacher while all of this was going on?'

'Looking at her phone.'

'*What?*'

'We had a sub, Mom. She wrote her name on the board, and then told us to read the next chapter in our Social Studies books and answer the questions. Then she didn't even look up till the bell rang at the end of the period.'

My blood, which had been simmering for the last couple of minutes, was now boiling. Any second, steam would come out of my pores, cleansing them from the inside out.

'What was this woman's name?'

'Miss Birdsong.'

'And did she remind you of a bird?' I demanded. 'Did she have legs like sticks, and did she chirp when she talked?'

'Yeah, I guess.'

'Well, I'll be a lemur's auntie! That was Susan Birdsong from our church. I taught her Sunday school ten years ago, and even then one would have thought that a phone was grafted to her hand. Well, I'll see to it that she doesn't substitute teach in this school system anymore.'

'You can do that, Mom?'

'You bet your bippy, I can. I'm not only on the Board of Education, but I bring the doughnuts to the meetings.'

That brought a 'snurfle' out of Little Jacob. For those unfamiliar with our family lingo, a 'snurfle' is the sort of chuckle one might produce after a hard cry.

I clapped my hands. 'Well, we should be getting you home, so that you can shower and change.'

'But Mom—'

'Sweetie, your daddy isn't going to care that you – uh – lost control of your bladder when some older boy hit you, and you were taunted by half your class. Your daddy's on your side.'

'Mom, there's one more thing. This kid Rodney was showing a picture to the other kids for five dollars a peek of Daddy's you-know-what.'

'No, I don't,' I said. 'What?'

Little Jacob's face turned crimson. 'His downstairs parts. How would Rodney even get that picture?'

'Because your daddy ran outside to investigate some noise on Hertzler Road the night that Aaron Miller drove into town. Unfortunately, your father forgot to put on a robe. Did you look at that picture?'

He managed to turn even more red. 'Yeah. I had to, didn't I? I needed to see if it was all a bunch of baloney. Mama, they were making jokes about Daddy. They called him names like Superman and Bigfoot and King Kong. But Mama, I ain't never going to grow up to be like Daddy.'

I hid my smile. 'All things in good time, dear. But I'm sure it will help a lot if you eat all your vegetables.'

I reached over and patted him lovingly. Then I started the car and put us back on the road. Gabriel was not a macho monster of a father who would deride his son for wetting his pants. Therefore I saw no reason to sneak our son into the house. In fact, doing that would be sending Little Jacob a wrong message, one that his accident had been something shameful.

'But Mom,' he practically shrieked, before I had driven a hundred yards, 'I didn't tell you the rest of what happened.'

I slammed on the brakes so fast, that my pocketbook, which I'd set on the console between us, hurtled to the floor of the car, its contents spilling everywhere. If we hadn't been belted securely in, the Hernia Rescue Squad would have been scraping our brain matter off of my windshield.

I pulled over and parked on the edge of a drainage ditch. 'What else happened, dear?'

'This,' Little Jacob said. He leaned over and pulled a pamphlet from his backpack, which had been wedged between his legs. It was three glossy pages, in colour, which he'd folded accordion-style, and then over once in the middle. When I opened it, I could hardly believe my faded blue eyes.

The cover page showed an artist rendering of the completed Armageddon amusement park, with its towering pavilions, and ant-like people milling about outside waiting to gain entrance. In bold red words across the top of the page were the words: The Worlds #1 Attraction Needs You! As if those words weren't provocative enough, when I opened the pamphlet, my dentures nearly fell out – and I have all my own teeth, mind you – for there followed multiple listings for 'actors wanted to play parts of screaming heathens consumed eternally by hellfire in Biblical drama'. They differed only in their requirements for age and gender. There were listings for actors to play the parts of 'Believers and Unbelievers in the End Times battle'. There was even a listing for an actor to play the part of the Whore of Babylon.

'The Whore of Babylon!' I said, reading that last listing aloud. 'That man has gone off the deep end.'

'That's what he called you,' Little Jacob said.

I jiggled pinkies in both ears to make sure they were both working. 'What?'

'Rodney called you the Whore of Babylon, Mom. He said that you didn't even need to try out for the part, because that's what you already were. That's when I punched him in the nose.'

'So then you each got a punch in?'

'Yeah. Are you mad?'

'No, dear. Just don't do it again. Hey, I thought Rodney called me a seductress.'

'He called you that too. Mom, what does "whore" mean? I didn't have time to look up the meaning, and everyone was laughing so hard.'

'It means a woman who does the mattress mambo for money.'

'You mean sex?'

'To put it bluntly, yes.'

'When you sex it up with Daddy, do you do it for money?'

'Why, Little Jacob, if I wasn't a practicing pacifist, and a loving mother, I'd have a mind to box your ears. What kind of question is that?'

'Well, Rodney Miller claims that you made his father pay you for sex.'

'That does it! I'm going to clobber that man – the father, not the son. But the son needs to have his mouth washed out with soap. An entire bar of soap, like one of those brands that they make for workmen, the kind that contains pumice.'

Little Jacob cheered weakly. 'But ya know, Mom, anything that ya do, will be taken out on me.'

'How so?'

'Most of the kids in the school already hate you.'

'*Me*? What did I ever do to them? Besides maybe tell them to shush if they were in my Sunday school class. Do you think that it's because I'm on the school board, and we've decided to extend the school year into the summer a full week, because of all the snow days we had to take this past winter? Because if that's it, I'm not willing to take the fall alone. Bobby Rittenhouse's father is also on the school board, and he wanted to add *two* more weeks to the term.'

'Calm down, Mom. It's not that. Mom, it's because you have too much power in the village, and they're afraid that you will find a way to stop Rodney's father from building this awesome amusement park. A lot of them want summer jobs as actors, or at the concessions stands, or working in the gift shop. Some of the girls are talking about this being their big break. Ya know, for their modelling and acting careers.'

'Right,' I said. 'Like playing the part of a heathen, screaming in agony, is going to make them a movie star.'

Little Jacob laughed. 'Yeah, that's kind of stupid, isn't it? But still, it could be fun, and they're looking for actors of all ages over seven. And look at it this way, ya wouldn't have to pay me no allowance if I got one of those jobs.'

'That's "any" allowance, but no was the right word in any case, because that's what the answer is. It's a big fat no! You are not working at Armageddonland, not as long as you're living under my roof.' I paused to reflect on something he'd just said. 'Why no actors under seven?'

Little Jacob stomped a bare foot on the floorboard of my car. 'Mom, ya know that!'

I bristled since I was already in a bad mood. 'If I knew – oh, I get it. It's because seven is the so-called "age of reason". Theologians give a free pass to children under seven, so there won't be any small children running around and shrieking in Armageddonland's Hell.'

'See Mom, ya ain't so dumb.'

'Young man, your grammar is getting worse by the minute. So here's what we're going to do: we're going home, where you're going to take a nice long shower, and then you're going to introduce yourself to the nice pair of atheists that will be joining us as your father's guests this weekend.'

'No way, Mom!'

'Way.'

'Honest-to-goodness, real, live atheists?'

'Rats, you got me there. These two have been dead for three years, but the taxidermist did a great job on them. Just be gentle when you're shaking her hand, because the instructions on the delivery crate said that her right pinkie was brittle. I don't want sawdust spilling out on my clean floors.'

When I saw the look that crossed his face I brayed like a she-donkey in heat. I have searched the scriptures diligently, and never found a verse that states that laughing at one's own jokes is a sin. Besides, as my friend Iris once said, "as long as you can tickle yourself, you can laugh whenever you please", so I often tickle myself with my own jokes.

Little Jacob was not so easily amused. 'Mom!'

'Well, at least part of what I said was true, sweetie. They really are atheists, but unfortunately they are still quite alive. Not that I wish them ill, it's just that I wasn't looking forward to guests this weekend. Hey, maybe you can help keep them entertained for me. Let's say I double your allowance – but you have to promise me something first, if I'm going to give you this assignment.'

Boy was that job offer a mood changer. 'Yeah? I'll make that promise, Mom, just tell me what it is.'

'You'll have to promise me you that you won't ask them any questions that have to do with God, or why they don't believe in Him.'

'Hey,' Little Jacob shouted, 'that's not fair, that's against my freedom of religion!'

'Little Jacob,' I said calmly, 'you have no freedom of religion. You're still a child.'

'But I'm a senior in high school! And you don't even make me go to church, because Daddy doesn't go to church.'

'More's the pity.'

'What is that supposed to mean?'

'We'll talk about it later,' I said.

We said not another word to each other until I pulled up next to the kitchen door. Then I reached over and smoothed his hair before unbuckling my seat belt.

'So, dear,' I said softly, 'what will it be? Would you like to charm these guests for some extra spending money, or would you . . . uh, prefer not to do so?' I'd been tempted to suggest that 'sulking' was the alternative.

My dear son leaned as far away from me as he could. 'I want to play in my room.'

To play in his room. Perhaps that was not a normal response for someone who was about to complete his senior year of high school and go off to university in the fall. However, it was not out of character for a boy of ten, even one with a genius IQ.

'Okey-dokey,' I said gently. 'So, how about I go in first and make sure that you have a clear shot into our bedroom, so that you can use our shower. If they're in the kitchen, I'll lead them into the parlour, or at least keep them in the dining room. Then while you're in the shower, I'll run up to your room and get you a fresh set of clothes. Does that sound like a plan?'

'Yeah.'

'Any special requests on the clothes?'

'No,' he mumbled.

I have a special request, I thought. Would it be too much to ask for you to thank me for dropping everything to run out to the school, and then so matter-of-factly handling your embarrassing situation? I know that's what mothers are supposed to do, but a lot of them don't, and anyway, that doesn't mean that one shouldn't thank the ones who do the right thing. And why should I be blamed because my ex-husband, who technically wasn't even my husband, had called me the Whore of Babylon?

But even worse than the besmirching of my name, was distributing those pamphlets in high school. That brilliant move by Aaron was going to tear this community apart. What Hernia parent was going to deny their child the opportunity to act in a Biblical drama? Especially when so many children don't want to go to church these days. To deny one's child this opportunity, would seem positively un-Christian. After all, acting the part of one doomed to eternal torment, just might scare someone back into the loving arms of Jesus.

But oh, what a terrible price my beloved village was going to pay for their children's religious education. Hernia would be subsumed by the culture of commercialized religion. Tourists would choke our quiet streets, and even if they hadn't already sold their farms, our Amish would still flee for the Dakotas, Nebraska, and Kansas – the rectangular states, so to speak.

As I saw it then, the battle against Armageddonland was all but lost. When I burst into the kitchen and saw the two atheists and the Babester gathered around the table, I quite forgot that his guests were on my side, and I forgot to think before I spoke.

'I'm going to kill Aaron Miller,' I shouted.

Rarely has this phrase passed the lips of a Mennonite woman who has been neither drugged, nor hypnotized. Immediately I regretted saying it, but of course it was too late to take it back. Little Jacob later told me that he heard me all the way out in the car. Unfortunately for me, I was to find out later that four people too many had heard me blow my stack that afternoon.

FIFTEEN

One of the things that really big feet are good for is killing lots of cockroaches with one stomp. Another thing is that they sometimes offer one the opportunity to think fast on them.

'I'm going to kill Aaron Miller,' I said again, just not as loud as before. 'That's what a lot of parents are going to be saying when their daughter goes acting from like a tormented pagan, to a Hollywood hussy.'

'Oy vey,' the Babester said. 'I can't wait to hear the rest of this story.'

'It's a doozy,' I said. 'Tell you what, sweetheart, why don't you entertain your guests in the parlour while I whip us up an afternoon snack? A Jewish nosh, an English tea, something for them, for you, and for me.' I was beginning to babble like the brook that ran through our woods.

'Mags, look at the table. That's what we've been doing.'

'Isn't that lovely,' I said. I waggled my sparse eyebrows at Gabe. 'Well, then maybe you'd care to take them into the parlour to meet Granny.'

'I've already done that,' Gabe said. 'Did you know that you're having eye spasms, babe?'

'Miss Yoder,' the handsome and virile-looking Jim Barker said, 'I actually *saw* your great-granny. Can you believe that? As well as heard her. Me, an atheist! I communed with a real, live ghost! It was the most unbelievable thing.'

Tammy Faye snorted. 'Yes, it is unbelievable. You saw her because I told you that I'd seen her. But on second thought, I really didn't. In my case it was an optical migraine. In your case, it was the power of suggestion – that's all it was. Gabriel, here, says he's never seen her, and he's a reasonable man – a man of science.'

'What about Miss Yoder?' Jim Barker said. 'Does that make her a whackadoodle?'

'If the doodle fits,' Tammy Faye said, and snickered.

Now, that hiked my hackles, but I didn't have time to throw a proper hissy fit, not when I had a ten-year-old sitting out in the car who was much in need of a shower. I have sometimes been accused of being a bossy woman, but a *whackadoodle*? Now that was a new one. Well, they say that if the shoe fits, then wear it, and since it was hard to find shoes to fit comfortably in my size, I decided to go for it.

'Cock-a-doodle-do!' I crowed, as I flapped my arms. 'Cock-a-doodle-do!' Roosters don't flap their wings while they crow, but I reckoned that city folks wouldn't know the difference.

The Barkers eyed me warily. 'Uh, Gabriel,' Jim said, 'if it's all the same to you, Tammy Faye and I could use some alone time in those splendid rocking chairs of yours on the front porch. Wouldn't we, darling?'

'Yes, yes, absolutely,' Tammy Faye said, and shot to her full height, on her perfectly shaped legs, in an indecent amount of time. It was a wonder that she didn't then immediately tip over, given the size of her upper body assets, because they far outweighed her well-proportioned bottom gifts.

When I was quite sure that they were out of earshot, I instructed Gabe to avoid eye contact with Little Jacob when he first saw him, and that I would explain later. Then I opened the kitchen door and beckoned our son to come in and head straight upstairs to his room, and his own shower. After that I was free to tell my husband everything that had transpired since I'd seen him last.

I wasn't even finished when the dear man pounded the old wooden table so hard with his fist that he cracked it. The table, not his fist, although that got pretty banged up as well.

'*I'm* going to kill that man!' he roared. 'Mags, you're going to have to wait in line.'

Quite unfortunately, that was the moment that our new house-help stepped in from the dining room. Allow me a moment to explain myself: Jonathan Hostetler cannot be called a maid, and I was going to refer to him as a houseboy, until the Babester explained that the term now has a sexual meaning. Anyway, Jonathan, who is eighteen, is the grandson of my kinswoman, Freni. After Jonathan made Rumschpringe, that period of finding oneself permitted to Amish youth, he decided to go secular. As a result, he is banned from his community.

Freni alone would not turn her back on him. Since she lives in a small widow's apartment that we've built for her attached to our house, there really is no room for her grandson to live there. However, we do have another finished space in a section of the barn where our previous housekeeper stayed. While Jonathan sorts out his life, he takes care of my livestock, cleans for us, and even cooks – a skill that Freni taught him.

Gabe's outburst left me unfazed, but I jumped when I saw Jonathan. 'You didn't see that, dear.'

'Yah, Cousin Magdalena, I did.'

'Well, maybe you did, but Cousin Gabe might have been playing a game on his phone.'

'There is no phone,' Jonathan said. 'He was talking about Aaron Miller, yah? The same man that you want dead. Shame on you for telling this lie.'

'Why I never!' I huffed. 'The nerve of young people these days. I would never have spoken to an adult like that when I was your age.' It's been said that the best defence is a good offense, and I can be quite offensive if need be.

'Cousin Magdalena, my mother taught me never to lie.'

'You mean Too-tall Barbara? What did her outspokenness get her? She had to move back to Iowa with your father and siblings because she was a square peg in a round hole, and she always shot from the hip.'

Jonathan looked like a sheep that had been asked an algebra question, or in this case, an Amish lad who'd been asked an algebra question. In either situation, neither sheep, nor Amish boy, would know the answer. This is because Amish children are exempted from attending school after the eighth grade. Too much education, the Amish believe, will lead their children to stray from the faith.

'Jonathan, have you heard about Armageddonland?'

'Yah, Cousin, it's in the Bible. It's the place where sinners will do battle with the saints of God in the last days.'

'That too, but it's also coming to Hernia.'

Jonathan had a beautiful smile that revealed perfect teeth. His height he got from his mother. The rest of his looks were either from her side of the family too, or else inherited from distant ancestors of mine. Frankly, Jonathan was far better looking than any boy that I knew of in Hernia, and I knew them all. I should think that Jonathan Hostetler would be a shoo-in as a male model, and he might do well to try his hand at acting.

I grabbed one of his large, strong hands – the other was holding a feather duster – and made him sit next to Gabe. Instinctively he looked down, as a good Amish boy should do when a woman not of the faith, and a distant relative to boot, is standing in your space. However, I snapped my bony (but still rather elegant) fingers under his nose which caused him to look up with a start.

'Pay attention to her,' Gabe ordered.

'Yah, Cousin Magdalena,' Jonathan said.

'Jonathan, this Armageddon, the one that's coming to Hernia, is an amusement park. Like Disneyworld. You have heard of Disneyworld, haven't you?'

His face coloured. 'Yah. I went there on my Rumschpringe. It was like magic. It made me happy inside.'

That wasn't at all the reaction I'd hoped for. 'But it was huge, right? With lots and lots of people.'

'Yah. And it cost a lot of money. I couldn't see everything that I wanted to see. They would not let us sleep on the street, or take food from the trash cans. Even if someone throws away half of a pizza, it must stay there. In the trash! Can you imagine that?'

'That's plumb outrageous,' I said. I patted my non-bosom a few times in sympathy, and then I plunged back into my nefarious plot of manipulation. 'The amusement park that's coming to Hernia is going to destroy this community. With our two-lane roads clogged with thousands of tourists cars, how will Amish buggies get around? That is if any Amish are left.'

'Ach, what do you mean?'

'Well, they want to buy up your farms for the space that's needed. They already own the old Bontrager place. They also made Sam Yoder an offer to turn his food market into a massive new superstore in order to serve the tens of thousands of employees that will be needed to run an amusement park this large.'

Poor Jonathan appeared gobsmacked. He swallowed hard before responding.

'How many employees?'

'Aaron Miller claims it will be bigger than Disneyworld, Florida. They will have over sixty thousand employees.'

'Then he must be stopped,' Jonathan said, his handsome jaw clenched. 'But without violence.'

'Of course not, dear,' I cooed. 'That was just a few seconds when the Devil got the best of me. But it won't happen again, I assure you. I have been in the slammer, the hoosegow, the house with bars for walls, and I have no intention of ever going back. Of course, my reticence to perform my bodily functions on a cold metal seat in full view of others, is not my primary reason. Murder is a sin, plain and simple, I cannot deny that. On the other hand, the Good Lord does fill part one of the Holy Bible with thousands of seemingly justified killings. I'm just saying.'

'Watch it, Mags,' Gabe said in his most disapproving tone, 'your tendency to overthink and over-rationalize things might undo any hope of rapprochement here.'

Jonathan smiled. 'Cousin Gabe, I don't know what you just said, but I agree with Cousin Magdalena. I see too much violence in the Holy Bible. Both parts. I too do not want to see an amusement park where people can take pleasure in watching others suffer, even if those who suffer have been condemned by their own sins in the eyes of God. The hearts of those tourists who take pleasure in this will be become hardened to the suffering of others in the real world. That is what I think.'

I clapped vigorously. 'Bravo, bravo! That's it in a nutshell. Jonathan, I need you to make a video for us saying exactly those words. Don't you agree, Gabe?'

'Yes, darling, I couldn't agree more.'

'Excellent. Then that's settled.' I strode over to our massive industrial-size refrigerator and perused its contents. Spying a clear plastic Tupperware container of fried chicken, I tucked it under my arm. 'OK, I'm off to see Aaron while you two stay here and make that video. Post it on YouTube and send it to all the TV stations in Pittsburgh and Harrisburg. Check and see if Little Jacob had a chance to eat his lunch before I picked him up at school. If not, feed him; that goes without saying. Oh, and don't hold dinner for me; I can put together a sandwich or bowl of cereal when I get home, but make sure that Little Jacob eats. He's a growing boy.'

'But Mags, you can't just—'

'But I can, dear. I love you. Bye.'

Then I was out the kitchen door faster than a cat in heat.

SIXTEEN

To get from the PennDutch Inn to the Bontragers' old farm was maybe just five miles as the crow flies (since they are monogamous, they always fly in pairs, unless some cruel person decides to shoot one). But crows fly over our numerous hills and creeks, and they ignore property boundaries. That said, it's a twelve-mile journey by car, and will take the faster driver (i.e. moi) eighteen point seven minutes to get there without doing damage to man, beast, or machine along the way. It can also take a lot longer if one gets behind an Amish buggy to two, or in this case, a string of Amish buggies headed to a funeral.

'Geez Louise,' I found myself swearing, and then slapped my mouth for having uttered a profanity. 'But can't you clop along any faster?'

The Amish hearse – and yes, there is such a thing as a long, black, hearse buggy – which led the procession to the cemetery, and therefore setting the pace, was moving so slowly that I feared the horses pulling it might fall asleep in their traces. I was sorely tempted to get out of my car, run ahead, and give one of the two horses a slap on one of its haunches. It wouldn't be a hard slap, mind you, but just enough to startle it, and move it along. After all, if this funeral procession played out the way it was going, then there stood a chance that the body ahead could badly decompose before it was put safely away in the ground.

I could see the road clearly because it curved substantially to the left, before disappearing between two hills. Because of this curve, and the topography which made the curve necessary, the road warranted two double yellow lines down the middle. Twenty years ago those double yellow lines might not have prevented me from pressing the pedal to the metal, and passing twenty-two horse-drawn buggies in one fell swoop. But I have matured a wee bit since marrying the Babester, and most especially since becoming a mother.

During my reckless driving days, one of my sister's kooky friends (Esmerelda believed in astrology and reincarnation and was a Presbyterian to boot) told me that she 'just knew' from looking into my faded blue peepers, that I had been a charioteer back in the days of the Roman Empire. Even crazier was Esmerelda's supposed memory that she had been my Greek wife, Epiglottis. You can't beat that with a stick, can you?

Now where was I? Oh yes, I was doomed to have to wait patiently while an Amish funeral cortège of twenty-two horse-drawn buggies crawled along for at least another one point two miles until they reached the turn-off for Weber Road and the Isaiah Weber Cemetery. Since suffering in silence is not my forte, I could sing – but that might spook all the horses, and they could bolt any which way, including loose. I could pray aloud – but that was sure to put both the Good Lord and myself to sleep, or I could check my phone for texts, and maybe even make a call. I decided on the last option.

Sure enough, there was a text from Cousin Sam. The Amish bishop had been horrified to learn about Aaron Miller's plan to build Armageddonland, and had promised to tell his flock not to sell their farms. After that I called my daughter.

'Hey Mom,' Alison said, 'I can only talk a minute because some friends of mine are stopping to pick me up. Then we're going out to eat.'

'Oh? Who are these friends?'

'Monique and Gary.'

'Alison, I hope that you're sitting down, because you're never going to believe what I just learned.'

'Mom, I have to hang up. They texted; they'll be here in, like, two minutes.'

'That's nice, dear, but this is something that Aaron Miller did, and you're not going to believe it.'

'Mom! We still have to make the bed in case one of them needs to walk through and use the bathroom when they stop.'

'We? Alison, who is the *we* that has to make the bed? When did you get a roommate?'

'Uhm – we is Terry.'

'Is that Terry with a "y" or Terri with an "i"?'

'It's Terree with two "ee"s.'

'Well, this is your mom, with four "mm"s and two "o"s, and your brother, Rodney, is alive and well and attending Hernia High School, where he is harassing your other brother, Little Jacob. Remember him? And who's behind all this? Why none other than Aaron Miller, that's who!'

Stunning someone into silence is only satisfactory if one can see the victim's face. After an interminable length of time, during which my fingernails grew back to clipping length, my smart-mouthed daughter responded. 'I'm going to kill Aaron Miller, if that's the last thing I do.'

Alison has not subscribed to my pacifist beliefs, but she stoops to help stranded earthworms off the sidewalks following heavy rains. She was no more of a killer than Mother Theresa was, or than Hillary Clinton is, or than I am.

'Listen dear, I'm on my way to see him right now, to set a few things straight – oh, thank heavens, at last!'

'At last what, Mom? Did your rupture finally happen?'

'That would be *rapture*, dear, and it most certainly won't be a joking matter for those who are left behind and face eternal damnation. No, I've been stuck behind an Amish funeral procession that hadn't been moving, and apparently they were waiting for Sheriff Stodgewiggle to come and stop traffic in the opposing lane.'

'If it's the Isaiah Weber Cemetery, everyone knows to look out for buggies when approaching from the west side. There's even a sign with a picture of a buggy on it. But why the heck did the Amish even put a cemetery there, on a blind curve.'

'The cemetery dates back to 1836, dear. At that time it was pretty safe to assume that there wouldn't be any cars racing around that curve. Anyway, we locals know what might await them around that bend, so we do mind the speed signs. Tourists, however, don't. So far there have been five fatalities there – three humans, and two horses.'

'Hey Mom, they're here – our dinner partners for tonight. Gotta go. Love ya!'

'Wait! Does Terree with too many "ee"s remember to put the seat down? Can you at least tell me *that*?'

Well she could have, if she'd been cooperative and stayed on the phone. Instead I was dropped like a hot potato. Maybe it was just as well, because by then I had reached the old Bontrager place. But to tell you the truth, I, who was most definitely not a tourist, almost zipped right past it with my lead foot.

It wasn't my fault, of course, because the landscape had changed drastically. Gone were the large pin oak set back on the house's right and the two silver maples in the front yard and the giant Colorado blue spruce that stood like a sentinel directly in front of the living room. Mable Bontrager planted that tree herself, never guessing that she would regret placing it so close to the house, and that it would eventually leave the sitting room dark, even on the sunniest days, much less fill the gutter with needles.

Now the house reminded me of a plucked chicken. I felt strangely embarrassed. I also felt like I wanted to cry – although there was no possibility of that. As I have an allotment of only seventeen tears a year, I need to save them up for the next death in the family. The year that my parents were killed, squished to death between two trucks in the Allegheny Tunnel, I'd already used up my quota by foolishly weeping over Nelson Burrell, a college boyfriend, who dumped me for Sherry Larson.

The house had been given a fresh coat of paint, and all the doors and windows that I could see, had been replaced. It is a wonder what one can do with an army of men in a short period of time if one has enough money. Instead of the banner that Alison had described following her visit, a brass plaque had been imbedded in a tall marble slab (rather like a tombstone, I thought, and fittingly so). In essence, the words on the plaque announced that the former Bontrager house was now the headquarters of Armageddonland, Inc.

Not being quite the timid soul that some might expect me to be, I marched right up to the fancy new door and walked right in. That's right, I did not bother to ring a bell or knock. And why should I? These people were out to destroy everything Hernia was about, and that made them my enemy. I'm not a betting woman, but if I were, I would wager that even the very polite English (the politest people on the planet) don't knock when invading an enemy camp. Taking the enemy by surprise, is to catch them with their pants down – not that I wanted to see Aaron Miller with his pants down again, mind you. The sight of *that* on our wedding night made it impossible for me to ever again look at a turkey neck without residual feelings of horror.

What I did not expect was to be greeted by a young redhead in a tight-fitting blouse, and a skirt so short that I immediately looked away, lest the Devil lead me down a new path of temptation. But as one must know what one is up against, to truly understand the gravity of one's situation, I decided that a close examination was in order.

Well, I am no expert in this matter, except for my many decades of assessing other women's looks and comparing them to my own, but this woman's bazoombas, as Gabe is wont to call them, had to be ninety percent silicon. Surely the Good Lord would not create a woman with a chest like that, and a waist so small that she could wear one of my napkin rings for a belt. But it was her hair that caused my appraisal to go from mere fact-finding to out-and-out judgment. Although this woman had red hair, she was no natural redhead. The black part down the middle of her do, as well as her black eyebrows, should instantly confirm this to any sighted man. Oh why, oh why, don't men see through this silly deception, and why do some women perpetrate it? Surely a quick peek on one's wedding night is going to reveal that the bride's drapes don't match her carpet. Plus, whenever such a woman forgets to groom herself on a regular basis, her significant other is sure to be surprised by what would appear to be black Persian kittens snuggling in her armpits.

'Are you here for the secretary position?' this fake redhead asked.

'Why would I be here for anything else?' I said, and nudging her gently aside, sailed past her and into a huge room, only part of which was once the Bontragers' living room. Then I remember Alison describing the presence of large-scale models of Armageddonland in the room. However, nothing Alison could have said would have prepared me for seeing these models with my own eyes.

'*Excuse* me?' the young woman said. 'Because if you are, I

feel that I should tell you right up front that Mr Miller likes his employees to be attractive.'

'Were you just about to leave then?' I said.

'Look, lady, I was referring to old women like you. And don't take it personally, because even my grandma couldn't get a job here because of her age, and she has a lot more going on than you do.' As she spoke she fluffed up her unnaturally red locks, and wiggled her hips seductively.

'Why I never!' I said. And then not to be outdone, I patted the mousey brown braids that coiled around my head, and wiggled my hips as well. Who knew that hip-wiggling was supposed to be sexy? I always thought that it meant one had something uncomfortable in one's britches. If I'd learned that this was the way to attract a man, back when I was equally as young as this gal, I could have been a grandmother by then, the matriarch of a large, inbred clan.

'Aaron, honey!' the young woman practically screeched.

'Tiffany,' I heard a man's sharp rebuke, 'you're supposed to come and get me – what on God's glorious earth is this lovely surprise doing here?'

And there he was, the horrible man who was committed to ruining Hernia, just because I'd flushed him from my marital bed – to coin an apt expression. In all truthfulness, the sound of his voice still made my legs quiver, and when I saw his face again, my first feeling was not revulsion, or even mere anger. It was more akin to nostalgia for what we had had together in the beginning, followed by a second or two of pining for what might have been. I am a God-fearing woman, one who takes the Bible literally (well, in most cases), and thus I believe that marriage is forever. So when I pledged my troth to this handsome man with a voice that could calm the Bosporus Straits, I meant it.

I made a promise before God that I would love and protect him forever. Then when I discovered that we weren't legally married, I was not only devastated, but confused. How does one 'un-love' another person, even a person who had hurt one so deeply? There isn't a switch that one can just turn off. Suppose that one realized that there was still an ember somehow glowing in the heart that had once been broken clean in half? The astonishing thing was that the ember had not been extinguished over

the years, despite the fact that one practically hated the man.
By the way, to actually have hated him, would have been the
same thing as murdering him. Those are Jesus's words, not mine.

But introspection is a luxury that I am rarely afforded. That
afternoon was not to prove the exception.

'Why Magdalena, what a wonderful surprise. As ever, Babe,
you are a sight for sore eyes.'

I was of half a mind to say 'same back at you', while the
other half was wishing there was a way to draw and quarter
his handsome torso (his beautiful head with its strong jaw and
high cheekbones, I would leave intact). Instead I slapped my
own cheeks as a way of knocking me back on the track. Besides,
the temporary sting was sure to put some colour into my old
cheeks.

Then I cleared my throat. 'First of all, Aaron, I am not your
babe, and I'm certainly no longer a sight for your sore eyes. Not
when you have Miss Universe standing here.'

The woman-child laughed. On closer inspection her face looked
remarkably familiar.

'Oh honey,' she said, 'I weren't no Miss Universe. But I was
second runner-up to Miss Teenage Hog Slop Hollow down in
West Virginia.'

'You can take comfort in the fact you weren't third runner-up,'
I said kindly. 'Now if you will excuse us, dear, Mr Miller and I
are going to have a private conversation.'

'Oh, he don't mind if I'm here, do you Sugar Bear?'

'This is an adults-only conversation, Poopsie Woopsie,' I said.

Aaron chuckled. He has a deep voice, and if a bear could
speak, it might well sound like him.

'Tiff,' he said addressing the girl, 'why don't you go upstairs
and type up the notes from this morning's meeting?'

'You know that I can't type, Sugar Bear. Besides, we didn't
have no meeting this morning.'

'Sugar Bear wants you to get lost, dear,' I said helpfully.

'Fine!' Tiff stamped a foot, and given that her shoe had a six-
inch spike heel, it was not a good move. The poor child toppled
sideways, in my direction, and as a good Christian woman, I saw
it as my duty to catch her. It is important to know that my long,
gangly arms are not equipped with tentacles, because I was not

at fault for her slipping out of my arms and landing a wee bit
hard.

'Ow, ow, ow! She pushed me; this old bag of bones pushed
me. You saw that, Sugar Bear, didn't you?'

'I did not,' I said hotly. 'If you weren't wearing those ridiculous
shoes, and lost your temper, none of this would have happened.'

'Ridiculous shoes?' Tiff hissed. 'I'll have you know that not
only do high heels make a woman's leg look longer, they also
show off her calf muscle. And for your information, these *ridiculous* shoes are genuine imitations of the ones that Jennifer
Anniston wore to the Oscars.'

'That may be, dear,' I said, 'but if you wore sensible brogans
like I do, you wouldn't topple over like the Leaning Tower of
Pisa is bound to do some day.'

'Uhg! Your shoes are clodhoppers and they're gross, just like you.'

'Thank you for the update, dear,' I said, even as I helped
her to her foot – the one that still had an intact heel. Interesting,
I thought, that Sugar Bear had made no move to catch her, or to
stand her upright.

'Go upstairs and do whatever you want, Tiff,' Aaron said. Then
as soon as she'd hobbled out of earshot, he grabbed my arm, and
steered me to the largest model across the room. 'This one is
going to be a real game-changer,' he said.

I stared mutely, while I tried to comprehend the scene before
me. When at last I understood what I was looking at, I turned
slowly to Aaron as I struggled to find the right words.

'This time you've gone too far,' I whispered. 'Alison told me
about these models, but apparently she hadn't seen this one. I
promise you that nothing like that will ever be built in Bedford
County.'

SEVENTEEN

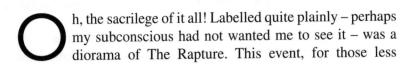

h, the sacrilege of it all! Labelled quite plainly – perhaps
my subconscious had not wanted me to see it – was a
diorama of The Rapture. This event, for those less

informed, precedes the Second Coming of Jesus. At the sound
of a trumpet, and in the 'twinkling of an eye', folks who have
been 'saved' will rise up to meet Jesus in the sky. The Bible
states quite clearly that no one will know the date of this occur-
rence. Therefore everyone will be caught by surprise. This means,
for instance, that any Christians who are driving down the
road – perhaps on their way to do a bit of shopping – will be
plucked out of their cars, and said cars, which will then
be unmanned, will subsequently crash. The same thing holds true
for pilots, train engineers, and boat captains. They'll be whisked
away from their jobs. However, their passengers, if not saved,
will be in a bit of a pickle – and that's an understatement.

'Mags, so what do you think?' Aaron said.

'My name is *not* Mags,' I said. 'Not for you, it isn't. *You* may
call me Mrs Rosen. As to what I think – it's an outrage.'

'Calm down,' Aaron said, and lightly touched my elbow. I
must confess that I felt both a thrill, and a deep sense of loathing.

How could I react like that? I wondered. What was the source
of power behind this lying, cheating bigamist? How could he lay
claim to any part of my heart, unless he was the Devil himself?

'Get behind me, Satan,' I cried, and jumped away from the
evil man.

Aaron had the temerity to laugh. 'Same old Mags,' he said.
'I bet you take the Bible literally, that you think every word was
dictated by God.'

'You're darn tooting I do – oops, sorry about the swearing.'

'You never have any doubts?' he said.

Of course I had my doubts – from time to time. I am human,
after all. But I wasn't about to share my spiritual journey with
this man. Neither do I share the details with Gabe, because then
he would think that he had made a convert of me with his so-called
rational way of thinking. Even my pastor, Reverend Wilbur
Utterall, wasn't privy to my inner thoughts. Only Agnes, my pal
from infanthood, knows how I struggle sometimes to keep my
feet on the one true path.

'You'll never get away with this,' I said to change the subject,
as I pointed to the diorama.

What lay before me was a detailed replica of the main
street running through a small Midwestern town. The flat-roofed

buildings included a pharmacy, a ladies' dress shop, a barber shop, a florist, and an antique store, among others. There was writing in the shop windows, and a pair of pansy-filled urns stood on either side of the door to the florist shop. Figures of people, finely crafted from resin, dotted the sidewalks. Details of small-town life were everywhere – pigeons roosting on window ledges, and even a shaggy white dog relieving itself against a yellow fire hydrant.

Of course, no town would be complete without automobiles on the street. The toy cars I beheld before me appeared to be of the highest quality, perhaps even special editions made to order. They certainly were nothing I'd ever seen, and I had a ten-year-old son who collected model cars. However, all of these cars had been purposely damaged to some extent, to make them appear as if they had been involved in various automobile accidents. Two cars that were 'totalled' had supposedly been involved in a head-on collision. There was a pile-up of cars as a result of a rear-end wreck, and one much damaged car had ended up on the sidewalk and was 'wrapped' around a lamp post.

I shook my head as I beheld what lay before me on the display table. 'I realize that you have based this diorama on the Book of Thessalonians, but—'

'Chapter four, verses thirteen through eighteen,' Aaron said proudly. 'I had the same religious upbringing as you did, Mags. Like you, I know my scripture.'

'Yes, but are we to take pleasure in watching these non-believers wreck their cars? Don't you think we will have other things on our minds, seeing as how we will have joined Jesus in the clouds?'

Aaron grunted. 'This is a teaching moment for all non-believers. In fact, all of Armageddonland is meant to inform those who are still lost, to come to terms with what awaits them if they do not convert.'

'Ha!' I said. 'Armageddonland is meant to make you even richer than you apparently are. Besides, how could The Rapture be turned into a ride?'

'"Oh ye of little faith",' Aaron said, quoting Jesus out of context. 'This will be our most expensive ride – although actually it will be billed as an "experience", not a ride. For three hundred and fifty dollars, and some change, participants will ride in facsimiles of cars along a track that takes them through the village resembling this one. The cars will be made of flexible material that can be crushed, and then pop back into shape when the ride is finished. The participants – we call them guests – will be wearing harnesses – like the ones actors use when they supposedly fly on stage. The roofs of the cars will consist of thin paper that has been pulled taut over a framework to give them shape, and of course the paper will have been coloured the exact shade of the car. When the trumpet of the Lord sounds, the guests will be lifted straight up, right through the roofs of the cars. Mags, you have to admit that it's a brilliant idea.'

'No, I do not! First of all, you'll be promoting the idea that it's alright to ignore the pain of others, in this case the crash victims.'

'The *others* made their choice, and it was the wrong one. In this case, however, the so-called others will be represented by "crash dummies", but realistic ones. Plus, there will be a soundtrack of tires screeching, people shouting—'

I shook my head. 'You're a greedy, sick man, Aaron Miller. In any case, I didn't drive out here this afternoon to argue with you about your hare-brained schemes. I want to know why you lied to Alison about the whereabouts of her brother.'

Aaron smiled slowly. 'You're a smart woman,' he said. 'Why don't *you* tell me?'

'All right, then I will. You didn't want your daughter to throw a monkey wrench in your plans. You were afraid that if she met Rodney, and they got to know each other, she might be able to convince him not to cooperate with you.'

Aaron winked. 'Like I said, you're a smart cookie.'

'Stop it,' I said. 'Don't you dare wink at me. I'm furious at you, Aaron. Do you know that your son harassed Little Jacob today at school, to the point that I had to come and get him? If this happens again, I'm going to do everything in my power to see that Rodney gets expelled.'

Aaron reached for my hand, but I snatched it away. 'Mags, you're beautiful when you get angry. Has anyone ever told you that? You look mighty fine up there on your "high horse". Come back to me, sweetheart, and we can blend our families. Then Little Jacob will have a big brother, not an adversary.'

'Little Jacob is not your son's adversary!' I shouted. 'And I wouldn't come back to you, even if we were the only two people left on earth. Aaron Miller, you are the slime beneath the scum on the pond across the road from me.'

His eyes danced. 'You mean the Miller Pond, the one I used to own when I lived there. It was on the banks of that pond that I first kissed you.'

Ding, dang, dong, darn him, for remembering that moment. It had been my first kiss, and the thrill of it sent sinful shivers of delight throughout my body. I mean *everywhere*. Not that this is any of your business, of course.

'The pond has been renamed, buster,' I said. 'We now call it Dead Skunk Pond, after what we found floating in it last spring.'

Aaron laughed. 'I'm telling you, the more you get worked up, the more beautiful you become. Kiss me again, Magdalena, and let me die a happy man.' He grabbed my left arm and tried to pull me close.

I slapped his hand and managed to jerk my arm loose. Frankly, I would have slapped his face if not for a brilliant thought.

'I think that you should allow the people of Hernia to see your well-executed models. I mean, perhaps if they see how much effort you've put into their construction, some of them – I mean us – might start to think about your project differently. They might start to see you as a serious investor in our community – vis-a-vis employment opportunities. Who knows, some of them might even be persuaded that such a theme park might actually do more good than harm. Maybe then one of them will be able to convince me of the same.'

Aaron regarded me warily. 'You're up to something; I can tell it. What's the catch, Mags?'

I coughed and cleared my throat, in order to give myself more time to think. 'There isn't a catch: it's just that all of a sudden, I feel resigned to this travesty happening. But before I give up entirely, I want my fellow Herniaites to weigh in with their opinions. Their informed opinions. If enough of them welcome your – uh – project, then maybe I might become convinced that Armageddonland will be more of a blessing than a curse.'

'You don't mean that for a second,' Aaron said. 'Liar, liar, dress on fire. Still, I think your idea might have some merit. I suppose that I could hold an open house here and let the peasants tromp through.'

I feigned horror. 'Not after all the work you've down to remodel this old house. I assume that these displays are transportable. Am I right?'

'Yes,' Aaron said cagily. 'I did bring them down from Minnesota with me.'

'Great! Then it's all settled, you can bring them down to Beechy Grove Mennonite Church and set them up in our new social hall. We can make this a two-day event. The first day, we'll invite the pastors and board members from all our churches, as well as the town council. I'll see to it that the ladies from church supply some light refreshments, and we'll have you give a speech. Then the second day the general public will be invited, which will give you a chance to peruse the crowd for potential actors. You can speak again then, if you like, but of course there won't be any refreshments. I can't con— I mean convince my church ladies into putting themselves out for *that* many people. I'm sure you understand.'

Aaron grinned, showing teeth that were unnaturally white in my opinion. After all, if the Good Lord wanted us to have blindingly white chompers, then he would have created us that way. He certainly wouldn't have given some folks, like me, pleasingly yellow smiles.

'What I understand, Mags,' Aaron said, 'is that you are up to something, but hey, I'll bite. I think it will be worth the inconvenience of moving these dioramas to your church, just for the chance to see what you really have up your long, modest sleeve.' He winked again. 'As your former husband, I can attest to the fact that you have lovely arms under your sleeves.'

'Ha,' I scoffed. 'These spindly things? They look like broken golf clubs with elbows.'

'Mags,' Aaron said sharply. 'Stop putting yourself down. There was even a psychiatrist in Bedford who stated that you suffer from body dysmorphia. Your arms are lovely. Period.'

Compliments are my undoing. First of all, they are extraordinarily rare, and are usually said with sarcasm. Therefore, it is understandable that when I am complimented, I either refuse to hear them, or else I'm given to irrational behaviour in response. In any case, I should not be held responsible for what I did next.

'Lovely, are they?' I said, as I pushed back a sleeve an inch to reveal a slender wrist.

'I think I'm going to swoon,' Aaron said in response.

Of course he was being sarcastic, but nonetheless I enjoyed his gentle teasing. Who knows, I might even have rolled my sleeve all the way back, had it not been for the sudden intrusion of a third party.

'Aha, so you are here! Your secretary lied.'

I whirled and found myself practically nose to nose with Sam Yoder's wife. When it dawned on Dorothy who I was, she emitted a yelp of displeasure.

'You can't choose her,' she said to Aaron. 'Magdalena does not have an ounce of sexuality, and Heaven knows that she can't act. Magdalena can barely say her own lines without fluffing them.'

Aaron beheld his newest intruder with a look of amusement. 'How nice to see you, Dorothy, after all these years, although I can't imagine you share this sentiment. Weren't you one of the folks who came after me with tar and feathers when news got out that I seduced Magdalena into a fraudulent marriage?'

'Not me,' Dorothy cried. 'When I found out that you were a lying cheat, I kept my mouth shut. I didn't say a word to anyone about what a scumbag you were. And I could have been gossiping like crazy, given that everyone in Hernia walks into our store sooner or later.'

'She's right,' I said. 'Back then Dorothy was confined to her room above the store by four-hundred-and-sixty-five pounds of . . .' I let my voice trail off before saying the 'F' word, lest I be accused of shaming her.

'In that case, Dorothy,' Aaron said, 'tell me why you're here.'

'I want to play the part of The Whore of Babylon.' She thrust a coloured brochure at Aaron, which he reluctantly took. 'One of your flunkies dropped off a passel of these things at our store. I know that it says to sign up for an audition online, but what is the point of that, when all it takes is one look at me, and you can see that I fit the part exactly?'

Aaron shook his head. 'Actually, you don't, Dorothy. The woman I have in mind is . . . well, let's just say "not of your generation".'

Dorothy stared open-mouthed for an uncomfortable length of time.

'He means that you're too old, dear,' I said.

Dorothy glared at me, and then pointed a painted talon at Aaron. 'You'll pay for this,' she hissed. 'Mark my words: you will both pay for this.'

EIGHTEEN

When I returned to The PennDutch Inn I found my 'menfolk' and the Barkers sitting around the kitchen table playing Scrabble. I didn't need to ask the score to learn who was ahead. Last year, when he was nine, Little Jacob made it a goal of his to memorize every entry in the *Official Scrabble Dictionary*. He succeeded at this task in just six months, and now the game is no longer fun for his father and me. But obviously neither of my guys had bothered to inform our guests that they were at a disadvantage.

'Who's ahead?' I asked, just to boost my son's spirits.

The three adults groaned in unison.

'Sweetheart, what took you so long?' the Babester asked. 'You *did* tell us not to hold supper, but I have a plate for you in the fridge.'

'Thanks.'

I plodded over and retrieved my dinner and heated it in the microwave. After wolfing down a couple of bites, I felt revived enough to talk.

'I don't suppose any of you four can quote the Gospel of John, chapter three, verse twenty,' I said with a chuckle.

To my utter astonishment both Barkers raised their hands. Leave it to the two atheists to know the scriptures.

'Tammy Faye,' I said, 'be a dear and tell us what you think the verse means.'

'It means that evil people don't like having their actions scrutinized closely, because they won't hold up in the light of day.'

I nodded approvingly. 'Well said. This afternoon I got a close-up look at Aaron Miller's plans for Armageddonland, and they were even more shocking than I'd been led to believe. He wants to scare people, like the four of you, into converting.'

'That will happen when Hell freezes over,' Jim Barker growled.

'But hon,' the Babester said, 'don't you want the same thing?'

'Yes, dear, I do,' I said. 'But I want you to convert out of love for Jesus, not out of fear of Hell.'

Gabe said nothing, and I didn't push. I knew his reasons for his beliefs; I'd known them before we got married.

'Anyway,' I said, 'I made a unilateral decision that the best way to get this community to band together and do something to stop this amusement park from being built next to our village, is to make everything about it public. To that end, I have invited Aaron Miller to bring his detailed models and dioramas and put them on display at Beechy Grove Mennonite for a gathering of the local church councils, as well as the town council. He will also be giving us a lecture that will provide us more details on the park. After that, we will serve refreshments.'

'Mags, you didn't!' Gabe said. He regarded the Barkers anxiously.

'I think that it's a brilliant strategy,' Jim Barker said. 'But only *if* the townspeople aren't seduced by looking at the evidence.'

'I agree,' Tammy Faye said. 'These simple villagers might wish to see these model-size exhibits actually built, in order to add some excitement to their otherwise dull lives.'

'That is so insulting,' the Babester said. 'I'll have you know that some of us lead very exciting lives.'

'Indeed,' I concurred. 'Why just last week I won Hernia's one-hundred-and-fifty-sixth annual Watch the Paint Drying Contest. Not counting the birth of my son, those eleven hours were the most exciting I've spent in my entire life.'

'Please accept our apologies,' Jim Barker said. 'But I have a question: when is this happening at Beechy Grove Mennonite Church? And would it be possible for Tammy Faye and me to wrangle invitations?'

'It's Saturday, and yes, you can be my guests. But be

forewarned, there will be prayers, and maybe a hymn or two sung. It's at a church, after all.'

'Mom, can I go too?' Little Jacob asked anxiously.

I gave him what I thought was a meaningful look. 'You-know-who might be there, dear.'

'If he is, then I'll punch him in the stomach,' Little Jacob retorted instantly.

I glared at his father, whom I knew to be the guilty culprit. Although secretly, and I'm ashamed to admit this, I was glad that Gabe had given back his son a spirit of confidence.

'Hon,' Gabe said, 'in today's mail there was a fancy brochure from Armageddonland. It was just like the one Little Jacob said was distributed around his school. But besides describing the place that's coming, they were listing a slew of employment openings. Most of them were for entertainers and actors. Do you have any clue why Aaron is advertising these jobs so far out in advance, when the place isn't even built?'

I gulped down another enormous bite of food before answering. Yes, it was rude of me to stuff so much food into my mouth at one time, but it's also a bit rude to perish from starvation in front of guests, if one has a plate full of food in front of her.

'I do know the answer, because I asked Aaron that exact question. He gave me an evil grin and said it was a "hook" to get young people on his side. I asked him what he meant by a "hook", and he said that most kids these days dream about being famous, and that it was common knowledge that acting was a proven path to fame. He said that when kids see that there are acting roles for them, they will have dreams of being discovered by Hollywood types. This means that these kids are going to pressure their parents to side with Armageddonland, if it comes down to a communitywide vote.'

'Wait a minute,' Gabe said, 'the Conservative Mennonite kids from your church don't care a frozen fig about acting, or worldly fame – or do they?'

'You're right,' I said, 'but there will be hundreds of other job opportunities for them. Remember this will be a huge theme park, and it will require concession stand employees, greeters, a large janitorial staff, groundskeepers, parking lot attendants—'

'I get it,' Gabe said.

'And we have five other churches in town that are more liberal than mine,' I said.

'Yes,' Little Jacob said, 'like Auntie Agnes's Mennonite church, right? Why can't your church be like hers?'

I gave him a loving mother's version of the evil eye. 'Because we're not the same denomination, dear. You know that.'

'Schisms, and circumcisions,' said Jim Barker. 'Two good reasons not to like religion.'

I turned to Gabe's atheist guest. 'Mind your own beeswax,' I said kindly. 'Now, where was I?'

'You were speaking of the five other churches in town,' Gabe's other atheist guest said.

'Yes, dear. Normally I wouldn't expect many would-be actors coming from the liberal Mennonite Church, or the church with sixty-six names, but since the theme of this park is based on the Book of Revelation – well, that's a horse of another colour. And of course Armageddonland is going to need actors of all ages, including senior citizens, and with the unemployment rate being what it is – well, if we're going to save this town, we've got our work cut out for us.'

Little Jacob's hand shot up, as if he were still in school. 'Is Daddy a senior citizen?' he asked.

'Bite your tongue,' Gabe growled, while the rest of us laughed.

Then we all jumped a bit when we noticed, quite simultaneously, that there was a little grey man standing in my kitchen not five feet away from where we sat. I am sad to report that this intruder was not an alien from another planet, because I have always wanted to know if some of those folks also believe in the one true God and His son Jesus, and if so, have some of them been saved. Think about it: will I see aliens in Heaven, and will Hitler encounter aliens in Hell? Alas, this dingy munchkin was actually my very own pastor, the Reverend Wilbur Utterall. Not only was he the spiritual leader of Beechy Grove Mennonite Church, but he was the improbable husband of that firebrand, Prissy Utterall.

Reverend Wilbur Utterall is barely taller than ten-year-old Little Jacob, and like my son who has not yet reached puberty, Wilbur has narrow shoulders. Unlike Little Jacob, my pastor has grey hair and eyes, large round ears, and a curiously grey cast to his skin. Unfortunately, he draws attention to the latter condition by wearing rumpled grey suits, with matching grey shirts and grey ties. Even his suede shoes are grey. On the plus side, Reverend Wilbur Utterall lacks an overbite and a visible tail. Therefore, when he's up in the pulpit preaching, only a bored parishioner with an overactive imagination would come to the conclusion that this little man resembles an unusually large mouse.

I must that confess that I was head of the search committee for the new pastor. Not only that, but I advocated strongly for the candidate, Wilbur Utterall. For one thing, despite his appearance, the man is only thirty-five. That means he is young enough to connect with our youth, but still 'old enough to know better'. Well, one hopes so, at any rate. But mostly I liked that he came from a village similar in size to ours, with similar demographics. And yes, it didn't hurt that he was the only candidate that didn't flinch when I mentioned the salary that we were willing to pay.

'Reverend!' I cried, when I saw him standing there ghostlike in my kitchen. 'Where did you come from? I mean, how did you get in?'

'Your front door was unlocked, Magdalena,' he said softly. 'What a lovely custom. It gives me goose flesh to think of all those times that you might have entertained angels unawares, just like it says in the scriptures.'

'Or serial killers,' Tammy Faye said. 'Keeping one's door unlocked is a stupid custom.'

'Hmm,' Reverend Wilbur Utterall murmured. 'To each their own, I suppose.'

'Reverend,' I said, 'you've met my husband and son, but allow me to introduce you to Tammy Faye and Jim Barker. They're friends of Gabe.'

'So,' Reverend Wilbur Utterall said, 'you are of the Jewish faith, I presume?'

Jim extended his hand. 'No sir, my wife and I are atheists.'

The reverend who'd also extended his hand snatched it back. I'd like to think that he did it subconsciously.

'Atheists in Hernia. Imagine that.'

'But don't worry,' Little Jacob piped up. 'Mom said that they ain't alive anymore. She said that they've been dead for three years, and that a taxidermist stuffed them with sawdust. But you got to be careful shaking hands with them, because you don't want to go breaking off any of their fingers, and getting the sawdust to spill. You see, my mom's kind of a neat freak.'

'L.J.!' I said sharply.

'But it's true, Mom. You said every word of that, didn't you?'

'Yes, but you knew I was joking.'

The little rascal shrugged. 'Did I? I'm just a kid. I'm supposed to take adults at their word.'

'Oh, come on,' I said. 'I explained right afterwards that I'd been only kidding.'

He shrugged again. 'Maybe that was the time when you were joking.'

'This is no longer funny,' I snapped.

'Well, anyway,' Reverend Utterall said in his soft, sibilant voice, 'I came to talk to you about that message you left on my phone this afternoon.'

'Excellent,' I said. 'Pull up a chair, Reverend. That's what we were just discussing ourselves.'

The grey eyes looked startled. 'With atheists?'

'Indeed. They're every bit as much against having Armageddonland built as we are. Maybe more so.'

'You don't seem to understand, Magdalena,' Reverend Wilbur Utterall said, this time avoiding eye contact. 'I'm not against the project. I'm actually very much in favour of it. That's why I'm here. Not only do I approve of having this event happening at our church, I want to offer my assistance in any capacity that I can.'

Oh, what a let-down, what a complete betrayal. Pastor Utterall had utterly gobsmacked me. His sermons had always been mildly inspiring, but they had never once touched on hellfire and brimstone.

'But Aaron Miller is an evil man,' I said vehemently. 'He was still married when he seduced me into marrying him, and me, an innocent virgin, who had never even been kissed. Then, even after that sham of a marriage was legally declared invalid, Aaron refused to leave me alone. I had a restraining order put on him, but it wasn't enforced, because back then our Chief of Police was Melvin Stoltzfus, who was so incompetent, that his name appears in the dictionary as part of that word's definition. Finally, I took matters into my own hands and I paid Aaron Miller to leave Hernia.'

'Mags, you didn't!' Gabe said.

'I had to, dear. I gave him fifty thousand smackeroos on the condition that he never show his hiney in Hernia again.'

'I'm sorry to hear you talk this way about Aaron Miller,' my pastor said quietly.

'You're sorry?' My voice rose two octaves, in keeping with my indignation. OK, so perhaps I was a mite shrill for a mild-mannered Mennonite, but I didn't break any lightbulbs.

'Actually, if I may speak freely . . .' Pastor Utterall had begun and ended his request by mumbling at a frequency inaudible to the human ear.

'Speak freely, by all means, but speak up! Pretend that you're in a shouting match with your wife Prissy, and that I'm her. Go ahead, now yell at me.'

'Prissy,' my pastor hollered, 'I don't want to have sex twice a day; it tires me out!'

NINETEEN

I t was President Theodore Roosevelt whose foreign policy was 'speak softly and carry a big stick'. That was Reverend Utterall's church policy as well. If it was also his marital policy to speak softly and carry a big stick, that would certainly explain the gleam I saw in Prissy's eyes from time to time.

At any rate, by the time he left the PennDutch that evening he'd browbeaten me – with his soft voice – into accepting two conditions. The first was that Aaron Miller be allowed unlimited time to speak about his 'wonderful new theme park'. The second condition was that Hernia's five churches were to compete in a baking contest. The pastries were to be baked by each church's sisterhood and they were to be sold in the parking lot of my church on the day of the event. The money would be given to charity. The sisterhoods were all to be given the exact same recipe for custard tarts, although they were free to add their own flavours and even fruit. This would turn it into a game to see which church had the better bakers. It was all in good Christian fun, and surely I could see that. For the record I didn't see that; I thought it was a horrible idea.

But on the bright side, the weather on Hernia's ultimate 'Show and Tell' day was sunny and pleasantly warm. I was pleased, but not surprised, when nearly a thousand people showed up. That happens to be nearly half the population of our village. I had expected about as many, and so had stated on the internet, and on the posted flyers, that attendees had to reserve either a morning or afternoon visit. For the most part, folks were cooperative.

Aaron's horrible exhibits were on display in our new social hall, and upstairs in our sanctuary. Aaron gave two lectures, one in the morning, and one in the afternoon. Outside, under a brightly coloured tent a variety of freshly baked tarts and fruit punch were served, courtesy of the participating churches. The church bathrooms were off-limits to the public, but a row of porta-potties lined one side of the parking lot, and they were courtesy of Aaron, of course.

The valet parking was also courtesy of him. While it was necessary, given the number of cars and the size of our lot, many of our citizens found it baffling, and refused to turn their vehicles over to strangers. Finally, my sweet, urbane husband volunteered to sit outside in the parking lot all day and explain the process to the townsfolk.

I am normally an even-tempered woman, slow to anger, and even slower to judge, but I will confess that my hackles were immediately hiked when I spotted the human tart who was Aaron's secretary, Tiff, prancing around on stiletto heels in one of the refreshment tents. Again, she was wearing clothes that no God-fearing woman would be found dead in. As for her make-up, well, no self-respecting clown would wear that much paint on his, or her, face.

'Good morning, Poopsie Woopsie,' I said. All right, I will admit that there was perhaps a tinge of malice in my voice, but I am human after all.

'What do *you* want?' Tiff retorted. 'And just so you know, I have a right to be here. I came as Aaron Miller's guest. Plus,

I brought these.' She held up a plate of tarts that looked delicious, certainly far better than the burnt offerings that I'd brought with me.

'Harrumph,' I said.

'How's that?'

'That's English for "whatever". In any case, you're not a church, dear. Only churches were invited to bring tarts.'

'Not so, *dear*,' Tiff said. 'Your cute little minister called me personally and invited me to bring some. Lucky for me, that old farmhouse still has its kitchen. My Sugar Bear has to eat, doesn't he?'

'Speaking of your Sugar Bear, did he bring that bully of a son along?'

'Rodney's actually a very sweet boy once you get to know him,' Tiff said.

'I've heard that said about attack dogs,' I said. 'Is the boy here?'

'No, of course not. He's seen all this stuff before. He's back at the headquarters playing video games like any normal kid – well, any normal kid, except for maybe yours.'

That did it. That hiked my hackles so far they pricked my armpits. I was tempted to say something really untoward to the fake redhead with certain manmade attractions. Instead, I mumbled, 'Get behind me Satan,' as I stomped my way to my church's social hall.

As the day progressed my temper cooled, but the temperature in the social hall rose, due to the hundreds of bodies inside it radiating heat. I flitted about on my boat-size shoes to take in the temperature of the room. OK, to be more precise, only the top part of me flitted; my feet unfortunately stepped on a good many toes. Also, I wasn't checking the air temperature; I was assessing people's reactions to the various displays. Much to my dismay, they were mixed, perhaps even skewed in favour of Aaron Miller.

While I was taking my informal poll, Prissy Utterall, bless her heart, was flouncing about the room in a frilly frock, denouncing Armageddonland in a voice so shrill it made my ear wax melt. Meanwhile her hubby, pastor of the very church in whose social hall we were, followed close behind murmuring messages that contradicted hers. As this was going on, the cause of it all, the despicable Aaron Miller, was up on the stage, ensconced in a throne-like wicker chair. A line of people, controlled by my dear friend Agnes, had queued to ask him questions. Folks were allowed one question each, and for the sake of expediency, the answers were to be 'yes' or 'no'.

Mid-morning, Betsy Whitaker, from St Mark's Lutheran Church, brought in a selection of tarts for Aaron, and set it on an ugly little round table next to his chair. The table had been purchased at a thrift store by yours truly, and had been thrown out twice by others with more discerning taste, and always rescued by me. But you see, it did come in useful, just like I said it would. At any rate, that was a signal for Agnes to shoo the townsfolk off the stage and let Aaron have a nosh, maybe even get up and use the men's room (of course *he* was allowed to use the church facilities).

I was quite ravenous myself by then, and was about to dip into the pockets of my sensible denim skirt and retrieve one of the goodies I'd baked the day before. This is why I can clearly remember the exact moment that Aaron Miller picked up a tart, and took a tentative bite. The time was 10.32, as per the enormous analogue clock on the wall behind him. Next he licked his lips, smiled, and crammed the rest of the tart into his mouth. He chewed slowly, as one does when they wish to savour the experience. After swallowing, he licked his lips again.

Then Aaron immediately reached for a second tart and stuffed it into his mouth. As I watched, I held my breath, hoping foolishly that it might have been one of the tarts that I had baked. As much as I despised the man (but still loved him, in the 'God has commanded me to' way), it's always flattering when a man wolfs down one's handiwork.

There are some finger foods that can be described as 'more-ish', meaning that one just has to have *more* of the treat. For me, it's shortbread cookies. I can eat an entire box while I'm relaxing with a good book (leaving it with butter-stained pages). Apparently Aaron Miller found someone's tarts to really hit the spot, because a third one was soon crammed into his mouth. I can only imagine that he supposed that there were many more tarts where those had come from, so that it was no longer necessary to savour each bite. But had he never heard of gluttony?

Not that it mattered, because seconds after Aaron Miller swallowed the third tart, his tanned, handsome face paled, and his forehead beaded with sweat. What happened next I will not describe, because the details are extremely unpleasant – gross, in the vernacular. Suffice it to say, Aaron had just ingested a lethal amount of poison.

However, he did not die immediately, so I shouted for Gabe. It is a shame that in a village of 2,173½ people (Cindy Shtupheimer is pregnant again, even though she's unmarried), we have no working doctor. By the way, I'm not gossiping about Cindy, because everyone already knows about the baby. This happens to be Cindy's fourth child out of wedlock – not that I'm judging, mind you – but that gal ought to spend more time on her knees praying, and less time with her knees in the air.

Gabe came running, but there was nothing much he could do there in the social hall, because he didn't have a stethoscope with him. By then Aaron was shivering and sweating profusely, and even more worrisome, was unable to speak. There, I've said too much. Anyway, Hernia doesn't own an ambulance, but Timmy Hecht, who volunteers on the Rescue Squad was in the crowd, and he said that he would take Aaron into the Bedford County Hospital. Timmy keeps one of those revolving red lights that he can clap onto the roof of his car, and it comes equipped with a siren that can make even a statue cover its ears. My Sweet Baboo proved yet again what a mensch he was when he insisted on accompanying the men to the hospital, although I wish that he would have asked my permission first.

At any rate, Gabe called exactly sixteen minutes later to say that Aaron Miller had 'expired'.

'What do you mean he *expired*?' I shrieked. 'He's not a can of tuna fish!'

'He died, Mags. He died on the gurney, as he was being wheeled into the emergency room. They did everything they could to revive him, but . . . well, you know what this means, don't you?'

I sighed so hard that it blew twin clouds of dust off the stage curtains twenty feet away. Then my heart started pounding, and I too broke out in a cold sweat.

'Mags? Mags? Are you still there?'

'Yes, unfortunately.'

'So,' my beloved said, 'which one of us is going to call that poor-excuse for a lawman, Sheriff Stodgewiggle?'

'Does it *have* to be either of us?' I wailed.

'Yes, it does,' Gabe said emphatically. 'That is if we want control of the narrative from the get-go. Not that we can hang on to it, but believe me, it could be a lot worse if someone with an axe to grind started off with a tall tale.'

'I hear you, dear. Then I'll do it; I saw it all happen. I watched him stuff those tarts in his mouth like there was no tomorrow – oops, bad choice of words, given that for Aaron there won't be a tomorrow.'

'You don't think that Aaron's going to Heaven?' Gabe said.

'Oops again, because that's not for me to judge. I meant he won't have another tomorrow living on earth.'

'Gotcha. But hon, don't you think we should start clearing this place out. Aaron's project is dead in the water – uh, bad choice of words – still, you know what I mean. There's no longer any reason for anyone to be here.'

Truer words were never spoken, so I clambered on to the stage, tested the microphone, and just as I was about to open my yap, I felt a vice-like grip on my wrist. Imagine my surprise when I beheld the small grey hand of Reverend Utterall. Rest assured that this hand *was* attached to his arm, which was in turn attached to his body.

'Whatever you were going to say, don't!' he whispered.

Since the microphone was open, even his whisper was heard by most folks, and many turned to look at the stage. Reverend Utterall must have been embarrassed, or unprepared for the sudden reaction, for he dropped his hand, which gave me the upper hand – so to speak.

'Go home folks; the show is over, and in more ways than one. And if you stop to take photos of the stage on your way out, you'll be given a ticker for rubber-necking.'

'Liar!' George Hillcross yelled from halfway down the room.

'I was only joking about the tickets,' I shouted back. George is a lawyer, and a petty one at that. He once sued an ice cream store for keeping their frozen treats too cold; he said that they hurt his teeth.

Then I felt the microphone leave my unguarded grip. 'Please, stay,' Reverend Wilbur Utterall said, this time speaking quite audibly. 'I feel that we should take a few minutes to honour the recently departed with a few words and a prayer, so please bow your heads.'

Now the residents of Hernia are, in the main, a pious folk, but they are not a naive people. They all know that there is no such animal as 'a few words' from a clergyman, no matter which denomination he belongs to. Even the prayer is bound to turn the meal cold, if it is offered at a dinner table. Thus, it was as soon as Reverend Utterall had uttered the words 'Our Heavenly Father,' the village folk stampeded for the doors. And windows.

There were resounding shrieks, and even curses, as people shoved and stepped on each other, relinquishing any sense of shame. Herd mentality, one might call it. There was only one thing that I could think of to do to put an end to the madness, and that was to sing. In all honesty, I have a terrible voice. I sound like a goat that could sing (after inhaling helium from party balloons). Oh, I am tone deaf as well. Nonetheless, I do try my best to make a joyful noise unto the Lord every Sunday at church.

All that is to say that my voice can be rather distracting. Therefore, I began to belt out our very difficult to sing national anthem yet again. Many folks attempting to reach its highest note sound like constipated canaries first learning to warble. That morning half the fleeing citizens of Hernia stopped in their tracks out of respect for the anthem, hands on their hearts, while the other half stopped, and remained frozen in place, waiting breathlessly to see what I would do when I reached the impossible note.

Well, you can bet your bippy that as I sang, I prayed for inspiration. This old goat couldn't even hit a note an octave *below* the highest note in our national anthem. I was just a few bars into it, and already one could call it 'The Star-*Mangled* Banner'. The only reason that the crowd hadn't resumed their rush for the doors is that my singing was so awful that it was, in its own way, great entertainment. Of course, all good things must come to an end, and just as I hit the last pathetic note, my prayer was answered with an idea.

'Good citizens of Hernia,' I said, 'either you will now line up in an orderly fashion, just like you did when you were in grammar school, or I will pick up Thelma Nuenschwander's old accordion, over in yon corner, and start playing hymns. You may not know this, but I have never played any musical instrument before in my life. Then again, judging by the way dear, departed, Thelma played, it was hard to believe that she did either.'

'Boo, boo!' Reverend Utterall said with surprising force. Then again, he had a microphone attached to his lapel.

But his was the kindest comment hurled at me, and I certainly deserved it for having spoken ill of the dead. However, my threat served its purpose, and within minutes the auditorium was emptied of everyone save me, and both Utteralls. Then it was merely a matter of waiting for Sheriff Stodgewiggle to show up.

Believe me, I would much rather that our own Chief Toy Graham had been the officer summoned, even though he and I were no longer on the best of speaking terms (my fault entirely), but Beechy Grove Mennonite Church lies just outside the Hernia village limits. However, Sheriff Stodgewiggle and I are on the *worst* of speaking terms, and I am just stating a fact, when I say that the reason for this, is entirely his fault. Another fact that I wish to share – no malice intended – is that when Sheriff Stodgewiggle enters a room, he is preceded by at least one of his chins. Again, this was in no way meant to be unkind. After all, take a good look at me; I would have to get an implant should I ever want to learn to play the violin.

'Yoder,' Sheriff Stodgewiggle snarled, as soon as he saw me standing next to the pastor and his wife. 'I knew it! I told myself on the way over here that I'd find you standing at the crime scene.'

'Fine,' I said pleasantly. 'Then I'll sit.' I walked sedately over to the nearest folding chair and plonked my pathetic patooty down.

'Did I say you could sit?' the sheriff barked.

I jumped to my feet and saluted. 'No, sir!'

'You will *not* salute me, Yoder. This is not the army.'

'Yes, sir!'

'And stop calling me sir, Yoder. Do you understand?'

'No, sir!' I said.

The muscles in Sheriff Stodgewiggle's forehead pulsated as his face reddened. 'Yoder, do you think that I'm an idiot?'

'Yes, sir! I mean, no, sir, I mean that I don't know, sir. Well, it's like this: how come I can't call you sir, but yet you can order me not to sit down?'

Sheriff Stodgewiggle turned to address Reverend Wilbur Utterall. 'Did you see what happened?'

'It's no secret, Sheriff, that Magdalena had it in for Mr Miller. She was gunning for him, so to speak.'

'Shame on you, pastor,' I said. 'That expression denotes violence and is not in our people's lexicon.'

Boy was that a mistake. Lacking a rifle, Reverend Utterall cocked his chin, and aimed it right at my civil liberties.

TWENTY

'Sheriff,' Reverend Utterall said, 'I'm sure that you know that Magdalena and Aaron Miller used to be sweethearts.'

'But we were never *legally* married!' I wailed.

'Tell me more,' Sheriff Stodgewiggle said, sounding hopeful.

'Well,' the reverend said, 'Proverbs 6:34 says: "For Jealousy is a husband's fury". It is my contention that jealousy is just as much a wife's fury, and that when Aaron left Magdalena, and returned to his legal spouse, Magdalena immediately started plotting his murder. Why, I wouldn't be surprised if Magdalena adopting that daughter of hers – uh, Adrian, is it? If that wasn't part of a plan to hurt Aaron.'

'Wilbur! How could you?' Even Prissy was appalled by what had come out of my pastor's mouth.

For the record, I only cry when I'm angry or frustrated, seldom when I'm sad or hurt. At that moment I was so angry at my pastor that I wanted to slap my own face so that I wouldn't be tempted to strike him. By the time I found my tongue (right where I'd left it last), tears were streaming down my face. Their presence made me even angrier.

'I'll have you know that I had to pay that man to leave Hernia.

And my daughter's name is *Alison*, not Adrian. You would know that, if you paid any attention to a word I ever said, and I'm your head deacon.'

'Aha!' Sheriff Stodgewiggle exclaimed triumphantly. 'You bribed your husband.'

'I didn't bribe him,' I said. 'I told him that I would pay him fifty thousand dollars if he would return to Minnesota, and stay there. I even had him sign a contract, which he has clearly broken, because his corpse now resides in the county morgue.'

'I'm with Magdalena on this, Husband,' Prissy said. 'Any man who would take fifty thousand dollars from a woman in order to get him to leave her alone – well, a man like that deserves what he gets.'

'I didn't say *that*, Prissy!'

Prissy patted my arm. 'It's going to be OK, Magdalena, let it all out. We know what you mean. No one is judging you.'

'Speak for yourself, Priss,' my pastor hissed, sounding like a bag full of cut snakes. 'It wouldn't surprise me to learn that the fifty grand that she gave to Aaron Miller – an entrepreneur who was willing to reinvest in his own community – why, I suspect that money was, in fact, payment for his daughter, Alice.'

'Her name is *Alison*!'

'Aha! So you do admit to a crime, don't you?' chortled he of multiple chins. 'Child-trafficking is a serious crime, Yoder. Even an amateur sleuth such as yourself should know that by now. How long have you been at this now? Forty, fifty, years?'

'Fifty years,' I said. 'I began when I was nine. I was a child prodigy.'

Prissy giggled. Suddenly I couldn't remember why I'd heretofore disliked her so much. So what if she was a terrible gossip? At least they made interesting companions.

Unlike women, men seldom weep when they get frustrated. Thermostats controlled by testosterone sometimes register extremely high temperatures which often, but not always, lead to 'boiling over', and a seizing up of the male engine. At times these seizures manifest themselves as a stroke, and at other times as heart attacks. Or, if the victim is extraordinarily fortunate, nothing more untoward will be observed than a few tremors and twitches.

In Sheriff Stodgewiggle's case, the blood drained everywhere from his face, except from his rutabaga-like nose. The effort he put into coming up with a clever comeback set some of his chins to quivering, and his dewlap to dance under the harsh fluorescent lights of our social hall. It was enough to make me feel almost sorry for the man. Believe me, I know the pain of being judged on my looks, and I wouldn't wish the same fate on my worst enemy. But try explaining that to the sheriff, bless his heart.

'Magdalena Yoder,' he said, 'I am arresting you for the murder of Aaron Miller. You have the right to remain silent. Anything you can and do say will be used against you in a court of law. If you cannot afford—'

'Moving right along, dear, on what grounds are you arresting me for murder?'

Prissy giggled again.

'Do be quiet,' Reverend Utterall said.

'I most certainly will not,' Prissy said. 'The sheriff is a bully, and our Magdalena is sticking up for herself. I didn't see her poisoning Aaron Miller, did you? In fact, the coroner hasn't even ruled it poisoning. That's just hearsay. In fact, if I recall correctly, I heard it from you. Did you poison Aaron Miller, dear?'

My petite pastor puffed up like a bantam rooster about to crow and glared at his wife. 'God created woman *second*, to be man's helpmate. When I went into the ministry it was with the understanding that you were to be a *help* to me, not a hindrance.'

Prissy did a fine job of puffing up as well. 'So *that's* the arrangement that you and Daddy made. He paid your way through seminary, and you took the last of eight girls off his hands. Well, too bad for you that neither of us believes in divorce.' Prissy paused in her diatribe to wink at me. 'I know that you are a wealthy woman, Magdalena, and I know that you can afford to pay for your own lawyers. But if you need me to run some legwork for you while you're in jail, just holler.'

Sheriff Stodgewiggle is not a corrupt or evil man. He is merely inept, and prone to holding grudges. He won his last election by a razor-thin margin, and dare I say, on name recognition alone. Stodgewiggles were some of our first English settlers. Today you can't swing a long-tailed cat and not hit a structure or sign with some variation, or at least part, of that name on it. (Not that anyone should ever swing a cat by its tail, mind you!) In Bedford, our county seat, you will find a Dr Stodge, a Dr Wiggles, a dentist with the surname Stodgewig, a grocery named Wiggs, a hair salon named Gewig, and a gym called Wiggles Stodge.

Five years earlier I'd also been arrested by Sheriff Stodgewiggles, again for murder, so I pretty much knew what to expect. I knew that I had to cooperate, but at the same time, I didn't have to allow the experience to be an easy one for him either. This time around I had knowledge on my side.

The second he unhooked the pair of shiny handcuffs from the loop that kept them half hidden by his prodigious underbelly, I vigorously shook my horsey head.

'Neigh, to those hobbles, master,' I said. 'You put those restraints on me, and I will freak out.'

'Is that a threat, Yoder?'

'No, dear. It is merely a fact. I will scream bloody murder.'

'That sounds like a threat to me, lady. That sound like a threat to you, Reverend?'

'It most certainly did,' my pastor said.

'You Judas,' I said.

'Traitor,' Prissy said, and jabbed her husband's shoulder with her index finger. 'Wilbur, if this horrible man puts handcuffs on our head deacon, then I'm going to scream. I'll scream just as loud as I did on our wedding night, and then every month since then.'

Reverend Utterall turned a greyish green. He closed his eyes, and his lips moved silently for a minute and a half, going by that clock above the stage. That can seem like an eternity for a woman in my position. I assumed that he was praying, but he might simply have been reciting that secret recipe that we Mennonites have for boiling water. Who knows what goes on inside the head of a man?

'Sheriff,' he said at last, 'it has occurred to me that Magdalena Yoder not only should not be handcuffed, she should not even be on your list of murder suspects.'

'Come again?' the sheriff said.

'Well, witnesses saw him cramming tarts into his mouth before he collapsed and started having convulsions. Trust me, he wouldn't have been stuffing anything that Magdalena baked into his mouth. That woman burns everything. He would have found a charcoal briquette tastier than anything she baked.'

'It's true,' Prissy said, nodding vigorously. 'At church potluck suppers, we call her dish "burnt offerings for the Lord".'

'Why I never!' I said.

Prissy winked at me, which made me feel a little better.

'I've never been a great cook,' I said, 'but I'm certainly not the worst cook. It's just that I prefer to eat food that has been fully cooked, not merely waved over a flame. If one is going to cook a vegetable, then that veggie should be boiled until one can mash it with a fork. It's good practice for when one is consigned into an old folk's home. And when it comes to meat, well, I want to make sure that the animal is really dead. If it bleeds on my plate – no thank you! Black on the outside, and brown on the inside, that's how I like it. I don't want my steak to "moo" when I cut it.'

'So you enjoy eating shoe leather?' Sheriff Stodgewiggle said. He was obviously not happy with Reverend Utterall reversing his position, so I let him have his little victory.

'Yes, sir,' I said.

'What a waste of a good piece of meat,' he said. Then that was it; no more was said to me that day about Aaron Miller. Sheriff Stodgewiggle simply put away the cuffs, then he huffed, and he puffed, and he waddled out of the social hall, and presumably drove back to his office. Or not.

The Utteralls, on the other hand, were not quite done with the morning's main event. More specifically, Reverend Utterall's nose was bent out of shape because Prissy had stood up for me. They began to argue in front of me, so I started to leave. Then one of them called me back, and tried to involve me in their quarrel, so I tried to leave again, only to get stopped before I could reach the door. This happened four times, because I'm like one of Pavlov's dogs. Call my name, and I'll come running. Pet me master, give me a treat and I'll wag my bony behind. I was finally able to break the cycle when Reverend Utterall's phone rang with a voice message from his mother, on speaker. Even as I fled through a side door I could hear the voice of a mother who was annoyed at her son for not keeping in touch as often as he should.

Then less than ten minutes later, when I pulled into my driveway back at the PennDutch, this mother was annoyed at her son for touching someone he shouldn't be touching.

TWENTY-ONE

I could hardly believe my faded blue peepers! Tammy Faye was ensconced in one of my rocking chairs on the front porch, and sitting cross-legged at her feet, was Little Jacob. The sight of that, alone, was enough to turn thirty-six hairs in my braided bun grey. But the little rascal had the left foot of the ginger vamp in his lap, and was in the act of applying nail varnish to her largest little piggy. Bright red, sinfully red, fire engine red, hot chilly red polish.

'Stop!' I cried. 'Put her foot down now.'

'Aw, but Mom, I'm doing a really good job, aren't I? Right, Tammy Faye? You see, first I put these cotton balls between her toes, and—'

'Don't you call her Tammy Faye,' I said. 'To you, she is Mrs Barker.'

'But Mom, she said that I should call her that.'

'And if she told you to jump off Lover's Leap up on Stucky Ridge, would you do that too?'

'Maybe.'

'Now you're just being a smart mouth. I told you to put her foot down, and I mean it.'

'But why?'

'Because I told you so, that's why. And because it's an atheist's foot, and you're painting it a harlot's colour. There, are those good enough reasons?'

Boy, did my explanation get Tammy Faye cackling like a shed full of hens when a fox pokes his nose in. She laughed so hard that she jerked her foot out of my son's lap, and knocked the bottle of polish and applicator out of his hands. The applicator with the harlot red tip grazed my skirt, leaving a streak the colour of sin, and the bottle rolled across my porch, impregnating the natural pine with the mark of Cain. I was not amused.

'Ding, dang, dong, and rough puff pastry!' I swore. 'Now look what you've done.'

'I'm sorry, Mama.' Little Jacob leapt to his feet and threw his arms around my waist. 'I really am sorry. Will you forgive me?'

'Always,' I said, and gave him a squeeze. 'Now run upstairs and get on your computer and research how to remove nail polish from pine floors, because that's what you will be doing with your free time until the job is done. Then I am going to teach you how to sew, and you're going to make me a new skirt.'

'Yes, Mama.'

After the screen door slammed behind him, I turned my righteous wrath on the painted tart in my rocking chair. If looks could kill, then Tammy Faye would certainly be ready for taxidermy. She, on the other hand, was smirking.

'So you think this is funny?' I said. 'Leading my young son astray.'

'Lighten up,' she said. 'We all have toenails, don't we? So what's the big deal? He was just adding a little colour to them.'

I prayed for restraint. After patience, it's my least answered prayer.

'If the Good Lord had wanted us to have red toenails, dear, then we would be born that way. Red is the colour of harlots. Haven't you read the second chapter of Joshua?'

'Miss Yoder, I may be a glamorous redhead, with curves that would drive a race car crazy, but I don't read those romance novels.'

I threw up my hands in dismay. 'Joshua isn't a romance novel; it's a book in the Holy Bible.'

Tammy Faye snorted. 'Well, I certainly don't read fairy tales.'

How is a mild-mannered, Mennonite woman like myself to respond to this insult on my faith. Here was this atheist, sitting in my rocking chair (impregnating it with her atheist cooties), and she didn't even have the decency to apologize for involving my little boy in her abhorrent agenda.

'Mrs Barker,' I said, 'can't you at least admit, that since your skirt comes only halfway to your knees, and my son was down there at your feet, he might have glanced up and seen something inappropriate?'

'Well, how old is the boy anyway?' Tammy Faye asked casually. 'Yesterday when we were baking tarts, he told me that he was a senior in high school.'

'*What?*' I said. '*Where* were you baking tarts?'

'Why in your kitchen, of course. It's not like I kidnapped him. You were at your church all day setting up for Aaron Miller's big reveal, so I asked Gabe if I might contribute to the tart effort. I must say, that was quite a show, Miss Yoder. I especially liked the ending. Correction: I *loved* the ending.' She laughed raucously.

'Why I never,' I fumed. 'My oven is not to be used by atheists, and atheist tarts are not to be consumed in a church building by the faithful. Even if it is just the social hall.'

Tammy Faye laughed even harder.

'Stop it,' I said. 'Just stop it!' What I wanted to do was to order that woman and her husband to pack their bags and hit the road. But on the other hand, Tammy Faye was now *numero uno* on my newly created list of suspects in the death of Aaron Miller. She had a motive (her reason for being here in the first place was to stop Armageddonland), and she'd just revealed that she'd had opportunity and means. It could well have been her tart that Aaron crammed into his mouth. A tart from a tart – how ironic can it get?

'All right, all right,' she finally said, 'I was just having a little fun with you. But you just demonstrated how rigid in your thinking you religious types are. I bet you think that atheism is contagious, like a disease. Well, I hate to admit it, but you're actually right on that score. You're going to have to disinfect this chair later, because now that I've sat in it, it has atheist germs all over it. Same thing goes for the dining room and parlour chairs. And oh, you're going to have boil the linens we've used.'

'Don't be ridiculous,' I said. 'But let's just pretend that is true, how long would I need to boil the sheets? I mean, theoretically.'

'Twenty minutes after the water comes to a hard boil,' she said. 'But you do realize that you'll have to chuck the mattress. Jim perspires a great deal at night, and seeing as how you don't have a moisture-proof mattress topper – well, you know what that means.'

'No,' I said tartly, 'I do not. What does that mean?'

'Oh, you're just pretending to be dense as well,' Tammy Faye said. 'It means that he sweated through to the mattress, and that the next person to sleep on it will unwittingly be influenced by our atheist agenda.'

'Ack!' I squawked and fled from my own porch. Rather than seeking out the loving arms of my husband, I headed straight for the thirty-six jets of Big Bertha. Now before you judge me, there are times when I use my whirlpool bathtub strictly for relaxation, forsaking any thought of stimulation. This has been especially true when I'm happily married, as I was then. Sometimes I even get so relaxed that I drift off into a state of semi-conscious bliss – but never sleep, mind you. To fall asleep in the loving arms of Big Bertha might result in me arriving prematurely at the Pearly Gates, without my work on earth having been completed, not to mention the work on my promised mansion in the sky.

But on that particular day I *know* it was not sleep. Therefore, when a sweet, angelic voice spoke to me from above, it was only logical for me to conclude that it was indeed an angel who was speaking, for I am a logical woman.

'Magdalena,' the voice said, 'how art thou?'

'I art not doing so well,' I said. 'It has been a long, hard day, and it is only half over.'

'Would thou wish to tell me your troubles?' the voice said.

'If thee wishes, Your Highness – I mean, is that what I call you?' I said.

'My name would be fine,' the voice said. 'It's Beautiful.'

'I'm sure it is, dear,' I said, 'but what is it?'

'Beautiful. That's my name. Just like Michael and Gabriel are the names of archangels.'

'Speaking of which,' I said, 'those are male names. Why aren't there any female archangels?'

'Well, you'll have to ask God, I suppose,' Beautiful said, sounding a bit wistful.

'Believe me, I will,' I said. 'But for now, here's something that you can tell me: beneath your robes, do you have a you-know-what?'

'No, I'm afraid I don't,' Beautiful said, sounding a bit peevish for an angel in my opinion.

'Do you mean to say that you are as smooth down there as a rag doll? Or that if I took a peek under Arch Gabriel Michael's robe I wouldn't find a – uh – thingy?'

'Now you've gone too far. You always go too far. Really, Mags,

I know the story of your adoption, Magdalena, but sometimes I wonder if your parents didn't bring you back from the pound – the dog pound. At times your ideas are so far-fetched, so sacrilegious, that for all the difference it would make, you might as well be an atheist.'

In that moment, I realized that speaker was not an angel named Beautiful. Oh, no. I had let my wild imagination run away with me again, and I'd been conned by none other than my bestie, Agnes Miller. She'd managed to do it once before, right here, when I had succumbed to the temptations of Big Bertha. On that occasion I had actually believed that Agnes's voice was the voice of God Almighty. Can you believe how stupid I was? God a woman? Now that will take you laughing to your grave. Everyone knows that few women can grow a beard like the Lord God Jehovah, and none of them are five thousand years old.

Having realized that my best friend had, yet again, taken advantage of my wild and wandering imagination, and thus made a fool out of me, I set my feeble mind to the topic of retribution. I had initially thought that the heavenly voice was coming from above; I now surmised that Agnes was perched on a bar stool directly behind my head. This meant that if I cupped my hands in front of me, and tossed the water over my head, I was sure to hit her with some of it. But it also meant Agnes had a view of me in the altogether, since I had no bubbles in the bath that day.

'Agnes,' I said sternly, when that thought dawned on me, 'close your eyes at once, for I am as naked as a new-born jaybird.'

My buddy had the temerity to laugh. 'Oh, Mags, you're a hoot. We've known each other our entire lives. Our mothers used to bath us together in the same washtub. I've seen everything of yours that there is to see.'

I was not amused. 'Maybe. But they were a lot smaller then.'

'Not much smaller,' Agnes said, and laughed again.

That did it. Not only did I splash her as planned, but I leapt out of the tub as she squealed and wrestled her into Big Bertha. Then I grabbed a large towel from an overhead rack and flung it over my heaving, if somewhat smallish, bosom and let it trail down into the water. By that time the two of us were laughing hysterically. It was one of those laughing fits that I'm sure that everyone has enjoyed, wherein just as one party winds down, the other party winds up. Thus, around and around we went.

After some time, we were aware of someone pounding on the door, but that made us laugh even harder. Then we laughed in unison – shrieked in unison is more like it.

Finally Gabe opened the door and stuck his head in. Upon seeing us both in the tub, one fully dressed, and the other covered with a wet towel, he smiled broadly.

'Perverts,' he said, and closed it.

'That's us,' I said.

'Speak for yourself,' Agnes said, and then giggled happily.

I found Agnes one of Gabe's robes, since clothes meant for my bean pole frame weren't an option, and tossed her dress in the dryer. As for her frilly underpinnings, she was going to have to hang them outside on the clothesline herself, where the whole world could see them. I would die of shame if I was her; her so-called brassiere was pink and decorated with lace. It even sported a tiny bow between the two cups.

At any rate, as I was dressing, Agnes kept up a steady stream of chatter, as she is wont to do, and I was only half listening, as is my custom when I am occupied in one task or another.

'And that's when heard I them arguing,' she said.

My left ear swivelled her way. 'Whom did you hear argue, dear?'

'Aaron and Alison, of course.'

'*My* Alison?'

'No, Prince William's Alison. Mags, haven't you been paying attention?'

'Of course I have, but to the situation at hand. I've been fastening the eye hooks on my sturdy Christian brassiere, and it's hard to get them all lined up correctly.'

'Understood. So I'll start over. I wasn't about to use one of those smelly porta-potties, and given that I am your best friend, and that the location is your church, I granted myself special bathroom privileges. So, I was headed back to use the ladies' room, and I heard these voices coming from one of the darkened Sunday school rooms. Both of the voices sounded familiar, but one of them was especially familiar, so I stopped to listen. You know I've always had a curious mind, Magdalena.'

'You'd be dead if you were a cat,' I said. 'Finish your story.'

'Anyway, the two people in question were indeed your Alison and Aaron Miller, and they were in the middle of a heated argument.' Agnes paused to lick her lips.

'What about?' I almost shouted.

'Well, I couldn't make out the words, because they were in the back of the classroom, but their voices were definitely raised, and then suddenly Alison yells, "I could just kill you", and storms out of the room. I mean, she runs right past me in that skimpy college girl outfit of hers, and out the side door. I don't think she even saw me.'

My heart started beating with the rhythm of a jackhammer. Quite honestly, I couldn't think of which issue to address first: that Alison had been to the church and not chosen to see me; that she had seen Aaron and fought with him; or that she come to my church dressed like a tart. In the end I decided to address the least important issue first. This is something that I often do, as a way to postpone dealing with potentially life-changing problems.

'What do you mean when you say "skimpy"?'

'Well, she was wearing a halter top, and her shorts were so short, that you could see where the curve of her buttocks began.'

'And you saw all that in a few seconds?' I asked.

'There wasn't that much to take in.'

I pursed my lips. 'So, what's a halter top exactly?'

'It's not much different than the bra I'm going to hang outside, except maybe for the lack of ornamentation. Then again, it might have even more.'

'*Ach du leiber!*' I said. 'The shame of it all. My mother must be spinning in her grave.'

'For sure,' Agnes said. 'With all those revolutions per minute, she'll make enough electricity to supply Hernia until the end of summer.'

'Agnes, you never liked my mother, did you?'

'That's not true; I liked her from a distance. But up close she was like a cross between a pit bull and a porcupine.'

'Why I never!'

'Oh, come off it, Mags. Enough with the fake umbrage. Are you going to follow up on what they were arguing about?'

That hackneyed expression about ice water running through my veins did not apply. Instead, I felt like I had a bowling ball inside my chest. I just wanted to sit down. No, I really wanted to crawl under my covers with a flashlight and a good book, and stay there until I fell asleep. Of course, at my age, my bladder would force me out to face reality sooner rather than later, and if I was going to live into my destiny, I may as well do it with my intrepid Dr Watson at my side.

'Go home, Agnes,' I said, 'and get a change of clothes, and your pyjamas, and your toothbrush. We're going on a road trip.'

Agnes's first reaction was to squeal with delight. Then reality for her set in.

'But Mags, my dress is still wet, and so is my bra. I'll be driving in Gabe's bathrobe.'

'You look fetching in my husband's robe, dear. Now scoot. I need to let Little Jacob out of his room and give Gabe dinner instructions. Just get home and back as fast as you can. We don't want to hit the rush-hour traffic in Pittsburgh.'

'But what if I have an accident on the way home? What if someone sees me in this robe? It's not even my colour.'

'Agnes, dear, you live less than five miles from here, and you have never had an accident in your life. I'm leaving in precisely an hour – with, or without you.'

She was back in twenty-eight minutes.

TWENTY-TWO

I made Agnes drive. Pittsburgh is a beautiful city, but it is hilly. It is so hilly, in fact, that a couple of them are called mountains. Mount Washington, on the south side stands at a formidable height of 367 feet. Should you doubt that this qualifies as a mountain, then chew on the fact that Mount Wycheproof in Australia stands at a mere 141 feet, and supposedly is the smallest mountain in the world. Pshaw, I say.

Two long tunnels had to be bored through Mount Washington to give commuters access to the city from the west and from the south. It's been said that those who get their first glimpse of the city as they exit from the Fort Pitt tunnel, are treated to a sight of incomparable beauty. Completely hidden by the mountain, and now suddenly right in front of one's eyes, are two large rivers that converge, squeezing the downtown, with its skyscrapers, to a point. The rivers are the Allegheny and the Monongahela, and where they meet at the point, they create the mighty Ohio River, which is the Mississippi River's largest tributary.

But Agnes and I were going to pass through a different tunnel that day. The dreaded Squirrel Hill Tunnel. I say 'dreaded', because Pittsburghers suffer from a weird disorder that I call 'tunnel syndrome'. Even though there are signs posted above the tunnel that read: *Maintain Speed*, and the highway through the tunnel is well-lit and every bit as wide as it was outside, traffic slows to a crawl. Cars creep through the tunnel at a toddler's pace, and then just as they emerge, they shoot out as if they're being chased by some cave-dwelling monster. Various suggestions have been offered to remedy this syndrome. The one I like best is installing a giant rubber band at the entrance and flinging cars through. True, there may be a few mishaps at first, but after a few days of that, most folks would be willing to maintain speed on their own.

Anyway, Pittsburgh was an hour and half away from Hernia, which gave Agnes and me a lot of time to chew the fat. But since we'd known each other our entire lives, and this was the new and improved Magdalena who now eschewed gossip, the fat was pretty lean – if you get my drift. We tried playing word games, but I'm not the brightest bulb in the chandelier, and so Agnes always came out ahead.

Thus I was quite pleased when the dear woman suggested a game of What If. It's a silly, fantasy game, really, but here are the rules. We get to ask each other three theoretical questions in a row, and the answers supplied must be honest ones. This time around, it was decided that Agnes would start the game. 'Mags,' she said, 'who would you be, if you could be anyone in the world, living or dead.'

'Easy peasy. I'd be Hitler.'

'*Hitler?*'

'Yes. On my twenty-first birthday I'd shoot myself dead.'

'Mags, be serious!'

'I am.'

Agnes sighed. 'I think you are. OK then, if you weren't already a fabulously successful innkeeper, what career would you choose to be equally successful in?'

'I'd like to be a mystery writer. I'd write the so-called cozy mysteries, but not those ridiculous ones that are supposed to be funny. And anyway, as I'm sure you're aware, I have no sense of humour.'

'Truer words were never spoken,' Agnes said. 'Now tell me, what would your protagonist be like?'

'Hmm. Well, I'd want to write in the first person, so I'd base her on me. Same personality, same looks. You know: house-sized feet, chest as flat as an ironing board, and long, horsey face.'

'My, we flatter ourselves, don't we?' Agnes said.

'OK, OK,' I said irritably. 'So I forgot my jug ears and nose like a ripe banana.'

'That's better,' Agnes said.

'Now it's my turn to play,' I said, feeling the need for a bit of revenge. 'What would you do—'

'I'm not done,' Agnes said. 'What are you going to do if your meeting with Alison is – well, less than satisfactory?'

'Do you mean, like, if she has a man friend stashed away there? I'm pretty sure that she does. So when I *do* find him, probably hiding in a closet, I'll drag him out by the scruff of his neck, then throw my gangly arms around him and cry, "Son!".'

Agnes laughed. 'You *would*, too. I can just see it. No, what I mean is, what if during your meeting with Alison, you begin to suspect that *she* is the one who poisoned Aaron Miller.'

'Agnes, how *could* you?' I said, as I covered my face with my hands.

'Sorry, Mags, she said. 'But if you really intend to be an objective sleuth, you need to ask yourself if Alison might have had a motive. Because speaking as your Dr Watson, I believe that she did.'

'That's not what I meant,' I wailed. 'I meant how *could* you know that's exactly what I was thinking?'

'Maybe because I've known you since you peed in my bathwater.'

'I believe it was the other way around,' I said.

'Was not.'

'Was so.'

Agnes punched me playfully on my bony shoulder three times, while keeping an eye on the road. 'Was not, not, not,' she said.

'Waaah,' I cried, and then we both laughed.

We rode in companionable silence until the first exit sign for Pittsburgh appeared. Agnes was right, of course. The murderer might have been Alison, and my motive for going to Pittsburgh was to somehow clear her name. But if indeed Alison was guilty, she wasn't going anywhere. In the meantime, several other people that I had in mind could already be on their way to the airport.

'Dr Watson,' I said, 'please turn your old jalopy around, and take me back to Hernia post haste.'

'Aye, Sherlock,' she said, 'but only if you promise never to refer to my sweet ride as an old jalopy.'

'I promise. I need to get my own jalopy, and drive over to Yoder's Corner Market for a chat with the Whore of Babylon, before she should decide to skip town.'

'Whoa!' Watson, a.k.a. Agnes, screeched to a stop on the shoulder of the highway, but not without almost causing a pile-up on the turnpike. For a few seconds the blaring and honking of horns was embarrassing, if not deafening.

'What in the Sam Hill?' I said. It's an old expression of aggravation my parents used, and I have no idea what it means, except that it's strong language.

'You've got that right,' Agnes said angrily. 'First of all, Sherlock, you're not going anywhere without me, your Dr Watson. And second, I haven't a clue as to who the Whore of Babylon is, and outside of you, I couldn't even guess at her identity—'

'Why I never!' I said, every bit as miffed as she was.

'Oh, take it as a compliment. I didn't mean it literally, for Pete's sake; I simply meant that there is more to you than meets the eye.'

'Then why are we sitting here, toots?' I said.

When Watson is properly motivated, she drives almost as fast I do. Before she'd been distracted by our game, and also worried about my state of mind, should I become convinced that Alison was the killer. Now she couldn't wait to see me put the screws to Dorothy Yoder. Perhaps a wee bit of that eagerness had to do with the fact that Watson and Dorothy got along about as well as two feral cats fighting over the same sardine in a dead-end alley. In this case the sardine was Sam. Watson had had goo-goo eyes for him from first grade, on up until the day that he married Dorothy – a day that will for ever live in infamy in poor Watson's heart.

Although speed-demon Watson pulled her car up in front of the store without incident, it took another minute before my shadow made it there. The first thing I did was say a silent prayer of thanksgiving for our safe arrival. Then quite audibly, for Watson's benefit, I asked the Good Lord for guidance, and the gifts of wisdom and patience.

'Wow!' Watson said. 'Is that a first, Mags? *You* asking for patience?'

'Oh hush. I do it all the time. It just never gets answered.'

'Or maybe it does,' Watson said. 'Maybe you're ten times more patient than you'd be if you didn't pray for it. And if that's the case – yikes, you better *keep* praying for it, because I'd hate to be around you if you stopped.'

I stuck my tongue out at her in that friendly way, which we sometimes do. But the minute that we stepped into Yoder's Corner Market it was clear that I should have prayed to have that tongue tied in a knot. When I saw Cousin Sam's wife Dorothy standing behind the register, and gussied up even more than Aaron's secretary, I had to clamp both hands over my mouth. In the meantime, Watson was punching me in the ribs, to let on that she too could see the tart behind the counter.

'What's the matter?' Dorothy said to me. 'Cat got your tongue?'

I nodded.

'That'll be the day,' Dorothy said. 'A mute Magdalena is like a garbage can without flies. If you're sick and need to throw up, do it outside. Then make sure that you scrub off the sidewalk. We at Yoder's Corner Market like to keep a spotless establishment.'

I uncovered my mug. 'That's nice to hear.' I turned and smiled at two Amish women who had come in behind us. 'You ladies might not know this, but I gave birth on this floor.' I pointed. 'Right there, between aisles two and three, and Sam Yoder who owns this store, was the one who delivered my son. He even cut the umbilical cord.'

The two Amish women turned and scurried out the door. Fortunately, Watson waited until they were out of earshot before bursting into laughter.

I'm quite sure that Dorothy's face was red with rage, even though her pancake make-up didn't show it. But her blazing eyes and quivering lips sure gave her emotional state away. She waved a finger with a scarlet claw attached at us.

'See what you've done?' she yelled. 'You've cost me customers with your grotesque story, Magdalena.'

'Calm down, Dorothy,' I said. 'Birth is not grotesque. We were all born – even you.'

'Maybe. But my husband never came close to – uh, that end of you.'

Watson giggled.

'Watson,' I said, 'go find Sam.'

'Who's Watson?'

'Agnes here is Watson, and I'm Sherlock, because we're working on a murder case. Anyway, Sam can verify that he was indeed close to that end of me. Go, Watson.' I gave Watson a gentle push, and off she ambled.

'No, Watson, no!' Dorothy called after her. 'Come back.'

'All right,' I said. 'We'll let you pretend what you want about my birthing day. But you can't pretend that you weren't there at my church this morning, when Aaron Miller got his one-way ticket to the Ever After, because I saw you. Were you the slouch who brought packaged cookies from your store, or did you bring homemade tarts like every important and respectable citizen in Hernia did?'

Dorothy's hands flew to her face, and her mouth fell open in an expression of pure horror. If this was acting on her part, then she certainly had been deserving of the role of the Whore of Babylon *if* Armageddonland had opened as planned.

'Ladies,' she said, addressing us both, for Watson had returned, 'I would *never* try to pass off the stale stuff that we sell here as something that I had baked. Magdalena, you are my husband's cousin; how could you stoop so low to even suggest that I might do such a distasteful thing?' She shuddered. 'And I mean that literally. I would never even taste any of the packaged baked goods that we sell here. Furthermore, everything I make for Sam is either fresh, or homemade. From scratch. Nothing but the best for my man.'

At that another Amish woman fled, dragging two small children behind her. A third child, slightly older than her siblings, paused in the doorway for a few seconds and stared. It was not an Amish thing to do, and I guessed that in a dozen years that girl would leave the fold during her *Rumschpringe*.

'My sincere apologies,' I said, not quite sincerely, since I didn't believe a word she said. I have eaten dishes that Dorothy had brought to family dinners. Straight out of the box, a can, or the freezer, they were. Oh, she may have added a dollop of ketchup here or there, or a sprinkling of parmesan cheese, and called it 'a la' something or another. Even I do that, and I'm the world's worst cook.

'I know you're being snide with your fake apology,' Dorothy said, 'but I won't let that stop me taking the high road. So I'll be the grown-up here, and make polite conversation. How is your family, Magdalena?'

'Fine.'

'Are you sure? I didn't see that bratty boy of yours at the church this morning.'

'*Bratty?*' Watson said. 'You call that polite conversation?'

'Boy!' I said. 'I've been a terrible mother!'

'I'm sure you have,' Dorothy said.

'Not my boy,' I cried. '*His* boy!'

I turned and ran from the store.

TWENTY-THREE

Watson practically stepped on my heels as she followed me out of the store. 'Mags, are you losing it again?'

'What do you mean by *again*, dear? According to some people I know, I've been whackadoodle, looney bin, cuckoo-clock crazy since the day I spoke my first sentence.'

'Why, Magdalena, you sell yourself short,' Agnes said. 'But I'm asking if you are even more whacky now than usual, what with this talk about "his boy"?'

By then we'd reached Agnes's car, and I was anxious to get on the road again. 'Climb in, dear, and head out to the old Bontrager place. I'll explain on the way. If you ignore the speed limits I'll let you give me a nice long foot rub the first time I get a chance to fully relax.'

'Sweet deal,' Agnes said, and made retching sounds. But then after we were securely belted in, and had gotten out of town, she did indeed drive a few miles over the speed limit.

'So it's like this,' I said, keeping up my end of the bargain. 'Little Jacob is my son, and he loves his parents very much. If I were to die suddenly, he would be bereft, wouldn't he?'

Agnes giggled. 'I suppose that if you were you to die slowly, he would be bereft as well.'

'Agnes Miller, shame on you! You've turned into a stand-up comedienne. You know how I abhor humour.'

'Oh, get off your high horse, Mags, and get on with your explanation.'

'Very well, but it will cost you two foot rubs.' I took a deep breath. 'So anyway, it occurred to me that Aaron Miller's son, Rodney, is out there at the old Bontrager farm – a.k.a. the Armageddon headquarters – with no family to comfort him.'

'Well, you're certainly not family,' Agnes said. She sounded almost angry.

'No, I'm not, but Alison is, and Alison is family to me.'

Agnes snorted. 'Aren't you forgetting that this is the boy who bullied, and embarrassed, Little Jacob?'

'No, I'm not. But like you just said, he's a boy. Sure, he's a teenager, but he's still only a boy, and he's alone, and he's probably a bit afraid now. Besides, it was Aaron who put him up to the bullying. Who knows if he would have even done any of those things if he'd been allowed to attend Hernia High on his own terms?'

'Ha,' Agnes said.

'What is that supposed to mean?' I said.

'You're not going to like what I really want to say,' Agnes said. She cringed peremptorily.

'Stop with the drama, dear, and speak your piece. You know that I'm the most laid-back woman in all of Bedford County.'

'Ha,' Agnes said again. 'You're about as laid-back as a cat on a hot tin roof. I think that your interest in that boy Rodney is because he's the fruit of Aaron Miller's loins. The man you used to refer to as your Pookey Bear.'

'You take that back!' I said angrily.

'I will not,' she said calmly. 'I took Psychology 101 in Junior College, and that's my pseudo-professional assessment.'

'For your information, missy,' I hissed, 'I care about him because I have a son of my own, *and* because he is Alison's brother. That's the primary reason. Besides, shouldn't we all be looking out for each other in any case?'

'Yeah, you're right – as usual,' Agnes said. We were less than a mile from our destination when she spoke up again. 'Magdalena, I know that by now you must have a list of suspects drawn up in your head. Am I right? So tell me, are you on that list as well?'

'How dare you?' I screamed. 'Pull the car over right now.'

That's exactly what Agnes did. She stomped on the brakes and we skidded for twenty yards before ending up on the shoulder of the road, just feet from a pasture fence. A small herd of beefalo, a hybrid of cattle and the American bison (otherwise known as buffalo), were sent thundering off in the opposite direction. However, even before my long horsey head ceased to rock back and forth on my long spindly neck, I realized that Agnes had a point. I certainly had a motive for killing Aaron Miller, and by organizing a venue where all the refreshments were to be the same, I had indeed given myself the opportunity to do him in.

We sat there as the late-afternoon sun glared at me through the windshield. The sun visors that automobiles come equipped with are totally inadequate in my opinion. Especially when one is in a foul mood. Meanwhile a giant fly was buzzing around in the back of the car, but when I opened a rear window to let it out, it flew up front to buzz around my head.

Agnes was right, of course, except that she was wrong. I wouldn't be on my own list, because *I knew* that I hadn't killed anyone. But I might be on her list, just like I was on Sheriff Stodgewiggle's list. Finally I just bit the bullet.

'Agnes, do you think that there is any chance that I might have killed Aaron Miller?'

'No, not in the slightest. I was just trying to get you to see what it might look like to someone looking at the case from the outside – someone who doesn't know you like I do.'

I felt the tension flow from my body. 'I see,' I said. 'Believe me, I see how bad this looks for me. Now, I also see that farmhouse way over yonder. That's the Bontrager farm, and I want you to get us there, lickety-split.'

'Mags, you need to see an optometrist. That's a tree, not a farmhouse. And behind that tree, that's a hill, which we have to go around first.'

'Then that's all the more reason for us to quit yapping and get a move on,' I said.

So we did. We made haste, and when we pulled up to the Armageddon Inc. headquarters, we discovered that we weren't the only ones on the move. The place looked like an ant colony that had been disturbed. Men and women, but mostly men, were shouting and milling about. There were so many cars and trucks converging on the driveway from the fields, where work had begun, that a traffic jam had been created. The nexus of the problem was simple: no one wanted to yield the right of way. The din created by all the horns honking gave me such a splitting headache that I bit the fleshy base of my thumb to redistribute part of the pain. Of course, there was no place for us to park, except out on the road.

Once at the front door of the converted farmhouse we realized there was no point in knocking. A sonic boom wouldn't have been heard over that racket. But mercifully the door was unlocked, so we rushed in and slammed it quickly shut behind us.

'Well, well, look what the cat dragged in,' Aaron's sexy secretary immediately said. She was standing behind his desk. Its drawers were open, as well as the drawers of his two large file cabinets. There were papers and files piled willy-nilly on his desk, and more of the same scattered all over the floor.

'It was too hot on the tin roof,' Agnes said.

'And too noisy,' I said.

'It certainly is much quieter in here,' Agnes said.

'That's because Aaron replaced all those ancient windows with double pane ones,' Tiff said. 'Whoever buys this place will have lower energy bills.'

'Thank you for sharing, dear,' I said. 'Perhaps you'd be so kind as to tell me why you're rooting through Aaron's records.'

'That's none of your darn business,' Tiff said. She actually said a stronger word which I refuse to repeat.

'Those aren't your papers, dear,' I said.

Then Tiff let loose a torrent of cuss words that would instantly turn any other Conservative Mennonite woman's hair white – if she understood them, that is. The only reason that I am familiar with these filthy words is that I'm married to a worldly man from New York City, and my sister Susannah spent some time in the pokey. Even Agnes, who is a more liberal Mennonite (General Conference) didn't know what half those words meant.

'Agnes,' I said by way of explanation, 'Tiffany was second runner-up to Miss Teenage Hog Slop Hollow.'

Agnes shook her head. 'Why that's downright unfair; you should have won the crown!'

Tiff grinned. 'I knowed it. I knowed that someday someone was going to see things my way.'

'Well, of course,' Agnes said. 'Didn't we catch you rooting though Aaron's papers like a hog, and with all that slop that just came out of your mouth, I'm certain that you were robbed of that title. If you want, I can go back to the Hollow with you and straighten those judges out. You know, tell them that you have every right to be called a pig.'

'Oy vey,' I said. Now since both my head and my thumb hurt, I had no choice but to kick Agnes in order to redistribute the pain. (Yes, of course I kicked her gently.)

'Ouch,' she grumbled.

Tiffany, bless her heart, had only heard a positive message in Agnes's spiel. 'Yes, oh yes, please come back to Hog Slop Hollow with me! There's nothing I want more than that crown, on account of it was set with genuine glass jewels – none of that cheap plastic stuff that some other pageants use in theirs. Of course we can't go until I find Aaron's will, because I just know he mentioned me in it. I know it for a fact because he had me type it up for him.'

My land o' Goshen. She didn't sound one bit bereft. She might just as well have been reading items off her grocery list.

'Miss Runner-up Pig Slop,' I said tersely, 'so far you've expressed as much sentiment as a pork patty. One would think that you cared not one whit for your deceased employer, whom you called Sugar Bear.'

The woman blanched which, unfortunately, made her somewhat attractive. Take it from an expert who's seen everything before: the bloodless look pairs rather well with fire engine hair.

'Get out of here!' she shrieked. 'Both of you.'

'Even me?' Agnes asked innocently.

Before Tiff could answer, I heard a toilet flush, and from a room to the back, who should appear but my very own daughter. This surprise would have knocked my socks off, except that my sturdy Christian underwear includes a girdle that holds up my thick cotton stockings.

'What are you doing here?' Alison said.

'I came to check on Rodney. What are you doing here?'

'The same thing, of course,' she said. There was an edge to her voice. 'He *is* my brother, after all.'

'Of course he is, dear. But you could have called Daddy or me. Or Auntie Agnes. We live closer.'

'Yes, but he's my flesh and blood, isn't he? It's not the same if just anyone looks in on him.'

Just anyone? Were Gabe and I suddenly *just anyone*? We took her in, and later officially adopted her, after Aaron and her mother abandoned her. They actually kicked her out of their house when she turned nine! I can't accurately describe how deep her words cut into my heart, after all the things I'd done for her. After all the things that I'd given up for her.

'Speaking of him, how is he doing?' I said.

'Fine.'

'Agnes saw you at my church this morning,' I said. 'Why didn't you say hi?' I had tried to keep the judgment out of my voice.

'Because I wasn't there,' Alison snapped. 'Agnes was mistaken.'

'That's not true,' Agnes said. She turned to me. 'Really, it's not!'

'I believe you,' I whispered.

I'd temporarily forgotten that even my whispered words sounded like a sheep bleating, and that Alison claims to have the hearing of a bat. (Although I'm fairly certain my daughter is not able to use echolocation to navigate in the dark.)

'So you don't believe me, your own daughter?' Alison demanded angrily.

No, I didn't believe her, but what was I to say at this point? When one is stuck between a rock and a hard place, the only thing one can do is to amuse oneself and hope that the moment will pass.

'"'Twas brillig, and the slithy toves. Did grye and gimble in the wabe",' I said.

'"All mimsy were the borogoves. And the mome raths outgrabe",' Agnes added.

I felt irritated at Agnes for latching on to my private moment, but the feeling was short-lived when Tiff next spoke.

'"Beware the Jabberwock, my son! The jaws that bite, the claws that catch! Beware the Jubjub bird, and shun the frumious Bandersnatch!"'

I was stunned. Runner-up to Junior Miss Hog Slop Hollow quoting Lewis Carroll? Oh, had I misjudged her, and how! Shame on me.

Alison was stunned as well. 'What was that? Are you three speaking in tongues, or are you on drugs?'

'Didn't you take English literature in college?' Agnes said. Unfortunately, her tone was a bit snarky.

'I was pre-med,' Allison snapped.

'Now wait a minute, Alison,' Agnes said, 'I was just asking a simple question. You didn't have to bite my head off.'

'It sounded more like you were judging me, *Auntie* Agnes.'

I smiled sweetly, as is my custom. 'Ladies,' I said, 'let's put our tempers in our pockets for a minute and make arrangements for getting Rodney back to his mother in Minnesota.'

'I'm afraid that isn't possible,' Tiff said.

'What are you talking about?' Alison demanded.

'She's dead,' Tiff said, and went back to riffling through papers.

TWENTY-FOUR

There are times when I might embroider the truth in order to get a point across, but now I'm stating a true fact. Three of us women managing to say the word 'what' at exactly the same time, and with the same intonation, and the same strong emphasis. If you ask me, that accomplishment should be recorded in the *Guinness Book of World Records*. At any rate, it certainly got Tiff's attention.

'Well, if y'all cared so much about this boy, then y'all would have been following his story. His poor mama drowned in the Red Sea. Not the real Red Sea, but the one in the amusement park, Texas Exodus, that Aaron created just outside Dallas. Rodney's mama played the part of the Hebrew woman, Miriam, who was Moses's sister. Anyhow, it was a trial run for the production, but there was a computer malfunction, and the floodgates opened way too soon. Pharaoh's men and their chariots hadn't even reached the dry sea bed. Fortunately all the extras who played the parts of Hebrews could swim – all except for Miriam.'

Tears filled my faded blue eyes, proving yet again that I really am a big softie. 'When did that happen, dear?'

'A year ago this past May fifteenth. I can't believe y'all didn't see the news on TV, or at least read about it in the newspaper.'

'Maybe we did,' Agnes said, 'but every day there's a new tragedy somewhere in the world. And then the pandemic. After months and months of the newscasters listing the daily body counts, I started tuning things out. Finally I stopped watching TV altogether. I also stopped getting my newspaper.'

'So you live in a bubble of self-imposed ignorance?' Alison said.

'Whoa,' I said. 'Agnes Miller may not be your real aunt, but she is related to you through the tangled kinship lines of Amish-Mennonite genealogy. But more importantly, she has been there for you from the day you landed in Hernia. She loves you almost as much as your dad and I love you.'

'Oh yeah?' Alison said. 'Which dad is that? The one who has to stay at home and watch L.J. while you gallivant around trying to solve crimes, or the one possibly killed by you setting up the perfect murder venue?'

This time the hot tears that streamed down cheeks were for me. Since they were self-pity tears, they were the first of their kind for me. It was a good thing that I could swim, because I might have suffered the same fate as Rodney's mother.

Agnes grabbed my elbow like a Rottweiler on a bone. 'Come on, Mags, we're leaving.'

'But we didn't get what we came for.'

She tugged, putting all her weight into it. 'We got plenty.'

'I'm calling Child Services,' I said, as I was literally being dragged from the room.

Tiff raced around us and put her back against the door. 'You ain't doing that,' she said. 'I mean, you can't do that. Please, Miss Yoder, I'm asking you nicely. Don't call Child Services. They'll put him in foster care, because he has no other family, and he'll likely go from foster home to foster home until he's eighteen. We both know that he's a handful, and not likely to be adopted. Please, I'm begging you, there has to be another solution.'

Sometimes the Devil opens my mouth, and sometimes the Lord does. Or, to put it in my husband's Jewish perspective, sometimes I listen to my Evil Inclination, and sometimes I listen to my Good Inclination. They're like little angels, one good, and one bad, sitting on my shoulders, and whispering in my ears. That afternoon I listened to the angel on my right. It said the following.

'Do you think that Rodney would enjoy living on a farm with two cows, one horse, lots of chickens, and a little brother?'

'Mags, stop!' Agnes said. 'That kid's a bully. You said so yourself.'

I jerked free of her grip and stepped back into the centre of the room. 'Yes, there is no getting around the fact that he was very mean to your other brother, Alison. But if he promised to behave, with the understanding that he'd have to go into foster care if he doesn't – well, then I'm willing to give him a home.'

Alison gaped at me while her thoughts caught up with my words. 'And you wouldn't force feed him religion?'

'Did I force feed *you* religion? Although Lord only knows that I should have, because according to the model your birth father created of Hell – never mind, I've already said too much.' I slapped both cheeks, and not in a gentle way, either. I am such a slow learner.

Much to my relief, Alison merely smiled. 'You were pretty good on that score, Mom. You danced around the subject every now and then, even though dancing is a sin according to your faith. Anyhow, I think that your offer is a very generous one. How about you and Aunt Agnes head on back home, while I run your offer past him. Actually I'll do more than that; I'll try to convince him of its merits.'

'Me too,' Tiff said.

Then, what I can only call Divine Inspiration struck again. I say that because even though I have gigantic feet, I really *can't* think all that fast on them. Now, however, it occurred to me that without Rodney to care for there was no further need for Tiffany to hang around the area anymore (assuming she found what she was looking for in Aaron's office). But if she stayed at the inn, ostensibly to help the boy adjust to his new surroundings, then she'd be right where I needed her to be, if I turned up evidence that she was Aaron's killer.

'Tiffany, dear,' I said, purring like a one-hundred-and-ten-pound cat, 'how would you like to spend a free vacation in a lovely, genuine, reproduction, Amish farmhouse? And the only reason it's a reproduction is because the original was blown down in a tornado, which left me lying face down in a cow pasture, with my face mashed into a cow pie?'

Alison giggled, even though she'd heard that story countless times before. 'Mom, tell her about the six-seater outhouse that you used to have.'

'Oh yeah, well that miserable thing was built by my great-great-granddaddy Amos Yoder, whose motto was: "The family that sprays together, stays together".'

'I don't get it,' Tiff said.

'It's just as well that you don't. It isn't Christian to sit six in a row, first thing every morning. In fact, it's downright disgusting. I was glad when the tornado sent it twirling off to another state.'

'Yeah,' Alison said, 'but then you built a two-seater to add a touch of faux authenticity for your guests.'

'For which I paid dearly,' I lamented. 'A crazed killer dropped me down through one of the seats into the cesspit and kept me prisoner there. Fortunately for me, my guests were not fond of using that facility.'

'Miss Yoder,' Tiff said, 'I doubt that would have happened if you had weighed more than a hundred pounds, you being six foot six, after all.'

At that both Agnes and Alison howled like a pair of pent-up housecats in heat. Alison slapped her thighs, and Agnes clapped her hands.

'I'm five-feet, ten-inches tall in my thick and opaque modest stockings,' I said.

'Miss Yoder,' Tiff said, 'would you mind if I gave you some fashion advice?'

'No!' Agnes and Alison cried in unison, as they both cringed.

'What?' Tiff said. 'What was so wrong about asking her that? Clearly she – uh, could use a little help.'

'*No!*' My bestie and daughter cried even louder.

I cleared my throat. Loudly. Then I focused my faded blue peepers and affected what I thought was a look of severe disapproval.

'Tiffany. Miss Codswallop Hogwash Wallow Slop – dear. I do not now, nor will I ever need fashion tips from a woman who dresses like a lady of the night.'

'What does that even mean?' Tiff said.

'She means that she doesn't care for your style,' Agnes said, and winked at Alison.

'My friend is much kinder than I am,' I said to Tiff. 'Well, have you thought about it? Three square meals a day, and a roof over your head. You may even milk the cows?'

'Really?' Tiff squealed. 'I love cows! What breed?'

'Jerseys.'

'Oh, man. I've never seen one in real life – except at the Polk County Fair, and that was a two-headed calf, and it was, like, stuffed, so that don't count as real life, do it?'

'Not really,' Alison said. 'But I should warn you that the room my mother will be letting you stay in doesn't have a TV.'

'That's alright, I got me my phone.'

'Well, you will have to charge it downstairs. Also, there's a ghost in the parlour.'

'No kidding! A real life ghost?'

'I'm afraid not,' I said. 'Great-granny's been dead for over a century, but she is a *real* ghost.'

'And if you're lucky,' Agnes said, 'you might be able to see and talk to her. Magdalena can, and so can her ten-year-old son, Little Jacob.'

'Too cool,' Tiff said. 'You can definitely count me in. I can't wait to milk the cows and talk to that there ghost.'

'I think then that this is pretty much a done deal,' Alison said. 'If Tiffany stays with us for a while, I'm pretty sure that Rodney will agree to the arrangement.'

So on a relatively upbeat note we said our goodbyes and headed back to the PennDutch Inn. Of course, I still had to talk Gabe into yet another one of my nefarious schemes, and this one was getting more complex by the hour. If it wasn't for the comforting presence of Agnes – er, Watson – by my side, my ball of yarn would be far more unravelled at this point than it was. But just when I thought that I had this ball pretty much rolled up for the night, Watson found a loose strand and gave it a tug.

'Mags,' she said, 'what a brilliant idea you had to invite Miss Teenage Pickled Pigs Feet to come stay at the PennDutch, given that she's one of your suspects. Now you get to grill her like a weenie at your leisure. But what are you going to do about the pair of genuine atheists that no longer have a reason to remain? They came to discredit Aaron, and now that he's dead, they might as well pack up and leave tomorrow morning. That is, if they've not already left.'

I groaned. 'Watson, do you want me to cut a hole in the roof of my car, and then take it into Bedford and drive through a carwash?'

'What?' Watson said, momentarily confused. Then the light dawned. 'No!'

'Well, then why must you always rain on my parades?'

'Well, *excuuuse* me for just trying to help you see matters for what they are.'

'But now that you've brought up this potential problem,' I said, 'I suppose that I could pull the old Joseph and Benjamin trick.'

Agnes gasped. 'You mean Joseph in the Bible who hid a cup in his brother's grain sack, and then accused him of stealing it?'

'Pretty clever, huh?' I said. 'Only in this case, I'd have to sneak whatever valuable item that it was into one of their suitcases.'

'Mags, that's mean! Plus it's dishonourable, and probably illegal. It's certainly not Christian. Besides, you live very modestly. You make all those old-fashioned dresses that you wear, with their uneven hems, and your shoes are so old that they most likely walked out of Egypt along with the Children of Israel. Don't even get me started on your furniture. Your dining room table was hand crafted by your ancestor Jacob the Strong over two hundred years ago, and it's the only thing in the house that survived the tornado. The rest of your furniture you've picked up at yard sales and flea markets, along with their resident fleas. Three cheers for Gabe on insisting on a new bed when you got married, otherwise you'd still be using the same bed that you and Aaron—'

'OK, stop! You've made your point. Remember that my parents died when I was nineteen and left me a farm to run, as well as a sister to raise. But I do have something valuable: I have a flawless, ten carat diamond engagement ring that Gabriel gave me.'

'Oh yeah!' Agnes said. 'But you never wear it, because it isn't modest. Besides, you would never sell it.'

'You're right,' I said. 'It would break Gabe's heart if I did. Well, if I can't force the Barkers to stay, then I guess I'll just have to coax them to stay.'

I glanced at Watson just as her brows lifted and her eyes widened. 'Oh, really?'

'Yes, I'll ask them to tell me all about their beliefs.'

Agnes tittered. 'That shouldn't take long. They're atheists. They have none.'

'I believe you're wrong,' I said with conviction. 'One doesn't go to Hell without giving it a good deal of thought.'

TWENTY-FIVE

Agnes dropped me off at the PennDutch close to the dinner hour, but declined my invitation to come in and eat with us. It had been a long day for her, she rightly claimed, and besides, her favourite TV series was airing its finale that night. Toy and his husband were coming over to watch it with her, since they were also avid fans of the show. OK, I will admit here that I felt envious, but it wasn't just her friendship with Toy, it was that she was comfortable viewing such programs.

When I waltzed into my kitchen through the back door, I discovered Gabe, Little Jacob, and the Barkers had not waited dinner on me. In fact, they were so busy shoving slices of formerly frozen pizza into their maws that they barely looked up.

'Ahem,' I said.

Gabe swallowed. 'L.J. was starving, and we do have guests, so I moved things up a little. I put some extra mozzarella on this frozen pizza, so it's really not too bad. And see, I made us a nice big, tossed salad, and we're going to have ice cream for dessert, with fresh strawberries, if anyone wants them.'

I nodded. 'Sounds good. Hello, everyone.'

'Sit down, hon,' Gabe said. 'I'll warm up a couple of slices for you.'

'Thanks, dear, but I have an announcement to make first.'

Little Jacob groaned. 'Do I have to?'

'Do you have to do what?' I asked.

'Do I have to do whatever you're about to announce, or go to whatever stupid event you have planned? And Mama, you know how I hate funerals.'

I couldn't help but laugh. 'It's nothing like that. It's that we're going to be joined by two more guests tonight. One of them is a beautiful young woman. In fact, she was a runner-up in the Miss Teenage Hog Slop Hollow contest down in Hog Slop Hollow, West Virginia.'

Little Jacob and the Babester laughed so hard that tears ran down their cheeks, whereas Jim and Tammy Faye were anything but amused. They exchanged disapproving glances and clucked like a pair of hens getting ready to lay their daily eggs. Finally, Jim slapped the kitchen table with the palm of his meaty hand.

'It isn't right to make fun of folks from Appalachia on account of the quaint names they gave to their community generations ago. How would you like it if someone laughed when they heard that your village is named Hernia? Or that there is an Intercourse, Pennsylvania?'

'Don't get your knickers in a knot, Jim,' I said. 'I was merely stating a fact. This woman, by the way, would be really pretty if she didn't use a trowel to slap on her make-up. In fact, she looks very much like—'

'Like who?' the Babester said.

'Never mind,' I said. 'Anyway, this young woman, whom I will not refer to as a young lady, as there is a difference, you know, was Aaron Miller's personal secretary.'

'Oh, my gracious!' Tammy Faye said and acted quite surprised.

'You've got to be kidding,' the Babester said.

'Well, if you think that's shocking news, then hold on to your seats, folks, because it gets a lot better. And L.J., don't freak out. I've invited Aaron's son Rodney to come and stay with us for a few days.'

'Mama! *Why?* How *could* you?'

'Because his papa is dead, and as it turns out, so is his mama. He has no one, L.J. He's an orphan now, and if we don't give him a place to stay, he will have to immediately go into a foster home with people he doesn't know.'

'But he doesn't know us! Well, he knows me, and that's just to treat me like dirt.'

'That's true, dear. But Alison is making him promise to be nice to you.'

'Alison? What does *she* have to do with this?'

'Remember, dear, that Rodney is Alison's brother.'

'Yeah, but I'm just as much Alison's brother as he is,' Jacob said hotly. 'Besides, I've known her my whole life, so that makes me more her brother than Rodney.'

I saw my husband smile behind his clasped hands. It was sweet that Little Jacob claimed Alison as his genetic sister. He knew better, of course, but she had already been part of our family when he was born, so that's how he chose to view our family dynamics.

'L.J.,' I said, 'it's very important to Alison that you give this a try. If it doesn't work out – if he's mean to you – then out he goes. But keep an open mind, for your sake, as well as hers. Who knows, you might even wind up having a big brother.'

Gabe coughed. 'Now hold it there, Mags, are you possibly putting the cart before the horse? Maybe before a team of horses? Couldn't you have talked about any of this with me before springing this on the kid? And in front of our guests to boot?'

'Yeah,' I agreed.

'This isn't fair,' Little Jacob said. 'We got blinded.'

'I think you mean blindsided,' Jim said.

'I'll thank you for not correcting my son,' Gabe said.

'Yeah,' L.J. said.

'And mind your manners,' I said. 'That goes for both of you.'

'Well, you're right, Gabe. I should have sent the Barkers away for this conversation. Or taken the two of you away from your supper and spoken to you privately, so I apologize. But I didn't think I had the time, because I honestly didn't know how long it would take for Alison to persuade – oops, I hear her car crunching on the gravel outside. Barkers, please take your plates and skedaddle into the dining room. And don't you dare listen at the door either once they come in, because, as you know, it's a swinging door, and over my almost sixty years I've gotten rather adept at giving it a good hard push when I set my mind to it.'

'I'm going as well, Mama,' L.J. said. 'If I may be excused from the table.'

'Ask your papa, dear. He's the one who fed you.'

'May I, Papa?'

Gabe smiled lovingly. 'Yes, but you know the rules: no taking food up to your room.'

'Ah! Then I'm staying – I guess.' He took another bite of pizza and chewed loudly, just to be annoying, but he stopped when the back door opened.

'Hey Tiger,' Alison said. L.J. ran to give her a hug, knocking his chair over in the process.

'He's got pizza hands,' I warned.

Alison kissed the top of her brother's head. 'No pizza hands,' she said. 'This is a new blouse. Hi Mama, hi Papa.'

Much to my irritation, and I am a patient woman, mind you, the Barkers had not made a beeline for the dining room door. They were standing just inside the kitchen, gawking like rubber-neckers at a car wreck. When Alison spotted them standing there, her gaze seemed to linger for a few seconds on Tammy Faye.

'Hello, I'm Alison Rosen,' she said. 'I'm their daughter.'

Jim quickly wiped his hand on a paper napkin he was holding and extended it. 'Jim Barker, here. Guest atheist. And this is my wife, Tammy Faye.'

'Oh yes, I heard about you two,' Alison said.

'Nothing too good, I hope. You know, given our creed.'

Alison laughed. 'Actually, my father thinks rather highly of you.'

'You do?' I wailed, turning to Gabe. 'And since when have you been talking to Alison? She barely has time to talk to me, and I'm her mother?'

'Papa talks to her all the time,' L.J. said, and pulled the remaining topping off the slice of pizza he was eating and stuffed it into his mouth. Then, even though his cheeks were pushed out, making him look like a chipmunk, he reached for a fresh slice.

'Uh, uh, uh, sport,' Gabe said. 'You eat that crust on your plate first. Think of all the starving children in London.'

'In my day it was India,' I said.

'For me it was China,' Gabe said. 'There are starving children everywhere, possibly even here in Hernia, so London's as good a place as any.'

'I don't think we have any starving—'

'Shh,' Alison said. 'Did you hear someone knock?'

I hate being shushed. 'We have a back doorbell,' I said. 'It's even lit.'

But no, apparently some folks just can't be bothered to examine their surroundings before acting. Someone was definitely knocking at the door, and it was getting progressively louder, and exponentially more annoying. Fortunately for said individual, dear Alison went bounding off to answer. That gave me a chance to glance at my son's face when Rodney and Tiff entered.

'Everybody,' Alison said, 'this is Tiffany Anderson and Rodney Miller.'

Hallelujah. Tiff had a last name, and Alison had been circumspect in not introducing Rodney as her brother. There was one of us who would happily have Rodney magically, and permanently, disappear.

'And I'm Alison's brother,' Rodney said.

'Yeah, maybe,' Little Jacob managed to say, despite his mouth being filled with pizza, 'but you didn't grow up with her.'

'So what?' Rodney said, as he grabbed Alison's hand. 'You ain't even no kind of brother to her, because you ain't even related at all.'

Little Jacob spat out his pizza. His face was red with rage. He stood up, and might even have attacked the older boy, had it not been for Gabe's restraining grip on his wrist.

'I am so her brother,' he yelled. 'These are my parents, and they're her parents too. Just ask her. So that makes me her brother. So there! Besides, you and Alison never even had one parent together, because your daddy threw her away before you were born.'

'L.J., that's enough,' Gabe said sternly. 'Remember what you promised?'

'But he started it, Papa.'

'What did I start?' Rodney said.

'If you ask me,' Jim Barker said, 'these boys sound just like any old pair of brothers. My brothers and I fought all the time.'

'Nobody asked you,' I said pleasantly. Trust me, although I am a meek and modest Mennonite woman, I can be a wee bit unpleasant when pushed to my breaking point – or so I've been told.

'Don't speak to Sugar Bear like that,' Tammy Faye snarled.

'This is *my* house, and I shall speak how I want,' I said, in a not so pleasant tone.

At that, dear, sweet Alison burst into tears. 'Please, just stop. Everyone. Don't you realize that this boy has just lost his father? Today? L.J., I've known you since the day that you were born. I fed you, rocked you to sleep in my arms – you will always be my Number One Brother. But Rodney is my brother as well. All I'm asking is that the two of you get along. At least, just for a little while. Who knows, maybe someday, you'll really be . . .' Her voice trailed off, but she looked at me expectantly.

Too soon, I thought. This was way too soon. Like she'd just stated it was only today that my arch enemy had died, and now she was beseeching me with her eyes to welcome his orphaned son into my house as one of my own. What chutzpah! I know, it was my idea in the first place, but she was so quick to make it her own that I almost regretted suggesting it in the first place. Unless – and this is a big 'unless' – the Good Lord had put this idea into my head as payback to me for hating Aaron Miller, which in His book is the same thing as killing the man. Just read Matthew 5:27-28 and you'll get the concept. Come to think of it, if I really had free will, then I would say that God had chutzpah for sticking me with the fruit of Aaron's loins, for amongst those loins I'd never been fruitful. But I dare not say that, because it would be a major sacrilege, although now that I've just thought it, I might as well just come out and say it.

But before I had a chance to react to my daughter's impassioned plea, Little Jacob broke free from his daddy and launched himself at his sister. He threw his arms around her with such force that he would have knocked her over, had Rodney not grabbed her. From where I stood, it appeared as if the three of them were hugging.

'Don't cry, big sister,' Jacob wailed. 'I'll be nice to him; I promise I will.'

'Yeah, and I won't mess with the kid,' Rodney grunted.

Alison wrapped her arms around both boys and squeezed tightly. Over their head she gave me a coy wink.

'That's all I'm asking. I just want my two brothers to be nice to each other. You don't even have to speak to each other – just don't be mean to each other.'

My word, what a master manipulator that young woman had become, and all because she was able to become a human faucet at will! I shouldn't have been surprised, I guessed. Even as a girl, she could twist Gabe around her little finger just by shedding a tear or two. This ability to turn on the waterworks is just so ding-dang-dong unfair, if you ask me. Try as I might to squeeze out one tear in order to get my way, just one teensy, weensy, little droplet, my tear ducts have always remained as dry as the

Sahara Desert. The last time I tried that trick on the Babester, he asked if I might be feeling constipated.

Anyhow, my faith, as a Mennonite, is averse to taking oaths (the Holy Bible forbids it), but Alison is most assuredly not a Mennonite. She made her brothers swear a pinkie oath (which got everyone laughing) that they would treat each other kindly, and with respect. After that little ceremony the mood in the room lightened considerably.

The rest of the evening passed quietly. The Barkers took a long walk, and then did whatever committed atheists do in their rooms on Saturday nights (Oh Lord spare me any details!). After eating a slice of pizza, Tiff retired to her assigned room. Upon finding out that his room did not contain a television, Rodney reluctantly accepted Little Jacob's invitation to play video games with him in Little Jacob's room, or watch television there. Alison had to say her goodbyes and get back to med school. That was understandable, but it always left me feeling a mite depressed.

But before Alison left, the three of us worked out a tentative funeral service for Aaron Miller. It would be held at my church, Beechy Grove Mennonite Church. It used to be Aaron's church as well, and generations of his family have attended there, including his parents, who were married there (we were married in my barn). Anyway, I would ask Reverend Utterall to officiate, and Aaron's earthly remains would be buried at Beechy Grove Mennonite Church. Of course, all this depended upon what Aaron's will had disclosed, and so far neither Tiff nor Alison had been able to find it. Well, supposedly.

Anyway, before I turned in for the night, I had one more phone call to make. I needed to reach out to an old friend whom I had been treating rather poorly. When he answered, despite the late hour, practically the first words out of his mouth were to invite me to lunch the following day. I accepted Toy's warm invitation, but I went to bed feeling like a proper heel.

TWENTY-SIX

When I smell bacon the minute I wake up, I immediately thank the Good Lord that he didn't forbid Christians from eating this most delicious of all foods. Then it registers that my Sweet Baboo, the Babester, *my* Honey Buns, must be in the kitchen frying up Sunday morning breakfast.

I don't recall ever missing church, not once in my almost sixty years, so as Gabe cooked, I dressed in my Sunday best. First I struggled into my sturdy Christian underwear. Then my ultra-tan Sunday pantyhose. Next came a knee-length cotton slip. Over the slip, and over my head, I pulled a genuine polyester dress that hit me mid-calf. Unlike my weekday navy broadcloth costumes, this outfit was truly worthy of the Sabbath. It was a print, with a sky-blue background, accentuated by hundreds of tiny, almost microscopic, yellow flowers. It felt almost sinful to wear such a jazzy frock. And as it was the Lord's Day, I wore a freshly laundered white organza prayer cap atop my pile of mouse-coloured braids.

When I stepped into the kitchen, the Babester whistled. 'Hot dog! Aren't you a sight for sore eyes?'

'Oh, stop it,' I said, feeling myself blush. After all, there were five other pairs of eyes looking at me, including those of my son, and the runner-up to Miss Teenage Hog Slop Hollow.

'Mama,' Little Jacob said, 'I think that you're the most beautiful woman in the world.'

Rodney snickered. 'Yeah? What about Tiff here? Now *there's* someone worth looking at!'

I pasted on my kindest smile, given that I'd just been dissed. After all, the lad was grieving, and had apparently been mother-less for a while (not that his mother had been a shining example of good etiquette). Contrary to popular platitudes it can take a lot of effort to smile – well at least for some of us. Thank good-ness that the Babester spoke up before the cheek muscles collapsed, or, Heaven forfend, maybe locked into place. Magdalena Yoder with a smile frozen permanently in place would put the cows off milking and scare the horses – not to mention freak out the entire populace of Hernia, Pennsylvania.

'Sweetie,' Gabe said, 'the boys want to spend the day at Kennywood. You know, that amusement park just south of Pittsburgh. I said that I'd be happy to take them.' He winked. 'They want to stay for fireworks at closing, so it's going to be a *long* day. Of course, this all depends on if it's all right with you.'

'Please,' Little Jacob begged. 'Please.'

I glanced at Rodney.

'You're very attractive for a woman of your age, Mrs Yoder,' he said quickly.

'OK,' I said. 'But you boys put on sunscreen. I don't want you coming back looking like ripe tomatoes.'

'Yes, Mama,' Little Jacob said.

'Yes, ma'am,' Rodney said. His response might have knocked my socks off, but I was wearing pantyhose.

'And what will the rest of you be doing on this beautiful day?' I asked. 'If you have no plans, you're more than welcome to come to church with me. I realize that two of you don't believe in the Good Lord who made you, and from whose bounty you are partaking at this very moment, nonetheless, you might have an anthropological interest in visiting an Old Order Mennonite church. At the very least, it will give you more arrows for your quiver labelled "reasons to rebel against organized religion".'

Jim Barker laughed heartedly. 'That's a good one. Thanks for the invitation, Miss Yoder, but my quiver is jam-packed already. At any rate, I'm going to have to turn you down, because the three of us are going into town to visit the museums, and then the ladies want to do some shopping.'

'Oh?' I said. When was that arranged? What could Little Miss Piggyback Hollow possibly have in common with a worldly sophisticate like Tammy Faye, a genuine atheist? Besides their trashy way of dressing, and the pounds of putty they slap on their faces in their mistaken belief that they're improving God's creation?

Tammy Faye slid out from behind the table and tottered over

to where I stood. There she slipped a shapely arm around my
bony shoulders and gave me a gentle squeeze. The scent of her
perfume (lavender and week-old skunk spray) was so strong that
it made my eyes water, and my knees feel wobbly.

'Miss Yoder,' she said gently, 'we would love to have you
come with us. Surely your God wouldn't mind if you missed
just one church service. Would she?'

'God is a he!' I snapped.

'How do you know?' she said.

'Because it says so in the Bible,' I said. 'That's the book you
don't read.'

'Yes, but the book isn't in English,' Tammy Faye said. 'Do
you read Hebrew, or Greek, or Aramaic?'

'But God is the boss of everybody,' I said. 'It wouldn't do to
have a woman be the boss of everyone.'

'That's a load of horse poop,' Tiff said. 'A woman can be just
as good at being a boss as a man.'

'You're right about that,' I said. 'But enough with this God
talk; it's Sunday, after all. This is a day of rest, not quiet contem-
plation. So if everyone is happy with their plans for the day, and
if you are all through chowing down, trot on over to the sink –
which I will fill with warm, sudsy water, so that you can wash
your own dishes. And hon, you will wash the frying pan, since
you are the one who used it.'

'But Mama, we have a dishwasher,' Little Jacob whined.

'I'm preparing you for real-world contingencies,' I said. 'Like
for your bachelor days, or when the power goes out, and your
wife doesn't like washing up any more than you do.'

'And what are you preparing us for?' Jimmy Barker said.

'Nothing,' I answered. 'But you signed up for A.L.P.O, the Amish
Lifestyle Plan Option, and the Amish don't have electricity.'

'What about me?' Tiffany whined.

'Yeah, and me,' said Rodney.

'Folks under thirty don't get a choice,' I said.

'Hey!' Tammy Faye, said. 'You don't know how old I am.'

Chances were that I had sturdy Christian underwear older than
that woman. And anyway, the tiny fissures in her layers of
make-up betrayed her age, just like the rings in a tree trunk.
Tammy Faye was probably well into her fourth decade.

I simply ignored her protest, and by and by I had the house to myself – and Satan. Oh yes, the Devil is omnipresent. No sooner did the last bunch leave, than I started thinking about skipping church. Don't get me wrong, I wasn't about to return to bed, or lollygag on one of the two recliners in our private lounge and stuff bon-bons into my face. No siree Bob, I was thinking about doing some serious detective work, and in the process quite possibly securing my daughter's future. But skipping church to do so, even with the Devil's encouragement, was frightfully hard to contemplate. In fact, I would have to ask the oldest member of the family for permission.

That said, I slithered sinfully off to the parlour for an audience with Granny. Granny was already scowling when I entered the room, so I surmised that somehow she knew that I was coming.

'What is it this time, Magdalena? Did your cat get hit by that swinging kitchen door again? I don't know how many times I told your mama to get rid of that door. Someday, someone is going to get really hurt by that thing.'

'Granny, the incident with Kitty happened when I was four, and she survived just fine. Still, I'll thank you not to mention it again. No, I'm here to ask for your permission to skip going to church this morning.'

Granny howled with laughter. There is nothing more unsettling than an Apparition-American letting loose with a laugh that sounds human at the beginning, but then the sound morphs into something like the howls of Arctic wolves as heard on Gabe's massive TV screen. As Granny carried on, she rocked steadily in her ancient rocker, with her head thrown back. Any normal person observing her would have bundled her up and shipped her off to a home for the severely mentally disturbed – although not having a tangible body, that's easier said than done, I guess.

'I don't see what's so ding-dang-dong funny about my question,' I said, when she had finally worn herself out enough to listen to me again. 'You are the head of this family, aren't you?'

'Boogers,' Granny said. 'I don't even have a head. Or maybe I do. But it would be in my casket in Settler's Cemetery up on Stucky Ridge. I'm just a ghost, a phantom, or whatever that fancy name is that you like to call me.'

'Apparition-American,' I said. 'Anyway, Granny, I still value your opinions, and see you as the spiritual leader of this family – no pun intended.'

'What's a pun, child?'

'Let's say that a word has two different meanings, or sounds like another word. So for a humorous effect, one might—'

'Enough, child. You're boring me to death.'

'I hardly think so, Granny. That ship sailed a long time ago.'

'Don't get fresh with me, Magdalena. Now back to your silly question. What sort of advice do you think I would give you? Don't you realize that I've been skipping church for nigh on to half a century?'

'Has it been *that* long?'

'Well, you were ten when I passed – well, sort of passed. You get the drift, anyhow.'

'I'm still fifty-nine,' I wailed. 'I won't be sixty until tomorrow. Not that anyone has noticed. I mean, Gabe hasn't even mentioned my birthday. Every year he asks me how I want to celebrate it – even *if* I want to celebrate it. And he always asks me for gift ideas. If I left it up to him he'd buy me expensive jewellery, like diamonds, when everyone knows that a good woman much prefers household items like another cast-iron skillet, or a new toilet scrubbing brush and plunger, with their own plastic caddy in a refreshing shade of lime green.'

'Oh, quit your whinging, girl. That man is the best thing that ever happened to you. The next time he accidentally sits on me, I'm going to give him the ride of his life.'

'Granny!'

'Just hush, Magdalena. You're always complaining. If you wanted perfection, then you should have married your mirror. But back to your stupid question about skipping church. Have you ever skipped it before?'

'No,' I said. 'Not once in my life. Even when I had the chicken pox, measles, and mumps, Mama bundled me up and made me go. She said that she was doing the other mothers a favour by letting their kids get exposed all at once. Something about herd immunity. But the truth is that she didn't want to bother staying at home with me.'

'Well then,' Granny said, 'you have a lot of "get out of jail free" cards built up in Heaven, if you ask me. So, whatever trouble that you're planning to get into today, I say go for it.'

'I don't plan on getting into trouble,' I said hotly.

Granny chortled.

'Well, I don't!' I said.

'Child, trouble follows you, like flies follow the rear end of a horse. But I'm not saying that ought to stop you from skipping church. Less praying, and a little more playing, might loosen you up a bit. Lord only knows, you were always wound so tight that a body figured you'd snap at the slightest unexpected sound.'

'Well, since you don't have a body, it couldn't have been you doing the figuring.'

'Don't be mean, Magdalena; it doesn't become you.'

'Sorry, Granny.'

'Then come give me a kiss to prove that you mean it.'

I actually took a step closer to the rocking chair before I realized I was being had. As real as my granny is to me, one cannot actually kiss an Apparition-American. Believe me, I've tried – twice. Both times when I took aim at her face, I took care to avoid the grape-size mole, with the inch long whisker waving merrily from it. Both times my lips encountered only air. After my second attempt I decided that I was no longer the brightest bulb in the chandelier.

Having taken that step closer to Granny this time, I blew her an 'air kiss', which set her off laughing hysterically again, whereon I exited the parlour guilt-free, and with half of my dignity intact. This Sunday morning was now all mine. I could do anything that I wanted with it. I could indeed lollygag if I wished. I could return to bed, or even take a nice rewarding soak in Big Bertha, she with the thirty-six jet sprays. But oh no, Miss Horsey Face with a muzzle for trouble wasted no time in getting her fly-ridden behind into more trouble than even she, a pro, could handle.

TWENTY-SEVEN

For starters, my Sunday morning drive was embarrassing. I had decided to disguise myself by wearing a hat with a veil. I only had one hat, which was a wool, winter hat, and it lacked a veil. However, I did have an orange-coloured net bag, made of plastic that my onions came in at the grocery store. This I pinned to the rim of the black hat, and it looked curiously fetching, if not fashionable.

While it may have disguised my face, my car, with its vanity license plate that read PENNDUTCH, was a dead giveaway. It seemed that every driver I passed honked, and many of these cars were headed in the opposite direction, towards *my* church. At the social hour following the service, my ears were going to be burning so hot, it would feel as if the Devil had placed a lit charcoal briquette in each one.

It wasn't just the constant stream of cars headed in the direction of my church (nothings draws a crowd like a murder), but it was the handful of Amish buggies that I overtook on their way to their services. Amish traditionally worship in private homes (they rotate between homes), instead of buildings set aside for that purpose. I had no idea where these families were headed that particular Sunday, but it appeared as if they were going in my general direction. As I passed them, I saw these usually reserved people waving energetically at me.

All this attention directed at me puzzled me, it made me highly anxious. I will not claim to have an imagination, but all the waving and honking compelled me to pull over to the side of the road and inspect the grill, and the undercarriage, of my car. I once read a newspaper account about a drunk driver who returned home late from a bar one night, and then fell asleep in his car, without even going in to bed. When he awoke the next morning and exited the car, he discovered the body of a young woman stuck in the front grill.

I'm happy to report that I had not run over anyone, neither in a drunken state, nor while sober. And there were no animal carcasses attached to my automobile either. Instead, someone had taped a piece of cardboard to the front bumper, and also one to the back bumper. Printed on these message boards, in large black letters, were the words: JUST MARRIED.

'Ha, ha,' I said to myself as I ripped off the cardboard pieces. 'Your silly joke is over now.' But frankly, I was rather irked. Yes, my car is recognizable, since it is one of the more expensive models in Hernia, but it isn't the only one of its make. Who knows, I might have been able to drive out to the old Bontrager place in my clever disguise, without anyone giving it a thought, had it not been for someone's idiotic sense of humour.

However, one must keep a stiff upper lip, as the Brits say, and get on with the task at hand. Which reminds me, a former guest at the PennDutch, a gentleman who was contemplating a move to England, was so concerned that his upper lip wouldn't be stiff enough for his new compatriots, that he had stainless steel mesh implanted in it. Somehow this mesh became magnetized, and subsequently this gent was able to hang his car keys, and even his fork and knife from his stiff lip. He became all the rage at dinner parties, but was never able to find a woman brave enough to kiss him.

Anyway, upon my arrival at the old Bontrager place, now known as the Armageddonland construction site headquarters, I knew exactly what to do. More precisely, I knew how to gain entrance without smashing a window with a brick, and all this because I had been married to that monster, Aaron Miller. Yes, I know, one mustn't speak ill of the dead, but surely ex-wives get a pass on this rule. But back to easy access: there was a brightly coloured gnome sitting by the front door. It wasn't just any cute little garden gnome; this gnome was facing the wall and bending forward with his pants pulled down. This disgusting little figure had sat on Aaron's front porch in his bachelor days, but you can bet your bippy, that this graven image was not displayed during our so-called married life.

Before you make up your mind that I'm just being prudish about a pair of resin buttocks, please locate your King James Bible, and read Exodus, chapter twenty, verse four. It's one of the Ten Commandments, and it forbids us to make a carved image or likeness of *anything*. A gnome is definitely something. At any rate, this particular gnome, which Aaron had named Grimsby, had a shallow depression under its base. In his bachelor-hood days, Aaron used to tape his spare key up under there, on the theory that a thief would lift the stupid thing to look under it, but not turn it over to inspect the bottom.

The crazy thing was that was back in the day when we didn't even need to lock our doors in Hernia. However, Aaron had attended college in the big city, and had returned somewhat paranoid in my opinion. I refused to have the obscene gnome on my porch, where all of my friends and relations could see it. However, I did compromise to the point that I agreed to keep the front door locked, and hide the key under the front doormat.

So sure enough, getting into Armageddonland was easy as pie, but looking for his will was not going to be a piece of cake. That tart of a secretary, along with Alison, had done a good job of trashing his office. The contents of his desk drawers had been spilled out onto the floor and spread around. His file cabinet drawers had obviously been rifled through. It looked as if thieves had been at work in the room, rather than an executive secretary and a medical student.

Just getting to Aaron's desk took a bit of effort. Finally, I plopped my pitiful patooty in Aaron's comfy leather, swivel chair, and beseeched the Dear Lord for guidance. How could I possibly find a needle in a haystack that had been hit by a tornado and blown to smithereens? The last time I beheld a room in such disarray was when Alison was a teenager. Back then Gabe and I came to a mutual agreement that it wasn't in the best interest of our sanity to insist that she keep her room tidy. The agreement that we made with her then was that she had to keep her door closed at all times. She also had to wear clean clothes, which meant that she had to do her own laundry.

As I sat there in Aaron's office chair, ruminating about the past, my eyes drifted around the room to the various awards and degrees hanging on the walls. There were a few framed photos as well: Aaron holding a shovel at a ground-breaking ceremony, and a couple more of him shaking hands with smiling older men. However, there was only one personal photo, and I recognized the person in it immediately, even from across the room. Amelia

Yoder Miller, my father's second cousin, and Aaron's sainted mother!

Since Aaron grew up on the farm across Hertzler Road from us, we were playmates as children. The Millers had a pond, and we didn't, so I spent more time at the Millers than I did at home. Amelia was always very kind to me, and truth be told, more patient than Mama was, by a long stretch. She was also a much better baker, and once when I let it slip that Mrs Miller's chocolate-chip cookies were chewier, and not burnt, Mama whipped me soundly with a willow switch. Even though I was only six, I shouldn't have said that, so I deserved that whipping.

At any rate, Aaron adored his mother, who died at age forty-two from breast cancer. He used his mother's birthdate as his security code whenever one was required. Since it was used on our joint bank account, and to retrieve our telephone voicemail, that date got fixed in my memory. Also, during our four-year marriage, it was I who sent his beloved mother cards signed with his name on special occasions, because Aaron was too lazy to do so. Yet when she learned that he still had a wife up in Minnesota, after he married me, my wonderful mother-in-law turned on me as fast as milk will curdle if left out in the hot sun. When she saw me at church the following Sunday, she hissed at me as if she were a feral cat that I was trying to pet. I couldn't believe that this was the same, dear, sweet Amelia who used to give me chewy chocolate-chip cookies when I was six!

At any rate, I waded through the papers and files again to the free-standing safe, and tried what I thought sure was the correct combination. Nothing. Then I recalled a conversation I'd had with Aaron about how it wasn't a good idea to use the same security for all one's accounts, and that one should actually swap them out for new codes periodically. At the time Aaron had said he would think about it. That happened to be just days before I discovered that he had another family.

Well, maybe he had taken my advice. Knowing that he thought of himself as a bit of a sophisticate, and anything European was superior to anything home-grown, I tried swapping the day his mother was born with the month, in the European fashion. Click, and *voila*! The contents of the safe were mine to peruse.

Inside the safe were several packets of cash, in one-hundred-dollar denominations. There was a watch that appeared to be made of gold, but then what do I know? Also, there was Aaron's silly baseball card collection, in little leather-bound books. He used to claim that it was worth a fortune, and would joke that if our house caught on fire, he would get it outside first, and then come back and get me. And most importantly, as far as I was concerned, there was a file in the safe marked Last Will and Testament of Aaron Jacob Miller. (And no, I didn't name Little Jacob after my ex-pseudo-husband – not consciously, at any rate.) Bingo! I grabbed the all-important file, closed and locked the safe, and slogged through the mess back to the high-quality desk chair.

Now, people who know me well, can attest to the fact that I am a level-headed woman, not given to histrionics. Neither am I one known to exaggerate or go overboard with hyperbole. Sure, I may skilfully embroider a dull anecdote upon occasion, but who doesn't. And I literally never misuse the word 'literally', as virtually everyone else around me is wont to do. So believe me when I say that when I opened the file, and read that Aaron had left the whole of his estate to Yours Truly, I hit the roof! How dare that man! That was like accusing me of murder. The only conclusion that Sheriff Stodgewiggle could possible draw now was that I had killed Aaron in order to inherit his estate. But that's not the only thing that infuriated me; how could a father not include his children as his primary heirs? They weren't even mentioned in his will. They got nothing! Nada! Zip! Punishing me for exposing his bigamous ways was one thing but punishing his two innocent children in the process was unconscionable. And here I'd felt a flirtatious vibe coming from Aaron – or had my sinful heart just hoped that was the case? If only Aaron had aged into an ugly man, one so repulsive that he scared horses and made small children cry. Then maybe my body might have refused to recognize his pheromones when they came wafting my way in clouds so thick they were almost palpable.

Well, one thing was for sure: no one else was even getting a glimpse of this will until I had a chance to show it to my attorney. I wanted it on record that I planned to contest that ding-dang thing; I did not want to inherit a single penny of that man's money. By rights his estate should be split evenly between his children – however many that might be. Ever since learning about

Rodney, it would not have surprised me to learn that Aaron had deposited his seed in other wombs hither, thither, and yon, like a modern-day Johnny Appleseed, planting apple trees across this great country of ours.

As I pondered my next course of action, I picked over some of the papers that had been dumped on Aaron's desk. Now, while I eschew gossip, because it is hurtful to its subjects, and often inaccurate in the first place, I see nothing wrong in being nosy. Let me rephrase that: I see nothing wrong in being informed, for that's exactly what so-called nosiness is. It is nothing more than fact-gathering, and just as long as one keeps their big, fat nose out of my business, then I say go for it!.

Because of this tolerant viewpoint of mine, I got rather caught up reading some of Aaron's private correspondence with a woman who called herself 'Your Minx'. The letters were undated, and contained sexual innuendo, rather than anything explicit. If I were to be completely honest, I'd say that was rather disappointing. Therefore, I had no choice but to continue to read these missives, in the hope that one would provide me with new information about the sex act, and thus legitimize my snooping. Well, I certainly wasn't disappointed; the slattern who wrote those letters had the chutzpah to reference me, for crying out loud! She had written:

> My ample curves must be a welcome relief from that beanpole body of your wife. Still can't understand what you see in that bag of bones. Like I promised, if you divorce her, I'll divorce him.
> Love forever. D.

'D?' I said aloud. Did that initial stand for Delilah, or the Devil? Although there was no date on the letter, the writer had made it quite clear that she and my pseudo-husband were having an affair. Can a man sink any lower than Aaron Miller had? He'd been cheating on his wife with me, and during that time he was cheating on me with this trollop, this wanton tart. I was still recovering from learning the depths of Aaron's depravity when the front door to the building flew open, and I heard a woman's voice speaking on a cell phone.

'I can't believe that Magdalena skipped church,' Prissy was saying. 'It's not like her. She must be really sick. We need to call in on her this afternoon – no, I'll pay her a sick call. After the way you treated her yesterday, you're probably the last person she wants to see. Oh no, I just had a terrible thought. You don't think there's a chance that the reason she wasn't there is because she's joined another congregation because of you, dear, is there? Maybe the First Mennonite Church on Main Street where Agnes goes. I mean, Magdalena does seem to be sliding off into the liberal end of the pool, doesn't she, dear?'

There followed a period of mostly silence at her end, with a few feeble affirmations, but knowing Prissy, that meant she didn't agree with what was being said at all. When the conversation seemed to be ended she headed straight to Aaron's office and waded nosily across his paper strewn floor. Her approach could not have been made any clearer had she worn a cow bell around her neck.

Fortunately I had taken cover under Aaron's desk, and given my willowy frame, I had been quite able to hunch there, with my forehead resting on my knobby knees. In my panic, I'd also pulled the expensive leather chair close to me, as far under the desk as the armrests would allow. Unless Prissy had come into the office looking for a person, she could pass Aaron's desk repeatedly, and not have a clue that there was a five-foot-ten Mennonite woman under it, quaking in her clodhoppers. Or she could walk right up to it, and wishing to sit down, try to pull the chair away from the desk – which is exactly what she did.

I'm still not sure why I did it, but when she pulled at the chair I held it tightly in place. She tugged harder, and succeeded in yanking it about a foot away from me. She must have believed that the chair had been stuck on something, because when I reached out and jerked it back, she screamed like a nine-year-old boy. By then I figured that the jig was up entirely, so I scooted out of that confining space and unfolded my gangly limbs, only to find the office and the lobby deserted, and to hear a car racing away. I quickly thanked the Good Lord for deliverance, one I hadn't even prayed for, and I then also hopped into my automobile and pressed the pedal to the metal.

TWENTY-EIGHT

I had a lunch date to keep with Chief Toy and his husband Steven Lantz, but first I wanted to make a copy of the will and put it safely in my safe. There are two ways to get to the PennDutch from the old Bontrager place, the country way, and the short cut, which takes you through the village. But if you have a heavy foot, and I most certainly do, the country route is much quicker. That meant that even though I left before Prissy Utterall did, I arrived back home, and had just copied the document, when I heard her car coming up my long gravel driveway.

It occurred to my somewhat active imagination that I had three choices – no, four, actually. I could refuse to answer the door, but that would be stupid because my car was in the driveway. She might surmise that I was really sick, and call for an ambulance. I could answer the door and pretend to be quite ill, but not so sick that I needed medical attention. Or I could indeed pretend that I had attended Agnes's church – on sort of an 'exploratory' excursion. And lastly, just to shock the pantyhose off her, I could lie outrageously and claim that Gabe's visiting pair of atheists had finally convinced me that my beliefs were naive, and I had decided to become a secular humanist. But just imagining that last possibility gave me a deep pang of guilt, one that actually made my chest hurt.

In the end, I decided to say nothing. A woman just shy of her sixtieth birthday does not need to explain her absence from church – even to her pastor's wife. Besides, while it is true that 'loose lips sink ships', sealed lips can annoy the mashed potatoes out of the interrogator. Perhaps Miss Busybody would get so aggravated by my silence that she'd unintentionally divulge what she had been up to this morning. However, for me to keep my big fat mouth shut is like trying to stop Niagara Falls with a sieve.

The second I opened the door Prissy pushed past me and pranced right in. 'You believe in ghosts,' she said.

'Granny's my proof,' I said. 'What about it?'

'Well, the strangest thing just happened to me. Actually, it was downright terrifying. I was at this – uh – place, you see, and I was trying to move this chair out from beneath a table, when a ghost grabbed hold of the bottom of the chair and yanked it back.'

'You mean the ghost grabbed one of the chair legs?'

'Um, no. It was an office chair, one of the swivel types, but does it matter?'

I shrugged. 'Prissy, for all we know, there could be ghosts who have a thing for office chair legs, and then those who only hang out with lawn chairs. Or in Granny's case, with rocking chairs. Did you get a good look at this ghost?'

'I would say it was a fleeting look. You see, it was all hunched over beneath the – um – table. But it was hideous; that much I can tell you.'

'Four eyes? Horns? Vicious claws?'

Prissy plopped herself unbidden into one of my kitchen chairs. 'Don't mock me, Magdalena. Come to think of it now, it might have been the Devil. You do believe that the Devil can manifest Himself in any form that He wishes, don't you, Magdalena?'

'Indeed, I do. But I hardly think what you saw was the Devil.'

Prissy shook her head. 'Now that I think about it, I'm positive that's what I saw. And the smell, Magdalena. It was hideous.'

'Sulphur?' I guessed, for I'd had boiled eggs for breakfast.

'Exactly!'

'Prissy. Why would the Devil have a tug of war with you, of all people?'

'Because I was somewhere I shouldn't have been,' she said, and then clamped both hands over her mouth.

'Oh, you mean like Aaron Miller's office, for example. That was some shriek you let out.'

Prissy jumped to her feet. 'You knew all this time?'

'Of course, dear. What I don't know is, why you were there. However, I do know that you're just dying to tell me, so let's not waste time.'

Prissy scowled and tucked a stray lock of hair behind her left ear. 'Why on earth would I tell you?'

'Because if you do, I'll tell you about a scandalous love affair between Aaron Miller and a member of this community, and it all happened while he was married to me. In fact, I'll go one better.' I reached into my pocketbook and brought out a handful of letters. 'I'll let you read it for yourself.'

Prissy Utterall's eyes widened as she licked her lips. 'Hmm,' she said.

'You know what?' I said. 'Why don't you just keep these letters? I don't care what you do with the information in them. Maybe you can actually help me find the mystery woman.'

'Deal,' Prissy said. 'Now sit down.'

I set my pocketbook on the counter and obeyed her order to sit at my own kitchen table. As she spoke, I played with the packets of sugar and artificial sweetener.

'It was like this,' she said. 'Wilbur had made some bad choices, you see—'

'What kind of bad choices?'

'A quarter of a million dollars' worth. Every penny that my parents left to me.'

'Yes, now I do see. Go on, please.'

'So anyway, as you know, a Mennonite minister's salary is like—'

'Tread carefully, dear,' I said.

'Except for here,' she added quickly. 'On account of you're very generous, Magdalena. But most congregations aren't very wealthy; our previous congregation certainly wasn't. At any rate, Wilbur learned that there was a Mennonite – or at least a former Mennonite – who was going to build this awesome Biblical theme park just outside Dallas called Texas Exodus, and was in need of start-up cash. It was, Wilbur told me, a sure thing. But it was a strange contract; even I could see that, and I'm just a woman.'

'Piddle tosh, dear. There is no such thing as "I'm just a woman". God made Eve after He'd practiced on Adam. It says so right in the Bible. It gave Him a chance to correct His mistakes. Now tell me about this contract.'

'Well, there were to be ten different pavilions in Texas Exodus, each one representing a different plague, and promising a thrilling experience for park attendees. Then the peace of resistance – pardon me, my French is not very good – was the crossing of the Red, which isn't even one of the plagues, but it is very dramatic.' Prissy shook her head, and then paused further to wipe tears away from her olive green eyes. 'Wilbur was too trusting. I don't think he even read his copy of the contract. He certainly didn't show it to a lawyer. Anyway, it stated that all his money would be used as needed by the corporation as a whole, but that any profits would come solely from the plague pavilions. You see, they have separate entrance fees; there isn't just one entrance fee for the entire park. Can you believe that?'

'Yes,' I said simply.

'Some pavilions did better than others, but in the end, they all lost money. You're familiar with the ten plagues. Take the one about darkness. That one was nothing more than sitting in a totally dark room for twenty minutes – in a cubicle, by *oneself*. Then there was the one about locusts, where one was pelted with fake insects from all sides, and above, for twenty minutes. Oh, and get this, the cheesiest one was the "death of the first-born". In that, all one got for their money was piped-in sounds of wailing, such as I've never heard before. Although it was really gut-wrenching, that's all there was to it. No video of Pharaoh holding his dead son, like in the movie, *The Ten Commandments*.'

'I never saw the movie; I read the book instead.'

'Don't be self-righteous, Magdalena. I'm pouring my heart out to you while exposing my dear Wilbur's hare-brained investment scheme.'

'I apologize, dear,' I said.

'Thank you. Anyway, Texas Exodus exploded like a two-year-old bull from the starting pen. That means it really took off; it did well. But it didn't take long for word to get around that the pavilions were overpriced, and their so-called experiences were something that even a high school drama class would do a better job providing. The only department left standing was the truly awesome water feature called the Red Sea, so one by one Aaron bought the pavilions from his own investors, and converted those spaces into gift shops, restaurants, a Christian bookstore, and even more parking spaces.'

I held up my hand to signal that there was no need for her to continue further with this terrible tale. I would have offered her my shoulder to cry on, except both of mine are so bony, they can do serious damage to someone with such pale, white skin.

'I bet you wanted to wring Aaron's neck,' I said.

Prissy put a hand to her mouth. 'I beg your pardon?'

'Well, I certainly would have wanted to. It's only human to feel this way. I can only imagine how hard it was for your parents to save up a quarter of a million dollars.'

Prissy dug furiously into her purse, which was the size of an average suitcase. By and by she located her phone, which she then claimed had been ringing. To complete her ruse, she pretended to answer her phone, and followed through with a fake conversation. Unfortunately for Prissy, I have been blessed with exceptional hearing (it is one of the few gifts the Good Lord has seen fit to bestow upon me). I once heard a frog fart from the far side of Miller's Pond when I was standing on my own front porch, and that's with Hertzler Road between us. I can assure you that Prissy's phone did not ring, and that her conversation was entirely one-sided.

However, the gist of it was that she was needed back at the parish house immediately. Cora Neubrander, an elderly member, had shown up with a box containing eight kittens and a mother cat that had made their home under Cora's back porch. Silly Prissy, I knew for a fact that Cora Neubrander was visiting her daughter out in Phoenix, Arizona.

I suppose that I could have tackled Prissy, to stop her from leaving, but that would have been a very un-Mennonite thing to do. Besides, the woman was decades younger than I was, and no doubt as strong as a heifer. Anyway, she'd already given me a lot to mull over, and I had a lunch date to keep.

'You do know, dear, that lying is a sin,' I said to Prissy, as I held the kitchen door open for her.

'Why Magdalena, what an amusing thing for you to say, given that your pot couldn't possibly be any blacker.'

I smiled sweetly, and gave Prissy a gentle shove out onto the landing. It was time for me to boogie as well.

TWENTY-NINE

Toy's husband Steven is an excellent cook, but also something of an Anglophile. The main course was roast beef with Yorkshire pudding, and when I asked him how he learned to make the latter, he said something about me and a tube, which didn't make a lick of sense. Nonetheless, it was scrumptious, but when he announced that we were having tarts for the pudding, I pulled a long face, which is quite easy for me to do, given my equine features.

'Just joking,' he said, as he emerged from the kitchen bearing a magnificent trifle, which quite frankly isn't my favourite dessert. In my humble opinion, a trifle tries a trifle too hard to be something important. I much prefer a simple cake or pie that is obviously chocolate, or apple, and leave it at that. Dispense with the cream and all that nonsense, but then who am I, but a simple country woman?

As we lunched, I made my amends with the men for having snubbed them.

'Jesus didn't have a single bad thing to say about you,' I said.

Toy took a sip of water. 'Nor did he say anything bad about you, Magdalena.'

Steven snorted behind his napkin.

'I meant,' I said, 'that he didn't speak out against gays, like St Paul did.'

'There are scholars who say that the Biblical references refer to sex acts between male prostitutes at pagan temples, as was the practice at the time.'

'I didn't know that,' I said. 'So, anyway, please forgive me for being a bad friend.'

Toy got up and gave me a one-armed hug, and a kiss on my cheek. Then he sat back down.

'So, tell me all about your investigation,' he said.

That shouldn't have caught me by surprise, but I was disarmed by the one-armed hug and the smackeroo on my cheek. There was a time when I would have gotten all tingly you-know-where by this gesture of being forgiven, but that was before I got it through my thick skull that Toy, who was practically young enough to be my son, was no more sexually attracted to me, than I was to Steven's trifle.

'Well,' I said, when I'd regained a modicum of composure, 'there are far too many murder suspects, for one thing.'

'Oh?' Toy said. 'How many?'

'Five, including myself. And another possible contender.'

Steven Lantz chuckled. 'How can you suspect yourself? I mean, you would know whether or not you were guilty, wouldn't you?'

Toy reached across the table and put his hand on top of Steven's. 'I think that what she means, is that to an outsider – like Sheriff Lumberwarts – she would appear as guilty as all Hades. Am I correct, Magdalena?'

'Indeed, you are,' I said. 'But amused as I am by your rebranding of our notoriously incompetent sheriff, isn't that a little unprofessional of you?'

Steven pulled his hand out from under Toy's and grabbed one of mine. 'Miss Yoder, I'm not going to repeat the things that the sheriff has called my husband, in public, and the malicious gossip he's spread. Believe me, one nickname in the privacy of our home is small potatoes compared to all that.'

'I'm sorry,' I said, and I was. I was also sorry that I had never stuck up for Toy, because I had heard, and read, a lot of the ugliness fomented by the sheriff. As Mayor of Hernia, I was the unofficial dumping ground of gossip.

Steven accepted my apology, and released his grip. 'Do you mind giving us names?' he asked.

I took a deep breath. 'Dorothy Yoder, for starters,' I said.

'Motive?' Toy asked.

'Revenge. She wanted to play the part of the Whore of Babylon but was refused the role. She thought it was her ticket to Hollywood.'

'Hmm,' Toy said. 'I'm not sure that's a strong enough motive. The Whore of Babylon? I mean, really. Who would aspire to that role? And then to murder someone because you didn't get cast? This sounds like a high school drama.'

'Toy,' I said testily, 'you didn't know Dorothy when she

weighed over six hundred pounds. Now that she's down to one hundred and twenty, and has had all that surgery to remove excess skin, she really does look very pretty. Some might even say beautiful – if they squint. It's just all that extra make-up that she wears that makes her look so gross. I think that she wears it because inside she's still morbidly obese, and she's compensating for her weight.'

'Miss Yoder, the psychiatrist,' Steven said.

'Please call me Magdalena,' I said. 'Or Your Highness. Whichever moniker brings you the most joy.'

Steven winked. 'Then it's Your Majesty.'

'Quit flirting, you two,' Toy said, 'or else get a room.'

'Ach!' I squawked, and felt my cheeks burn.

'Go on, Magdalena,' Toy said, 'give me the lowdown on another of your suspects.'

'What else do you need to know about me?'

Toy grinned. 'I'm serious.'

'So am I. I had the strongest motive. People still call me an adulteress behind my back. Aaron ruined my reputation in my hometown, and he abandoned my daughter, whom I love.'

'But Miss Yoder,' Steven interjected, 'rational people can see that you were the victim in that sham marriage, so that strictly speaking, you weren't an adulterer.'

Toy nodded. 'Well said.'

'Men,' I groused. 'What you don't see is that it's the woman who usually gets blamed, and if not blamed, she's the one whose name gets remembered. The same thing goes for mothers – we're always the ones who get blamed when the daughter is a suspect, too.'

'Wow,' Toy said, 'I didn't see that coming.'

'Sorry, dear,' I said, 'but having laid that on you, does the chip on my shoulder look any smaller?'

'It's not only smaller,' Steven said quickly, 'but it switched shoulders.'

I wagged a long, shapely finger at Toy's husband. 'I think that I'm going to like you.'

Toy smiled. 'Magdalena, I'll concede that you could well be our killer. But surely not your lovely daughter. Alison has dedicated herself to saving lives, not taking them.'

'Alison was abandoned by her father,' I said emphatically, 'so that he could raise a male heir. When she saw him again recently, and tried to reconnect, tried to see her younger brother, she was rebuffed.'

'What about your other suspects?' Toy asked. 'What are their motives?'

'Actually, Toy, I'd rather not say any more on the subject, seeing as how I plan to grill them like sausages, in person, during a group confrontation.'

'Whoa,' Toy said. 'Do you think that's wise?'

'I do.'

'Shouldn't I be there with you?' he said. 'I *am* the police.'

'I won't be arresting anyone, dear. I'll be fact-finding.'

'Just the same—'

'Give it up, Toy,' Steven said. 'Her mind's made up.'

'But I do have a question you might be able to answer,' I said.

'Shoot,' Toy said. He pushed his chair back. Then he crossed his legs and folded his hand officiously in front of his flat, and very firm, stomach.

I cleared my throat. 'Let's suppose that a certain gal managed to find a will that everyone had been desperately seeking. What happens next?'

Toy slapped his forehead. 'Are you telling me that Sheriff Shamblebuster neglected to seal off the Armageddonland headquarters? No yellow tape? No guard? No anything?'

'Zilch,' I said, with a pie-eating grin. 'Nada. Just interested parties tearing the place apart looking for something, something which I think he kept locked up in the safe.'

'Magdalena Portulacca Yoder Rosen,' Toy said, as he raked a manicured hand through a thick head of blond hair, 'what are the odds that this certain gal, the one with the much-coveted will, is *you*?'

'I'd say that they're pretty darn-tooting good,' I said.

Toy shook his head. 'How did you manage to gain access to his safe combination?'

'Oh, that was easy; I was married to the man, so to speak. I knew what numbers were important to him.'

Toy sighed. 'Well, Steven here is a lawyer. He can tell you more about what to do than I can. Steven?'

I turned to look at Steven who was smiling broadly. 'Oh, Miss Yoder, you and I are going to be such great friends. You're such a firecracker, compared to Mr Stuffed Shirt here. At any rate, you are obliged to deliver that document to the county clerk first thing tomorrow morning. They will ask you how you came by it. Say you found it in the parking lot of your church next to Mr Miller's car.'

'Yes,' I said, 'but there may be another slight problem.'

Both men leaned forward but said nothing.

'You see,' I said, 'I read the will. The Devil made me do it. I mean sort of – really. I did it on Alison's behalf. I felt compelled to see if my beloved daughter had been excluded from her father's will, just like he'd excluded her from the rest of his life.'

'And?' both men said simultaneously.

'*I'm* the only one mentioned in the will,' I wailed. 'I'm supposed to inherit an estate worth millions of dollars.'

Now the men exchanged meaningful glances. I hate it when folks do that, unless I'm in on the meaning. Just thinking about their knowing looks, got me started on an unusually loud, and moisture-laden, crying jag.

'Quit being such an idiot,' Toy said, after snatching a box of facial tissues from the kitchen counter. 'There are billions of people in the world who would gladly have your problem, and Steven and I are two of them.'

I blew into a wad of tissues. 'It's not the money that I mind; I plan to give it all away anyway. I'm upset because that skunk of an ex – I mean, *pseudo*-ex-husband, didn't leave his children not even one thin dime! Can you imagine that? What kind of a father would do that?'

'A really bad father, Miss Yoder,' Steven said. 'A good father would have put money in trust funds for his children that they could access when they came of age. It seems to me that Mr Miller was more interested in punishing you with this problem than he was in the well-being of his children.'

'Bingo,' I said. 'I think that I'm going to like you right back. But stop calling me Miss Yoder.'

'Gotcha, Your Majesty. Hey, I have an idea: since this is your Sabbath, and your family is out of town, plus it's a perfect

September day outside, what say we head out to the deck and play a rousing game of Scrabble.'

My heart raced. I love the game, even though I invariably lose to Little Jacob. I have heard Scrabble described as many things, but I have never heard it described as *rousing*. This I had to experience.

'You're on,' I said.

So we repaired to the deck and the guys indeed showed me a rousing good time. Out of consideration for me, they sipped only non-alcoholic beverages, but they whooped and they hollered every time they were able to lay down all their tiles, or when they got a triple word score. Until that afternoon I'd been under the impression that I was a good Scrabble player, but by the end of our third game, and they had graciously extended a dinner invitation to me, I had to chalk the afternoon up to another lesson in humility.

'Thank you, but no,' I said about the invitation, 'but I would like to borrow your cell phone for a minute, Toy.'

'Does yours need charging?'

'No,' I said, 'but Dorothy Yoder won't pick up if she recognizes my number.'

'Magdalena,' Toy said, 'I'd just as soon be left out of your games.'

'Use my phone,' Steven offered. 'I love games.'

'Thanks, Steven, you're a pal.' I may be a mature woman, on the threshold of three score years, but I'm not so mature that I was above flashing Toy the tip of my tongue.

I walked across the yard a ways as Steven followed. Before calling Dorothy I made sure to put Steven's phone on speaker mode, so that he could hear the ensuing conversation.

'Hello,' Dorothy said cautiously. 'Who is this?'

'This is Mrs Dorothy Yoders' conscience calling,' I said in my best British accent. 'Is she at home?'

'Ha, ha, Magdalena, you sound like you have a mouth full of marbles. I'll give you ten seconds to state your business, and then I'm hanging up.'

'Aaron Miller left a will that might interest you.' That wasn't a lie, mind you, because when Dorothy learned that I was the sole beneficiary of his estate, she was bound to be *quite* interested. In fact, she was apt to go ballistic.

'I'm interested,' she said immediately.

'Then show up at the PennDutch tomorrow morning at nine sharp.'

'Can't you at least—'

I hung up. I also refused to answer Steven's phone when it rang immediately afterwards,

Steven laughed. 'Well played, and I, for one, thought you sounded exactly like Boris Johnson.'

'Thanks – I think.'

I thanked both men profusely for a delicious Sunday lunch, and a very pleasant afternoon, despite being roundly whipped (and whooped) at Scrabble. On my way back to the PennDutch I broke one of my cardinal rules, and made a couple of phone calls while driving. The first call was to Alison, and while the message was the same, the delivery was not. However, my daughter was nonetheless none too pleased.

'But Mom, I was just there! I can't just turn around and come back; I have an important lecture tomorrow morning and labs all afternoon.'

'I hear you,' I said. 'But this should take only a few minutes, and it's going to be life-changing for you. I promise.'

'Aw, Mom, you don't understand – how life-changing will it be?'

'Be there at nine sharp and see,' I said, and hung up.

The second call was to my husband. 'Hi darling, are you home yet?'

'Safe and sound,' the Babester said. 'Although all three of us are sunburnt and thoroughly knackered – that's British for *bushed*.'

'Yes, dear, I'm well aware of it.'

'Sorry, it's just that we got behind this English family in line for one of the rides, and their two teenagers seemed to have rubbery legs, and kept trying to hang on to their parents. Mum and Dad got rather annoyed, and Dad finally said, in a very firm voice, that if the kids were that knackered, then it was time to leave the amusement park. Both kids suddenly grew legs of steel.'

'Typical kids,' I said. 'How did your two charges behave?'

'Rather awesome, I'd say.'

'Are you being sarcastic?' I said.

'Not at all,' Gabe said. 'One would have thought they were

best buddies. They rode every ride together, and at lunch L.J. sat next to him, across from me. They're upstairs now in L.J.'s room playing computer games.'

'Did you feed them supper?' I asked.

'They said they don't want any; they're still full from all the junk food they ate at the park.'

'Well at least make them shower,' I said.

'Yeah,' Gabe said, 'that's a good idea. I should shower now as well; we all stink. When are you coming home?'

'In about two minutes. I can see the PennDutch from here.'

Upon arriving home, I felt as if I'd had a good day overall. It had begun with a shocking discovery, but it had also included making amends with an old and valuable friend. Now the day was ending with part of a plan already in place – one that would snap shut on Aaron Miller's killer, like a giant Venus fly trap, when she least suspected it. Oh yeah, and the boys seemed to have bonded. Maybe one day the boys would be brothers. But thinking any more about that now would just be tempting fate.

THIRTY

The Barkers and Tiffany returned close to midnight, and all three seemed startled to see me sitting at the kitchen table. As far as I was concerned, that was the clincher for me. Now I had all the information that I needed to put one of my five suspects away for murder.

I slept like a baby: with my eyes shut. Perhaps I cried out in my sleep a little, but Gabe is used to that. However, at no time did I demand to be fed, nor did I need to have my nappy changed – at least, as far as I can remember.

Right after breakfast my Dearly Beloved, who realized that I was up to something, but didn't want to know the particulars, cooperated fully with my suggestion that he entertain Jimmy Barker off our premises. There is a fabulous Frank Lloyd Wright house called Falling Waters, built over a stream, about a two-hour drive from here, and that's what Gabe thought would make a good destination. Jimmy Barker thought that was a wonderful idea, and as a consequence, the men cleared out well before the first woman arrived.

Prissy was the first. She was followed closely by Dorothy Yoder, who blew in like a hurricane with a number five rating.

'This better not take long, Magdalena. Monday is my day off, and I'm missing part of a Dr Pimple Popper marathon as I speak.'

'Zit will not take long,' I said. 'Just as soon as Alison arrives – and there she is!'

I waited a moment until my daughter was in the room and had pecked me on the check. Of course, during that time I had to tune out some griping, this time from Tammy Faye who had, of course, not had to do any traveling. All she and Tiff had needed to do was to slather glop on their perfectly sculpted faces, tug on some body-hugging doll clothes, and mince their way down my impossibly steep stairs. Except for a few fine lines around Tammy Faye's eyes, the two women were virtually inter-changeable. It was a realization that had dawned on me slowly, but which I'd become sure of the night before.

'OK, ladies,' I said, once we were all assembled in my spacious farmhouse kitchen, 'now we're going to troop into my parlour, where we will each take an admittedly uncomfortable seat for a very short, unofficial reading of Aaron Miller's will.'

I led the way, and knowing my furniture better than anyone, selected the only comfortable chair, except for Granny's rocker. I was, after all, the oldest person there. I have been noticing that some young folks these days show little respect for their elders. It seems to be a growing trend. Perhaps that explains why the curvaceous Tiff, by far the youngest of us, plopped her patooty right in Granny's lap.

Granny groaned.

'I didn't do that,' Tiff said, her face colouring. 'Honest, I didn't.'

For the record, Granny can't feel physical sensations, so although she could see Tiff, she couldn't feel the sudden weight of her. Granny was just having a bit of fun. After all, she's been dead for well over a hundred years, with nothing but the same flowered wallpaper to stare at for most of the time.

I clapped my hands twice. 'All right ladies. Let me begin by saying that, as you can see, there is a small table in the middle of the room with two manila envelopes on it. They are both labelled. In one is the name of Aaron Miller's killer, and in the second is a photocopy of his will. But first, I think that we should bow heads for a word of prayer, or, if we don't believe in God, which we should, although not all of us do, then at least said person should reflect positively on something, or someone, other than herself. Perhaps she might recall a spectacular sunset—'

'Enough blathering,' Dorothy said. 'Just get on with it, already.'

I swallowed my irritation, which fortunately has no calories. 'OK. So, there are five of us here. Each one of us had a motive for killing Aaron Miller, including me.'

'So that's what this is all about, huh?' Dorothy said. 'You're trying to pin his death on one of us by performing some cheap trick. I thought you'd found his will, and that you were going to read it to us.'

'I am. In a bit. I was also going to start explaining why it is that I am a good candidate to be his murderer, but—'

'Anybody who has lived here a week would know that,' Dorothy said. 'He turned you into an adulteress, and then left you a broken-hearted woman, who had to marry outside your faith, because no decent Mennonite man would look at you twice.'

'Shut up!' Alison shouted. 'How dare you talk to my mother like that? My parents' marriage is a beautiful love affair, unlike what you and Cousin Sam have.'

Dorothy's hands curled into fists. 'Oh yeah? What do Sam and I have, you impudent college kid?'

'I'm in medical school,' Alison said. 'At least I'm not a grocery clerk.'

I spread my open hands, on extended arms, in front of me in a calming gesture. I even flashed a smile that was intended to look beatific – although the odds were that I appeared to be suffering from painful haemorrhoids.

'Ladies, please,' I cooed. 'I can't stand to see two of my favourite people fight like this.'

'I was just sticking up for you, Mom,' Alison said, her dark eyes flashing.

'I'm certainly not one of your two favourite people,' Dorothy snarled. 'The minute you learned that your precious cousin, whom you always had a crush on, was marrying a Methodist from Bedford, your fangs dropped into place, and your claws came out.'

I laughed. 'That's a wonderful description of me, Dorothy. But that was me right up until I actually met you. Then it was instantly clear why Sam fell in love with you.'

Dorothy cocked her head. 'Yeah? Why?'

'Because you're extremely bright, and extraordinarily funny. There are very few people in this world who can make me laugh, and you're one of them.'

'More's the pity,' Dorothy said.

'I mean it. And your mind – besides being super intelligent and funny, you are original in your thinking. I could sit and listen to you talk all day.'

'Yeah?' Dorothy said.

By the tone of her voice, I could tell that Dorothy was beginning to soften. Surely hyperbolic flattery for a good cause is not a sin, even if it is insincere. I mean, there is a difference between lying for a just cause, and lying in order to get away with misbehaviour, isn't there? If not, then there should be. At any rate, it was time to bring out the big guns – so to speak.

'Yeah,' I said. 'And you know what, Dorothy? Now that you're back to your normal weight, you are drop dead gorgeous. Don't get me wrong – you were very pretty at six hundred pounds too, but now there isn't a starlet in Hollywood who could hold a candle next to you. But let's face it, dear, you're my age – pushing sixty. Aaron Miller didn't want a beautiful woman in her prime, like you, playing the Whore of Babylon. He was looking for some starving twenty-something, whom he could push around. Someone whom he could dominate. You were just too much woman for him.'

In a moment that shocked me and will stay with me the rest of my life, Dorothy Yoder, my erstwhile nemesis, burst into tears and jumped off her uncomfortable chair. She then stumbled her way across the room, weaving around the table upon which the two envelopes lay, and threw herself upon me.

'Oh Magdalena,' she blubbered, 'how can I ever thank you? What you just said has done more for my self-esteem than all my childhood therapy, and all the pep-talks I've been given since then. Magdalena, you are a wise, perceptive woman.'

Then, without another word, my cousin's wife extricated herself from my lap and limbs, turned, and departed the parlour. The two envelopes remained untouched, and it was time to select another victim.

'Alison, dear, I heard you say that you "could kill Aaron Miller".'

Alison, who'd been slumping, sat bolt upright. 'So did you, Mom!'

'Indeed, I did,' I said. 'But it was a figure of speech. *Did* you kill him?'

'Of course not!'

I studied her face. 'Then you are excused. Oh, on your way out, feel free to take a peek into one of the envelopes. But just one.'

That Alison had been incensed by my short interrogation was made clear by her body language. She leaped from her chair, strode to the table, and snatched up the envelope marked WILL. As she scanned its contents she snorted. Then she stuffed the papers back in without giving any thought to keeping them from getting bent or wrinkled. How rude can some people be, even if they are innocent? Anyway, having been apprised of the will's contents, my daughter sashayed indolently out of the room, acting more like a teenager than a woman in her early twenties.

'Well,' I said, 'it would appear that the young lass was disappointed. This could mean that the odds have changed in favour for one of you three. But that begs the question, why? If Aaron Miller did not leave his estate to his own flesh and blood, why on earth would he leave it to a preacher's wife, or his secretary, or' – I chuckled – 'an atheist, when he is building a religious theme park?

'This is the question that I've been asking myself. So, without getting our very heavy-handed sheriff involved, I thought that I would do some preliminary investigation. You are free to leave this room at any time, but keep in mind, doing so will make you look more than a mite suspicious.'

I rubbed my hands together. 'Prissy – I mean Priscilla Louise Utterall, I'll start with you.'

'Yes, ma'am.' Poor Prissy looked like I'd caught her with her hand in the cookie jar.

'I know for a fact that you rifled through Aaron Miller's office after he'd been killed. I know this because I saw you there.'

'But Magdalena, I didn't kill him! I was looking for his checkbook.'

'His *checkbook*?'

'Yes! I told you how he cheated Wilbur and me out of our lifesavings in Dallas. I was hoping to get away with writing a check for at least part of that amount and post-dating it. But of course, you ruined it.'

'Prissy, you can thank your lucky stars that I did ruin it. Trust me, with your complexion, you wouldn't look good in an orange jumpsuit.'

'What is that supposed to mean?' Prissy said. Clearly, my pastor's wife was not as experienced in the ways of the world as I was.

'It means the slammer. The hoosegow, the calaboose, the cooler, the crowbar hotel, the graybar hotel, the big house, the pokey. You savvy now?'

Prissy started to cry. 'I have no idea what you just said.'

'She means prison,' Tammy Faye said. 'Forging a check will send you to prison.'

'But you might get a lover named Hortense,' I said in an effort to comfort her. 'It would be a sin, of course, to have a female lover, but at least you wouldn't be lonely.'

'I don't even like the name Hortense,' Prissy sobbed.

'That was just an example,' I said. 'Her name might be Brunhilde, instead. Or Theodora.'

'But I *didn't* forge a check, because I didn't manage to find any, don't you see? And I certainly would never kill anyone – even in a figure of speech. That's your bailiwick, Magdalena.'

'Touché, dear. Well, then as far as I'm concerned, and I'm the only one that matters, since I convened this conference, you are excused as well. Please take a peep into one of the two envelopes on your way out.'

'No thanks,' Prissy said. 'I don't know why I even bothered to come.'

'You came,' I said, 'because I caught you snooping around a dead man's office. But you may go in peace, dear, because I am now convinced that you had nothing to do with Aaron Miller's murder.'

Without as much as a 'thank you', Prissy rushed from the room. I smiled at the remaining two women.

'Ladies, I thought that I would make this more of a joint interview, since you two are obviously related. I'm guessing mother and daughter – am I right?'

THIRTY-ONE

Tammy Faye did not react, but Tiff squirmed in her seat on the rocking chair, prompting Granny to groan. Tiff's eyes widened, and just to make sure that it wasn't some sort of trick chair, she wiggled her well-shaped posterior from side to side.

'Trollop,' Granny said. 'That's what we called girls like you in my day.'

'Hush, Granny,' I said.

'Who are you talking to?' Tiffany demanded.

'My great-grandmother's ghost,' I said.

'Boogers,' Granny said. 'You know I prefer to be known as an Apparition-American. Now tell this hotsy-totsy tart that she's sitting on my lap.'

I laughed. 'Hotsy-totsy? Did you just make that up?'

'Never you mind, child. Now go on and tell her like I said, before I try to pinch her.'

'Yes, Granny,' I said. I turned to Tiff. 'She said to tell you that you're sitting on her lap.'

Tiff shivered, and then practically catapulted across the room, where she took a chair adjacent to the one occupied by Tammy Faye. Meanwhile Tammy Faye still had not said a word.

'Another interesting titbit I discovered is that there is no such place as Hog Slop Hollow in West Virginia. You see, ladies, I may charge an arm and a leg for the privilege of staying at my full board inn, but one of the perks is that I will supply road maps of neighbouring states, free of charge, on request. The very detailed map of West Virginia, plus an internet search, came up with nothing. Young lady, you owe the Mountain State an apology for besmirching its reputation. In fact, you owe all of Appalachia an apology.'

Tiff glared at Tammy Faye. 'It was Mother's idea,' she said.

'Aha! Just as I thought; you are mother and daughter.'

'Which proves nothing,' Tammy Faye said.

'I beg to differ. But before I get into that, I just want to say that I think that the two of you are about the most beautiful women that I have ever known. Please don't get me wrong – I'm happily married. I'm just saying that when the Good Lord created the two of you, He pulled out all the stops – so to speak.'

Tammy Faye's eyes narrowed. 'Are you being sarcastic?'

I clutched the air, where a string of pearls would have laid, had I been so vain. 'My word, how can you say such a hurtful thing? Just look in the mirror, my dear. You have gorgeous eyes, a perfect petite nose, a pert little chin, classic cheekbones, and skin so flawless and smooth, that even compliments slide right off your face.'

Tammy Faye flashed me a smirk, which was at least something. Tiff, on the other hand, was nodding with the regularity of a metronome. It was time for me to carry the ball home.

'However,' I said slowly, 'as I studied your gorgeous profile, Tiff – and you are just as beautiful as your mother, make no mistake about that – I observed that there is nothing in your face, or even in your hands, or the way that you carry yourself, that comes from your mother's husband, Jim Barker. While on the other hand, there seems to be certain traits that you do share with my daughter Alison. Her biological father, by the way, was Aaron Miller.'

I paused for dramatic effect, and studied the women's faces. Tammy Faye's looked like polished marble, but Tiffany's face resembled chalk.

'Get on it with it,' Granny said. 'I love a good yarn.'

I glared at Granny, then turned back to the subjects of my interrogation. 'You, Tiffany, are also the biological daughter of Aaron Miller. You put yourself in the situation where he would hire you as his secretary, hoping that he would spot the resemblance. But of course, he never did.

'And I am guessing that you, Tammy Faye, had in the past notified Aaron Miller that he had a daughter, but cad that he was, he didn't give a rodent's behind. Perhaps you even sent him photos of your baby girl, and he never responded. Maybe you even went further—'

'I sent him Tiffany's class photos every year, starting with preschool,' Tammy said through gritted teeth. 'I did this all the way up through her high school graduation. We even drove out to Minnesota – we're from Ohio – to see him when Tiffany was eight, but he wouldn't even come to the door. But your Alison did.'

I leaned forward. 'How old was she then?'

'About the same age, I guess,' Tammy Faye said. 'Why does that matter?'

'That would be the year before Aaron kicked Alison out of the house.'

'My husband did that?'

'What do you mean by *your* husband?'

'We got married when I found out that I was pregnant. He gave me a big honker of a ring. Found out later that it was glass. Anyway, I didn't find out that he was married to that woman up in Minnesota, until I heard about you being his wife.'

'Oh, no,' I wailed. 'I'm not a bigamist, I'm a trigamist!'

'You're nuts, that's what you are,' Tammy Faye said. She stood. 'So, are you done with your flattery and suppositions, Miss Yoder? My daughter and I have better things to do with our day.'

'Sit back down, dearie,' I said in my Sunday schoolteacher's voice. 'I am far from done. Now comes the fun part, where one of you gets to confess to the murder of Aaron Miller. Motive? Vengeance. Opportunity? My ill-conceived tart buffet. Possible secondary motive? Killing Aaron, and then finding, and altering, his will to include Tiffany Barker.'

'Oh yeah?' said Tiffany, but her lips were quivering.

'Don't think that I'm foolish enough to accuse you without proof,' I said.

'That's exactly what you are,' Granny said.

'And of course I've already spoken to the police,' I said. 'At this point the game's pretty much over for you, so I suggest you go ahead and select an envelope. Silly me, what am I saying, just open the one marked WILL, because you already know what the one marked KILLER will read.'

'Don't mind if I do,' said Tiffany. She snatched up the envelope marked WILL and scanned the first page furiously, and then the second and third pages. I expected that reaction, but I was surprised when she ripped the first page into walnut-size pieces, tossed them on the floor, and ground them with her heel. While she was having this tantrum she howled like a bloodhound that had treed a family of coons.

'Mother!' she finally managed to say. 'She is the *only* one he left money to. Not to me, not you, not to his other daughter – Alison, I think her name is. Just this rude, obnoxious woman. Why, Mother, why?'

'I think I can explain that, dear,' I said.

'Shut up!' Tammy Faye said. She slipped her hand into her handbag and pulled out a handgun. Now, I'm no expert on fire-arms, but I think it was a cannon. No, I take that back. I'm quite positive it was a purse-to-air missile. Suffice it to say, I'm terri-fied of things that go 'bang', be they shutters knocking against the house in a storm, or body-piercing projectiles.

'Now that's just plain rude,' I said. My heart was pounding, but I couldn't help myself. Some people have no manners, scaring a sweet Mennonite woman in her own home.

'I said, shut up!' Tammy Faye advanced on me, waving her handgun as if it were a sword. As a Mennonite, I am not supposed to inflict bodily harm on anyone (although I did once use my bra as a slingshot to take down a giantess). At any rate, I tried to protect my head with my hands and my gangly arms, but apparently to no avail. Tammy Faye pistol-whipped me soundly, knocking me to the floor, whereupon she sat on me with her gun pressed right against my throbbing head.

'Go get some tape,' she barked to Tiff.

'Where do I find it, Mom?'

'In her junk drawer, where else?' Tammy Faye said.

'Where's that?' Tiff asked.

'In the kitchen, of course!' Tammy Faye hollered. 'Every house has a junk drawer in the kitchen. That's where one keeps their pliers, their hammer, their stuff to hang pictures, their string – you know what a junk drawer is. Now get!'

'Well, I do now,' Tiff whinged.

'Get a bag of frozen peas,' I called after her.

'I said shut up,' Tammy Faye said.

'You really are mean,' I said.

'Do you want me to hit you again, Miss Yoder?'

'Now that's a silly question, isn't it, dear? Put your gun away, and let's talk about this like adults.'

She hit me again. Harder.

'Ouch! Now that's not very Christian of you, is it?'

'I'm an atheist, remember?'

'Then you're giving atheists a bad name,' I said. 'I'm sure most of them are a lot nicer than you?'

'They are; I'm the meanest of the bunch. Tiff! Get your butt back in here with the tape now!'

'Dear Lord,' I began to pray in a loud voice, 'as you closed the mouths of lions—'

'I'll hit you again, so help me,' Tammy Faye roared.

'You can't hit a praying woman,' I said quickly. 'God will get you for that. Now where was I? Oh yeah, Lord, as you kept the hungry lions from killing Daniel when he was cast into their den, if it be Thy will, deliver me from this deranged pair of Barbie dolls who would likewise do me harm. But perchance if Thou wouldst have me battered to a pulp by the older villainess, the one with breath that could kill a badger at one hundred paces, then please consider this my last confession of sin, and forgive me all my trespasses.'

'That does it!' Tammy Faye said, as she sprang sprightly to her feet, and managing to grab a chair, she brought down upon my head and shoulders. How she managed to stand so easily while wearing sinfully high heels, is a riddle that only worldly women will ever be able to answer. As for me, the chair that she brought down atop my noggin, spelled 'lights out'.

It must have been at least an hour later when I awoke. Besides a blinding headache, I felt wet. I was on my back and lying in something, but definitely not water. In fact, the substance in which I was lying, felt much thicker than water. It felt more like porridge. Oh my stars! I was lying in cement, and the level was rising. Now it was getting into my ears. I lifted my head as high as I could. I tried sitting up, but my body was tied down to something. Maybe a beam? A board? Was I going to suffocate with cement in my mouth?

'Mom,' Tiff said, 'she's awake. Should I stop pouring now?'

'Nah, empty that bucket. Then we'll give her the good news.'

I felt the level of cement rise a wee bit when Tiff dumped the rest of her bucket. Then both women's faces appeared where there had just been sky.

'Well, well,' Tammy Faye said, 'fancy meeting you here. In a foundation form of all places. You know, once upon a time, this was going to be one of the corners of Armageddonland's main attraction. You know, Hell. Today, however, it's going to be your own personal Hell. How about them apples?'

'Yeah, how about them apples?' Tiff said. 'You should have minded your own business, Miss Yoder. I had it all under control. When Aaron Miller didn't recognize me, I told him flat out who I was. He just laughed, and then offered me a job. And when he still didn't acknowledge me, I started acting more like a girlfriend, hoping to embarrass him. That's why I called him Pooky Bear and stuff in front of you, so he would get mad and object.'

'Of course, she wasn't actually going to sleep with him,' Tammy Faye said. 'He was her father, after all. Yuk! So get your mind out of the gutter.'

Both women cackled.

'Good one, Mom,' Tiff said, 'but I think that is called a footer. Anyway, Miss Yoder, I started poisoning him my second week on the job. Just a little bit at a time. Then when he crammed some of my *special* tarts down his gullet – a fair-minded person would say that he did it to himself.'

'Yeah,' Tammy Faye said. 'That old buzzard gave himself a fatal tart attack.'

At that the villainesses cackled and hee-hawed like a barn full of livestock in a hailstorm. Although I found them both utterly despicable, I did admire the fact that they were so in sync with each other. *If* Alison and I ever committed a murder . . . no, I shall abandon that thought.

'What's going to happen to me?' I asked when I could get their attention.

'Well,' Tammy Faye said, 'we can't have you sending us to the hoosegow now, can we? Neither of us looks good in orange, do we, Tiff?' This set the berserk pair howling with laughter again.

'Stop it!' I hollered. 'I have a mother of all headaches. I'm quite sure that I have a concussion, since I see four of you, which is four too many. And another thing, I'm quite sure that they don't wear orange jumpsuits at the Funny Farm.'

'Oh, they're going to prison,' I heard someone say in a lovely Southern accent. 'Put your hands high in the air, you two. Now turn around. Sergeant, cuff them.'

Then, despite a tad of cement in my ears, I heard the click of metal – twice – and some angry cussing coming come from the mouths of the Barker gals as they were read their Miranda rights.

Meanwhile the strong arms of Toy Graham lifted me from my concrete grave. Then as gently as possible, Toy washed me with an industrial hose, until the point where he had to hand the hose to me and turn his back for the sake of my modesty. Believe me, the cement had gotten *everywhere*. I had just finished cleaning up when the ambulance arrived, but that's not where this saga ends.

THIRTY-TWO

J udge Gloria Van Derwimple found an opening for us on her calendar for August the eighth, which just happened to be Rodney Miller's fifteenth birthday. By then he'd been living with us for over a year and had integrated into our family like half of a zipper. By that I mean he had a lot of rough edges, and from his perspective so did we, but when put together, we fit rather well.

L.J. and Rodney started calling each other 'bro' within a month. One day about a month or two later Little Jacob was nagging me to take him into Bedford so that he could look for baseball cards in the antique stores. 'Please, Mama,' he said ad nausea. Then suddenly I heard, 'How about it, Mama,' from a boy whose voice had broken, and it shocked my stockings off. It also reduced me to tears.

It took about twice as long for Rodney to call Gabe 'Dad' or 'Papa', both terms that Little Jacob uses. The lag time is understandable, given that Rodney knew his birth father and once lived with him until he died.

But back to Judge Gloria Van Derwimple. She had Gabe, Alison, L.J. Rodney, and I all stand before her in her chambers. After introductions were made, she singled out Rodney.

'Young man,' she said, 'what we're about to do is more serious than even a wedding. If you say yes to my questions, then Mr and Mrs Rosen will be your parents for the rest of your life – not just their lives. And this handsome young man standing beside you, and this beautiful young woman, will be your brother and sister forever as well. Do you understand?'

'Yes, ma'am. I do,' Rodney said.

'And you, the Rosen family, do all four of you wish to adopt Rodney Kaufman Miller into your family, as your son or brother?'

'We do,' we said in well-rehearsed unison.

'And now to another item here. Do you Rodney Kaufman Miller wish to legally change your name to Rodney Kaufman Rosen?'

'No, ma'am,' Rodney said.

The judge raised a slightly over-plucked eyebrow.

'Ma'am,' Rodney said, 'I wish to change my name to Rodney *Yoder* Rosen.'

RECIPE FOR MINI TARTS

Serves: 6 (six three-inch diameter tartlets)

INGREDIENTS
Shells
    1 ½ cups (180 g) flour
    ¼ cup (50 g) sugar
    ⅛ teaspoon salt
    10 tablespoons butter (cold, unsalted)
    1 egg yolk
    2 tablespoons cold water
    ¼ teaspoon vanilla extract

Lemon Curd Filling
    2 large eggs plus 2 egg yolks (or 3 whole eggs)
    ¾ cup (150 g) granulated sugar
    1 tablespoon lemon zest
    ½ cup (120 ml) freshly squeezed lemon juice (2-3 lemons
        for both zest and juice)
    2 tablespoons heavy cream, optional
    ½ cup (1 stick/115 g) unsalted butter, cut into small pieces

DIRECTIONS
Shells
Prepare tart dough:
1. Using food processor, pulse the flour, sugar, salt to combine thoroughly.
2. Cut cold butter into small cubes. Add the butter into the food processor and pulse butter, flour, sugar and salt until the consistency becomes that of a coarse meal.
3. In a small cup, combine the egg yolk, ice water and vanilla and stir well together. Add the egg mixture to the food processor and pulse to combine. Shape the dough into a ball, wrap it with a plastic wrap and refrigerate for 2 hours.

Bake tart dough after it's been refrigerated for 2 hours:

1. Preheat oven to 350 F.
2. Divide the dough into 6 parts and roll each into a ball.
3. Grease each tartlet well. Flour the working surface, and roll each ball into a disk larger in diameter than a well of the tart pan, then place the round disk into a greased well. Because rolling each ball into a disk and placing it into a well usually takes time, keep the rest of the balls in the refrigerator and take each one out to work on one ball at a time. This way, the dough is kept cold, which will help the crust be soft and flaky. Also, it helps to put the tart pan into the freezer after filling the first two wells while shaping the next 2 disks. Then take the tart pan out of the freezer, place the 2 disks in, and repeat. Once you have filled all the wells in the tart pan, place the pan back into the freezer for 5 minutes before baking.
4. Prick the bottom of each tart with a fork 2 or 3 times. Bake the shells for 25 minutes until golden brown, not dark. Rotate the tart pan 180 degrees halfway through the baking time.
5. Remove the tartlets from the oven and let them cool completely.

Lemon Curd Filling

To make the lemon curd:

1. In a medium heatproof bowl, place eggs, sugar, lemon zest, lemon juice, and heavy cream, if using, and whisk to combine. Place the bowl over a saucepan of simmering water (bain-marie). Cook on moderate heat, whisking constantly, until mixture becomes thick (10 to 20 minutes). If you have a thermometer, it should register 170°F / 75°C; otherwise, it should coat the back of a wooden spoon and leave a clear pass if you run your finger through it. The curd will thicken more once cooled.
2. Remove from heat and immediately strain mixture through a sieve. Add butter, a few cubes at a time, and

whisk until completely melted and incorporated, and mixture is smooth. Take your time with it – the whisking makes for an airy and light texture. Allow to cool to room temperature before filling the tarts. (Lemon curd can be kept in an airtight container in the fridge for up to a week, or can be frozen for up to 2 months. To thaw, place overnight in the fridge. Whisk the mixture to smoothen it before using.)

Fill the tartlets:

Fill the tart shells with lemon curd, then refrigerate for at least 4 hours until chilled. Serve with berries or other fruit and whipped cream if you like.